Advance Praise

Ames finds tenderness lurking in even the most self-absorbed and self-deluded, in people we didn't think we needed to know. Gorgeous, affecting stories by a generous and capable writer.

- Linda Swanson-Davies, editor,
Glimmer Train Stories

The clarity and precision of language that illuminates the ordinary details of these stories, thereby exploring the meaning of the bumps and hesitations in our lives – that's why I read. You will not want to miss Brian Ames.

– Alex Kuo, author of *Lipstick*,
American Book Award

Funny, scary, sad, happy, the shifting moods of Ames' stories take you far and wide but always bring you back to the wilderness in your own heart.

- David Barringer, author of *American Home Life*

i

As Many Hands As God

Brian Ames

Pocol Press
Clifton, VA

iii

POCOL PRESS
Published in the United States of America
by Pocol Press
6023 Pocol Drive
Clifton, VA 20124
www.pocolpress.com

Publisher's Cataloguing-in-Publication

Ames, Brian, 1963-

As many hands as god / Brian Ames. – 1st ed. – Clifton,   VA : Pocol Press, 2008.

p. ; cm.

ISBN: 978-1-929763-37-5

1. God--Fiction. 2. Presence of God--Fiction.
3. Belief and doubt--Fiction. 4. Religious fiction--American. 5. Short stories. I. Title.

PS3601.M47 A8 2008

813.6–dc22   0804

Acknowledgments

Thanks to Kathryn Rantala, editor of *Snow Monkey* and Ravenna Press in Spokane, for this collection's title.

Reading her poem "Beijing Love Movie," I came across this gorgeous line: "as many hands as god." I had been turning about in my head the idea of a group of stories about how the Maker, by the actions of faith and love through people, makes its presence known. This phrase seemed perfect, first, for a story about a wife's faithfulness, and then as the work evolved, for this project.

I also wish to express gratitude to the editors of the following magazines, where some of the stories in this collection first appeared:

"Impala Desert," in *Glimmer Train Stories*; "Swept Through a Many Chambered Heart," in *Thought Magazine*; "As Many Hands as God," in *Night Train*; "Babe in Arms: A Still Life," in *Red Rock Review*; "The Confession of Titus," in *Scrivener's Pen*; "Damming the Carbon," in *Wisconsin Review*; "Displacing Water," in *Pierian Springs*; "Hughie and Moira Stand in Freezing Air," in *Literary Vision Magazine*; "Never," in *Windhover*; "The Last Living Elk in North America," in *North American Review*; "The Names of Moss," in *Bullfight Review*; "The Newark Marriott," in *Small Spiral Notebook*; "Hey Now, All You Sinners," in *Barrelhouse*; and "Viable," in *Thought Magazine*.

For my wife and best friend, Natalie

Table of Contents

Impala Desert

When my boy turned seven he was given a birthday gift from a rock enthusiast – a little geologist's collecting kit. This article comprised a small carrying case the size of a cigar box; within lay twelve cubbyholes formed by a matrix of cardboard separators. For placement therein, the kit came with a dozen stones representing the three geologic derivations: igneous, sedimentary, and metamorphic. The stones, alphabetically, were agate, basalt, feldspar, gabbro, granite, halite, obsidian, pumice, pyrite, rhyolite, schist, and shale.

My son would not have been more delighted if he had received a pony. A self-proclaimed future paleontologist, his boyish interests regarding vocation run to things dinosauric. He longs to grasp a small brush and clean flecks of soil from a prehistoric bone.

He held out each rock for me in his small hand, palm upward but cupped, pronouncing the names of the stones in succession. I noticed that his palms were the palms of a juvenile, that he had lost his toddler's subsurface adipose tissue. I wondered how many years it had been since I had looked at them so closely. The hands of my child.

"Pay attention in math," was my advice to him. He experimented with the word *gabbro*, his voice, the voice of my son, pronouncing the hard G, aspirating the A, lips together and larynx buzzing with the Bs and then mouth formed into an O off the R sound. "Gabbro." He played with the word, rolling the R: Gabb-*rrrrroh!*

"And science, too," I advised. His voiceplay amused me.

When I was his age, my career aspirations were this complex: baseball player, astronaut, preacher.

A royal blue Chevrolet Impala broke the speed limit on Interstate 15 across the desert floor between Barstow and the Nevada state line. My great-uncle was behind the wheel, a Winston drooping from his lips except when he sucked in and the cigarette's tip rose. Its length ran horizontal, like the near Mojave landscape behind his head out the window. He called the shrubs that we passed creosote bushes, Joshua trees. I liked the names of them. I sat in the front passenger seat, eleven years old, looking over at him. My sister and his daughter, both seven, were in back.

Uncle Hector wore sunglasses with black, opaque lenses and silver rims. We kids had none, and the bright air outside was stunning. We were driving into light, and from light. To the left and right of us was light, and enormity, and flatness, although beyond the curl of my uncle's smoke mountains could barely be discerned in a shimmer. We had passed the Calico Ghost Town thirty miles back and then, in the comprehension of children, we understood that surrounding us, outside the cloth and vinyl universe of the Impala and the odor of my uncle's cigarette, was nothing. We were asea, unaware that desert, like open ocean, possesses diversity urban people do not appreciate.

Hector was cycling two eight-track tapes, forty minutes of Charlie Rich, forty minutes of Frank Sinatra. He slowed on approach to a small settlement the green highway signs had told us would be called Baker. A dry, alluvial basin stretched out to the southeast. Morning sun leapt off it and drew the automobile coasting into Baker, where we were invited to arid commerce by a half-dozen souvenir shops. Wood billboards rose off their rooflines; they read SILVER and TURQUOISE.

Hector wanted to stop. My great-uncle was a collector, a saver of rare coins, cataloguer of stamps, displayer of antiques, jewelry and things of the indigenous cultures of the Southwest. Many years later, the Kokopeli and the gecko would become icons. White people would appreciate the beauty of the native craft of this region, would hear dry whispers of the Anasazi. Long before this, Hector was an aficionado.

Since we set out from San Bernardino that morning, we had been seeing signs that told us to turn north at Baker to get to Death Valley. The legendary place name intrigued and frightened me. I was relieved that we were headed for Las Vegas instead. Now that we had reached Baker, at the locus of the Mojave, we would keep heading east on 15.

Hector slowed, pulling into the dusty lot of the second structure in Baker. The girls reminded him they had to find a bathroom.

"We'll ask inside," he said. He braked to a stop in front of the

2

store, parked diagonally between the doors of two other autos. He lifted his doorlatch, paused, looked for us to follow suit. The opening of my door brought an inrush of airlessness, a parched vacuum of heat. Even as we emerged I could feel the desiccation of the skin of my hands, exposed arms, the back of my neck. The air was still. I looked out over the parking lot, disturbed by a sense that I would not see anything moving unless I got down on my hands and knees and examined, across the dust, the single inch of altitude above pavement. I could not name this discomfort; years later I would think back and understand that I was being drawn to the playan universe of that flat, near two-dimensional plane by something latent, something under the surface. It still is a mystery to me when I reflect, today, on the discomfiture I felt, which eased and vanished only with the sound of the Impala's doors closing. Only after my sister and cousin climbed from the back seat.

We followed Hector into the store. He inquired about facilities, sent the girls down a hallway alone, and engaged the shopkeeper in dialogue about things that interested him. I was left to explore. Fascinating – the rows and rows of bins with stones for sale: fire opals, agates, jasper, quartz, chrysoberyl, chalcedony. There was a section of inexpensive polished rocks, stones that had been tumbled in water and oil and silt for weeks, poured from a rotating-drum receptacle smooth-faced as glass. I plunged my hands into a half-barrel of these polished pebbles, enjoying the sensation of them against my fingers and palms, the backs of my hands. It was as soothing as a bag of marbles, cool, calming – it felt as if they were grouping around my extremities and touching back, the stones.

I saw from a cardboard sign that I could buy ten of them for a dollar. For seventy-five cents more, I could purchase a small suede pouch to carry them.

The store was dimly lit, a contrast to the hours of brightness outside. Sunlight filtered through dusty side-windows. Only the cashier's island where Hector lingered was awash in a drapery of light from a fluorescent tube. The glass displays and bits of silver and turquoise in jewelry were electrically backlit. But it was dusky away from these sources, in the corner of the store that had drawn me.

3

I pulled my hands from the polished rocks, moved on and stopped again, this time at a bin of cloven thunder eggs. I drew one forth, hefted the stony hemisphere in my hand. The geode was hewn in half; I could see the striations of carbon-tipped sawteeth on its cross-section. At the epicenter, like the core of a weighty melon, was a purple crystalline cavern. Even in the low light, the crystals refracted and shifted. I didn't know their colors; today I understand them: amethyst, violet, fuchsia, aubergine, magenta, lavender. At the edges, mauve. Deep at the core, lapis, plum.

It, too, went for one dollar. The fractal variations on purple pleased me. I grasped the thunder egg in my fingers, walked across the floor of raw boards to Hector, held it up for him. In the light, the crystals danced like fireworks.

"That's what you'd like, huh?" Hector took it from my hand, perused it. "It's pretty." The shopkeeper nodded as the girls half-skipped up the hall, only now noticing the shiny stones all around them. They, too, paused to discover tensile communion with the polished rocks and began the process of rejection and selection. They each brought Hector ten precious rocks.

"Polished them myself," the shopkeeper bragged, under the drape of fluorescence, one eye behind a jeweler's loupe worn more for effect than need. Neither my sister nor my cousin understood what he meant; they believed the rocks were born that way. Hector took them from the girls, laid our childish minerals on the counter. He added that he would like to purchase the 1922 silver dollar he and the shopkeeper had been talking about a moment ago, a coin missing from his collection. He tendered cash. The shopkeeper rang up the sale. Then the four of us – each with a treasure – left the store and emerged into heat, into gold white light.

We dropped out of a cleft between red and brown stone, jack pines, a mountain descent into the valley of Las Vegas. The city appeared ahead like a spaceport, bejeweled with lights and the anomalous structures of casinos – centered in the flat – strange there in the low back of the desert. Finite in its boundary. It was 2:20 in the afternoon by the dashboard clock. The sun was high, and its sky was blue at the zenith fading to white at a massif horizon.

As we neared, the density of buildings and fences grew, so that the impression from the cleft – that the city was all in one, bounded place – was revealed as an illusion. We began passing people, lone individuals at first, then groups, passing the first casino soon afterward. Then came a row of casinos, and chapels and pawnshops and the precursors of strip malls, attorneys outnumbering other tenants by three to one. And then great aggregations of people, crowding onto sidewalks and waiting at the doors of clubs.

The girls grew restless in the back seat, fidgeting and giggling. "What's craps?" my cousin asked. She stared out the window, delighted that this word was everywhere, on marquees, in neon, on posters.

"It's a game," Hector said. He pulled the Impala into a lot outside one of the casinos.

"You kids stay here," he said. "I'll be back to check on you in a while." And he left us to roll the windows down and pass the time with Keno placemats we had brought with us from the lunch diner where we'd stopped at the state line. We fabricated a game with these matrices of eighty numerals – some of them spotted with hamburger grease – using the girls' polished stones from Baker. We called out numbers randomly to each other, tried to form patterns – a childish algorithm exercised as we held our pee, and waited on the sizzling vinyl of the car seats.

As time passed, the three of us grew impatient, restless with our bladders. At one point we braved disobedience, left the car and relieved ourselves behind a dumpster in the casino's alley. After that, time seemed to move more quickly, and we waited for Hector with new stamina. Shadows cast by other cars parked near us grew longer. The number of people going in and out of the casino increased.

We had long ceased the Keno game, and were making up rhymes and songs in the heat, thirsty, when we saw Hector and a woman emerge from the casino across the lot. He stopped there at the approach to the door. She embraced him, kissed him on the mouth. As she pulled away her lips moved. He nodded, his hand still on her forearm, then dropping to his side. He turned and headed our way, walking differently, with side-bounce and an oiled, imprecise stride. Four cars away from us he stumbled against the rear-view mirror of a pickup truck. He stopped and looked at the mirror through his sunglasses as if from a distance. He tried to reconfigure it properly, rubbed his upper arm and shoulder, the point of impact.

He pulled the door open and dropped onto the seat, hands at ten and two o'clock on the wheel.

"You kids O.K.?" There was a smell like medicine from him as he spoke. I noticed, from the corner of his lips, a wiped smear of dry maroon.

"We're all right," I said.

"We played Keno," my sister said. "With our rocks."

"Good." Hector pushed his key into the ignition, pumped the accelerator twice, cranked the motor back to combustion. The dashboard clock blinked on and showed 7:14. "Good."

The Impala live again, he fished in his shirt pocket for cigarettes, pushed the lighter in with his right hand. When it popped he flared the end of the Winston. A drop of blood fell from the corner of his mouth. He wiped it away. There was blood on the Winston's filter. He saw me looking at this.

"Don't worry," he said. "Had a little problem in there."

Offering no further explanation, he backed out of the parking spot, negotiated the rest of the lot and roared into the Vegas street. Still, today, I wonder about Hector's blood: had he been discovered cheating at cards, taken out back, roughed up? Had he forgotten his manners at the bar, said something prurient to a woman and received her slap? Alternatively, had she accepted his line, gone up to a room with him, flailed out or bit his mouth during sex?

We ate supper at a Denny's then stopped at a liquor store. Hector bought a small bottle of whiskey, six bottles of Coke and more cigarettes. At twilight, we found lodging at a Motel 6. But enveloped in the glare of Las Vegas, it seemed as if the blue night never really fell.

Nightfall was mitigated, held back, by the constant flashing of colored bulbs, klieg lamps, neon. In the room, we children sat on the beds, watched TV, and drank the Cokes. Hector smoked cigarettes and drank the whiskey, laying on one of the beds with his back to the wall on some pillows. His feet formed a Y where they rested.

A long, straight aisle of Highway 95 stretched out in front of us as we left Vegas. The morning was somewhat chilly. The girls were in their jackets in the back seat, sleeping. Hector didn't put the tapes on for a while. We knifed through the clear desert air with only the sounds of wind funneling through the edges of the windows, the articulation of the cigarette lighter, the airburst when Hector would push the wing window open to exhaust smoke. The mountains rose around the Las Vegas Valley in fantastic, dazzling crenulation, holding the clarity of the desert there for us. The light made us ambitious to drive, my great-uncle and I, while the girls slept.

He drove north very fast. We passed thousands of acres pitted with sage plants. Reds, deep greens, siennas, browns, and the blue, blue sky hovered there, glowing, drawing. We passed signage about a wildlife refuge, then a test range. Hector must have known what this was all about, but I had no inkling until later of visored gentlemen – alchemists who turned sand into glass – who watched the violent rose of atomics bloom over the desert, pleased with themselves as we passed by on Highway 95 in a royal blue Chevrolet Impala.

As we neared the town of Beatty, Hector pointed out a group of wild burros off to his left. In Beatty, we stopped at a diner for breakfast. He woke the girls. We entered the place and they wriggled out of their hot jackets, hanging them near the door. We ate eggs and sausage. Hector dumped hot sauce from a tiny bottle onto his omelet.

After Beatty, the road opened up again. But the enthusiasm of the morning faded as we roared north on the blacktop. Near the highway, the land was flat. We passed the same creosote bushes and yucca plants we had been seeing for what seemed like thousands of hot, ironed miles.

Still to the east, the test site and a gunnery range, and to the west high ridges. As we were drawn northward, we began to see the nubs and outcrops of massifs: the Monitor Range, the Toquima, the Toiyabe. A few miles after Goldfield we had to head west on Highway 6 to pick up 95 again, going north.

All this passed by in an hour and a half or so. We sat in the car and said nothing, listening to the whistle of wind through the wing windows and Charlie Rich, whose deep-voiced cartridge Hector had plugged in after breakfast. We grew to anticipate the mid-song fade of the eight-track deck, the click of the next track engaging, the rise of music again. If I hear that music today, it is incomplete without this familiar interruption. It's as if we were imprinted in the desert.

Between Coaldale and Mina, I began to have visions. I imagined stones hovering off in the slow-moving distance, circling, grouping, forming patterns and kinetic glyphs. The rocks would float above the gravel and, in a rush of loess, assemble themselves into a stack, a beaded hoodoo, a mineral doll.
I imagined these eggs of the earth were engaged in a form of Brownian movement, that as the heat agitated their cores, they began to tremble and rise.

I imagined that light was the visible layer of time, and that the invisible forms of light, the infrared and X-ray, were other dimensions with other inhabitants.

I imagined I saw a dustdevil consume a pair of desert falcons who had dropped from Pilot Peak.

I imagined *objetos en el cielo*, motherships.
I imagined that the Impala grew wings, and that the four of us were flying but confined to the airspace one inch above the tarmac. I understood, at that moment, that the desert's final purpose, its teleology, was to hold us flat and move us along.

In a lucid interval from these mysteries, I glanced over at Hector and down at the Impala's instrument panel and speedometer. The red needle was pegged at 110 mph. I looked down; his right foot was fused with the floor mat. So he was feeling it too: the raw urge to be quit of the heat, the light, the crushing load of this place.

He broke the silence, told me that the sky above the desert is the eyeball of God. *In daytime, God's eye is rolled back in the socket; it looks at deserts on other worlds. At night, God's attention is focused on the arid places of this world. His dark pupil is the night sky, dusk and dawn the turning of his thoughts toward and away from us, respectively. Stars, in God's black pupil, are the reflections of the actions of men during the night, hogback deeds committed under blanket of darkness.* I stared at Uncle Hector throughout this monologue to see whether his lips were moving, whether the sounds really emanated from him. But his mouth was closed and did not open to form these syllables, not once during the time I heard him speak. His eyes, behind the shades, remained on the road ahead. I looked in the back seat. The girls were drowsing again. I shrugged it off, returned to watching the pass of landscape. I imagined that what Hector's voice said could be true.

Forward from us, to the north, toward a place to which we were quickly red-shifting, a black-silver mirage waited buoyant at the draw of my vision. It shook and shined and never grew closer, this lake. But I could barely discern a swimmer in its mercury waters. My first lover – her call and sigh and coil – and it pleased me, this harbinger up ahead.

We began to see signs for Carson City and Reno. This seemed to calm Hector. He eased off the accelerator, but still pushed ninety. For most of the day we had been alone on the road, passing only occasionally a sedan or eighteen-wheeler coming the other direction. We passed Walker Lake, moving through the vague boundary of the Mojave into the Great Basin Desert, and drove through the Walker River Reservation. We picked up speed again as we crossed a long, flat, low spot between the Reservation and the air base at Fallon, evolving from one desert to another.

Hector and I both saw the spot in the center of the highway simultaneously, and we closed on this blemish quickly. It sat exactly in the center of our lane. He slowed the car as we approached, discerned the object, pulled over letting the motor idle. "Stay in the car," he said. But I interpreted this as instruction for the girls and followed him outside anyway. He didn't object. We walked across the pavement a few steps and beheld the fractured carcass of a desert tortoise. The dead reptile was enormous, even for a tortoise, maybe fourteen inches from the front of its ruptured shell to the back. It was freshly dead, had crawled a little after being hit, bled a streak on the asphalt that was still deep black-red, wet. The carapace was split athwart the animal, cracked and open to the sky. Its guts were a mess inside. The head and beak lay sideways, well-muscled forelegs tucked under the shell. But the hind legs were mashed out mashed like those of a deflated elephant. Its gular horn was crushed and oozing.

"Damned shame," Hector said. "Look how pretty he was."
I nodded.

"Help me out with him."
My great-uncle and I grasped the tortoise by the shell and lifted him a few inches off the highway. The hind legs and gular horn rose from the hot road with moist noise. We carried the broken reptile to the shoulder, set him on the desert pavement behind a creosote bush. Hector thought we ought to bury it. He went back to the Impala to shut down the engine. He told the girls to hang tight and retrieved a tire iron from the trunk. He used this tool to dig on the hardpan behind the bush. I had the job of pulling the loose dirt out of the hole as it widened and deepened. A car passed every ten minutes or so, but none stopped. After about forty minutes, the grave was large enough for the tortoise. We put him in.

Hector started to scrape my dirt pile back over the tortoise with the tire iron. I reached down and scooped up the dry soil in my hands, letting it winnow between my fingers onto the reptile, the dust catching and soaking in the tortoise blood. When I was through sifting, I noticed that in my dusty hands were scores of seeds.

We left the tortoise's grave and pulled back out on the road. Soon we drove into Fallon and took a left onto Highway 50. Then we crossed the Carson River and saw a sign that read "Sparks 41 Reno 44." My sister discovered just then that she had left her jacket hanging in the Beatty diner.

"Too late to go back for it," Hector said. She started to cry. I pulled my thunder egg out of a brown sack on the floorboard, held it in my hands, looked into its purple cavern. Saw the entrails of the tortoise inside among the glistening crystals. Saw its torn case, the blood on the highway, the half geode, the fractured reptile. Uncle Hector accelerated.

   The memory of where my sister's coat hung sticks with me as a childhood milepost. I often surmise that were we again, as adults, to motor across the desert from Las Vegas to Reno, we would find the same diner at Beatty, unchanged, lucid and unmitigated by time. Here in this place, Hector never grasps his chest, alone, ten years after our trip across the Mojave, in his apartment as his heart explodes. Here in this diner, I possess a magical geode from which visions rise, a half-stone I misplaced somewhere over the intervening years. Here, compact discs never replace the metered music of eight-track cartridges. My sister's pink jacket hangs on the same chrome coat-stand of the diner, on the same peg, the pink dye of the fabric having waned in the bleaching sweep of eight thousand risings and settings of the Nevada sun. She puts the coat on and spins for us, the declination of hemispheres a clear line displaying where the coat faced the window, where the dark side was. She is a pink moon of quilted frosting, the revolving sphere of an orrery.

Swept Through a Many-Chambered Heart

There is nothing Esther loves so much as Patsy Cline music. But G'vieve wants to dance a snappy number with her new young man. The two women are bound to collide in a place you or I wouldn't understand. On a roadside just at the edge of town, in a different mid-America – it may have been in North Platte or Akron or Urbana, I can't remember and it and makes no difference anyway – there is this question: which is more relentless, ambition or love?

There is nothing Esther loves so much as Patsy Cline music.

Except, perhaps, the private view of her own future, that secret she tells no one but that places her, even now, irrefutably in a single place always. In front of the jukebox, and no one is going to move her, not with chidings, cluckings, no force of will is great enough. On a vinyl-covered chair with chrome legs, she sits facing all those blinking lights and colors. She feeds the Wurlitzer her nickels and pokes in selections. She practices the words to *Crazy* and *So Wrong*, and will do so again and again until she is good enough, herself, for Nashville. And while she is engaged in this preparation for the world she knows awaits her, she allows no one to come between her and the machine.

All of the sounds you hear in roadhouses or taverns at the edge of towns are around Esther. The clink of glassware and plates that have lost their polish. Tableware clacking against stained teeth. The pads of the waitress's shoes on hardwood, and the click of her ankles as she ferries hamburgers and beers from the kitchen and bar to tables. The front door opens and shuts, and there are bellows of greeting. All of this is subnoise. There is only Patsy's bell-clear voice of perfect pitch and the muted piano and steel guitar chords and tapping rhythm of the drums, this Wurlitzer of history spinning 10-inches through *I Fall to Pieces*, and offering no harbinger of the huge and horrific bashing and crashing rock and roll will one day become. This music is Esther's kingdom. She will defend it if necessary.

Esther permits no one access to the jukebox when she is practicing for her nascent Nashville career. Regulars know this and give her plenty of space. For months now her thighs have overhung the chair, this bit of furniture smallish under her. Her flesh rolls over the edges of the vinyl, but her voice possesses, indeed, such clarity that one wonders why she has not been discovered and whooshed away to a recording deal.

Those who come here often, growing weary of repeated administrations of Patsy's voice, have long since left off their complaints. But people unfamiliar with Esther and her ways, folks who happen on the roadhouse and want to hear other, more dissonant music, receive her sharp rebuke on approach, holding out their nickels. She waves arms at them, and flesh hanging from her moves without control. The waitresses bring her fries and milk shakes – you would think the shakes would gum things up in her vocal chords, but they do not – and she sings *Walkin' After Midnight*, knowing nothing of what she sings but the simple, compelling mechanics of it.

But G'vieve wants to dance a snappy number with her new young man. It is their third date and his name is Richard. He is an absolute dream, she thinks, and cannot believe her good fortune. Tonight they are planning a visit to the drive-in movies to see Natalie Wood in *Splendor in the Grass*, and she has run a brush through her hair more than a hundred times, and has applied very kissable lipstick in a mirror. G'vieve's skirt lays on her body exactly right, and her sweater is precisely taut so that, she believes correctly, Richard will want nothing so much as to come into contact, in some way, with her breasts. This she will allow – and even now, sitting down to supper with him, desires – perhaps as soon as moments away when she plugs the bright jukebox and they dance, bodies together.

"The woman there," G'vieve asks the waitress about Esther. "Odd that she sits so, hogging up the jukebox that way. Doesn't anyone here ever tire of it?"

"Sweetie, Esther's one of a kind." The waitress places their dinners before them, great, plate-spanning buns with meat at their cores, fries all red with catsup, and gigantic dill pickle slices. Coca-cola in tall tumblers, and red-piped straws standing erect from out of the fizz. "We

13

don't trouble her. People have tried, but I don't suggest it."

"The management allows this?" Richard says. "I mean, no one objects, and she's free to, to – monopolize the music?" He is pleased with himself for the intelligence, in front of G'vieve, of his inquiry. The long, impressive word. The waitress has turned to him during his question, which was really a pretty little speech.

"Hon, the management likes the fact Esther pops more nickels into that Wurlitzer than the rest of the town combined. And she ain't a bit hard to listen to. Now can I get you anything else?" She looks around to make the point there are other customers.

The pair nods overeagerly. "Oh no," G'vieve says. "This is perfect!" Her eyes make contact with Richard's and dance. She wants nothing to ruin their evening, and thus is of a mind to let this go, at least with their server anyway. After all, it is she and Richard's special night, one in which she plans delights for him, for them both. Things he surely desires, but will not believe his luck when they come true. For with a glance, she has made a discreet assessment of his auto's back seat and verified that it is wide. She transports herself, momentarily, a couple of hours ahead, to a largely ignored *Splendor in the Grass* casting movie light across them. Richard's trembling hands are warm on her. His fingers are perfectly shaped. There is the keen possibility of paradise.

Still, as she dabs fry grease from her fingers on a paper napkin and studies the knife line of Richard's oiled part, the repetition of the songs annoys her. And she has run out of clever dialogue with which to bewitch him.

"I can't believe that cow," she says, glancing toward the jukebox. The fat girl is just now singing a line, "...and then someday, you'd leave me for somebody new..." Her pudgy face is a mask of meaning and sorrow. Anguish is there, and a strange weeping without tears, and her neck is thrust forward toward the Wurlitzer so that the machine's dazzling lights illuminate her weirdly. Her flabby hands are clasped in her ample lap.

"Yes," Richard says. "She's definitely odd."

"Wouldn't you rather dance than listen to her moan?" G'vieve says. "I mean, really."

Richard says that he would dance with her if she'd like. "Let's be friendly, though," he suggests. But G'vieve already is up and over to the jukebox, and *I Fall to Pieces*'s last chords are drifting to a momentary silence. Esther digs in her small purse, which she has retrieved from next to her feet at the chair-legs, for another nickel.

"Excuse me," G'vieve says. "May I select just one song?" She has her nickel ready, out, displayed on her palm. Her intent cannot be mistaken. But Esther does not make any sort of acknowledgement. She feeds her own nickel to the machine – G'vieve watches the arc of her fist as she places the coin in the slot, hears it tumble and click through the jukebox's hidden chutes. There are only the two of them here, and G'vieve watches this as one would watch an accident form slowly, then happen slowly, then unfold its aftermath in the slow, unmetered absence of time. She cannot believe her own eyes, and the rudeness of this girl! What should she say?

"Didn't you hear me?"

Esther ignores the query as her fingers push the buttons whose algorithm will set in motion the machine's guts. Mechanisms click inside, an actuator lifting the selecting arm and moving to the indicated disk, selecting it gently – this marvel of robotics – placing the disk lightly on the platter. Spinning commences and the needle drops onto the outer edge. The tired opening strains of *You're Stronger than Me* spill like melted tin from the Wurlitzer's speakers.

"I heard you," Esther says. Then she begins to sing along.

Before G'vieve's eyes, the whole tableau blurs. Where she read WURLITZER, HI-FIDELITY across the top of the machine, there is now a jagged golden arc of electricity. The red lights that blinked merrily have now become a crimson wall. The golden W over one of the speakers looks like a malevolent scissors, or better, a blade. G'vieve could plunge it into this pig's heart.

"I..." she starts, and the word is bile on her lips. "I can't believe this!" She is shouting. Richard is somewhere behind her feeling foolish.

"Quiet!" Esther orders between the chorus and bridge. "Shhhh," she follows, "this is the best part. You'll like it, I promise."

But G'vieve is now like a locomotive, and slams herself into the

15

jukebox. The record skips. There is an abomination – the fracturing of Patsy Cline's voice and a horrible, subsequent amplified scratch that shears the roadhouse in half. Esther rises, as would Leviathan from a turbid sea. She faces this interloper while the record recovers and moves along with the song.

"You should'na done that," Esther says.

"You shouldn't pig up the music," G'vieve spits back. Esther dwarfs her, but G'vieve doesn't care. She wants justice and Richard's hands on her. The equation that will sum this is her own music – their special song, if it's on this machine – and a close dance of moist heat. All she wants is one song! It's a simple request, but it has all now gone far beyond what is reasonable.

Patrons have gathered around and are hooting. They'd like nothing more than to see the pair pull hair and send wallops bouncing off each other.

"Richard," G'vieve says, "tell this woman she shouldn't pig up the music." Her boyfriend stammers beside her, and there is no way to tell behind all the catcalls and hollering whether he obeys her command.

"You prissy little snot," Esther says. "Why don't you go back and sit down. I wasn't bothering you, not a bit."

"Yes," Richard says, "better yet, G'vieve, let's square away the check and leave."

His betrayal is like a blow. G'vieve studies him for a moment, his eyes, the intent behind them. She is disappointed – he is a meek man, something she had not known.

"Do as your boyfriend says," Esther commands. "He's a bright fellow."

But the crowd has tightened its circle. They want fisticuffs, or at minimum to witness some hair-yanking. "Come on ladies," someone yells. "Knock the shit outta each other, will ya!" The laughing becomes a tumult and G'vieve feels her face redden. Her neckline is hot. "Come on, Esther, slap 'er in the tits!" another voice shouts, lewdly, from the cover of anonymity. G'vieve's blood slams through the chambers of her heart, and the sides of her head.

"Go ahead," G'vieve says.

16

"Of course I will not," Esther says.

Having come to the precipice of brinksmanship, peered into the abyss and found it wanting, the two women take – inasmuch is possible – a step back from each other. G'vieve stumbles into Richard and they have made their contact. There is none of the pleasant shock G'vieve had anticipated. The crowd mutters a collective disappointment, and there is the voice of one of the waitresses imploring everyone to sit down, to go back to their seats.

"I just wanted to dance," G'vieve says, her confidence having fled.

"I just want to go to Nashville." Esther comes down off the balls of her feet.

G'vieve has the sudden notion that she has made herself silly in front of everyone, that she has ruined the evening for she and Richard. She searches for the appropriate way out of this. She makes herself conciliatory.

"You could, you know," she says.

"Could what?"

"Go... to Nashville, I mean."

"Yes?"

"With your voice."

Esther is suspicious. No one ever says anything to her by way of affirmation. She is wholly unfamiliar with the paths to reconciliation.

Is this what love is, G'vieve wonders as Richard fumbles across her body. The odor of carseat and man is upon her, and she is yielding with and without want. This goal of hers – to capture him in the back seat, to possess him, to make a hostage of him forever – is it this? His hands zealously under her sweater, on her breasts, her stomach, between her legs – is this it? The perfect fit of his fingers, slotted there – is it? Him inside her groaning – love?

Maybe, she concludes, and is still. There is only *Splendor in the Grass* and this lie.

In the chambers of G'vieve's heart this prevarication pumps until it is a false routine. Richard's touch is lukewarm on her skin. But she is determined to hold this captive. Believing against belief she has chosen right, that this will get better, that the movement of time will evolve their rawness into something refined and brilliant. She knows, already, that Richard is a clumsy fool. She understands that his betrayal at the roadhouse has given rise to resentment in her like the most remarkable poison. But, by way of repeated ministrations, she will change him. He is bound to come around.

Richard, for his part, is along for the fun. He enjoys, as would any man, screwing her. He's crazy for it. In his mind, it is he who possesses, and it is he who knows this is totally wrong and bankrupt. There is nothing of merit here.

"I love you," he lies.

"Oh darling," she says. "Come here."

And again and again he complies.

In the roadhouse, Esther's voice matches Patsy's with perfect fidelity. She is in her place as G'vieve enters. Not a soul notices, no one recalling the two at loggerheads months ago. G'vieve has been drawn here, wholly against reason and her wishes, with no intent in mind except to have an alcoholic drink and listen to the gorgeous mimicry of the fat woman. She cannot remember even that Esther is her name.

G'vieve has her drink – it's gin and some soda in a small glass. She decides to smoke a cigarette and asks for one from a kind-looking, barstooled older man whom she has never seen before. A safe man, someone who would not, by appearances, attempt anything beyond companionable conversation. Even that he doesn't muster, parting with the cigarette and returning to focus on the melting ice cubes in his own glass. She lights the smoke with a match from a book placed at the center of an ashtray on the bar. The fat woman's voice is rising in chorus. No one is paying any attention to her singing. She is a picture on the wall they have passed a thousand times on the way to the men's or ladies' rooms.

Yet for G'vieve, Esther's voice is like that of an angel's. In its plainfelt grief is succor and salve for G'vieve's fractured heart. And as well for the minuscule tributary heart that beats deep in her, the heart of her son or daughter, immaturely formed yet still passing the lie from chamber to tiny chamber, but at the same time distilling the lie, so that it becomes clearer and clearer as a lie with each beat.

G'vieve, after several alcoholic drinks and bummed cigarettes, suffers the need to commune with Esther, or, more properly, with the voice emanating from Esther. Tipsy, she totters from the barstool in the jukebox's direction. Esther is passionately in chorus, her fingers around a milk shake. Her voice washes G'vieve and is drunk in, much smoother than the gin and nicotine, like a great narcotic pleasant to both mother and child, and then the song is finished. As Esther reaches for her purse and a new nickel, she notices G'vieve's shoes. Her gaze travels upward to a forgotten but familiar face. The woman's arms are crossed under her breasts, held close, as one would carry a secret.

"I remember you."

"I wanted to say I'm sorry about that night." The apology comes out slurred from lips without lipstick. G'vieve waits, thinking, hoping, needing that everything will be all right, that forgiveness is forthcoming.

"You said I could go," Esther recalls.

"Go?" G'vieve dumbly echoes this word. Go? There is no sense in what she has heard. Her arms drop to her sides.

"To Nashville. You said I could go to Nashville." Esther remembers their altercation only for its finish, for its strange affirmation at the close of hostilities. "You and a man, the man who was with you."

G'vieve folds into weeping at the mention of him. If she could see through her burgeoning tears, she would see that Esther appears struck with question. What had she said to produce this flow? And though Esther may be simple, she is observant after a fashion, and can add two and two. Now that the woman's arms are down, Esther sees the rise of her belly. Sees that the woman wears no diamond band.

"He did this," Esther says.

G'vieve nods.

"And left," Esther concludes.

Not so much as left, but rather, simply walled himself off from her so that his indifference became intolerable. With a crawling desperation G'vieve had informed Richard of their pregnancy. She expected an immediate proposal, he in her grasp now forever. None was offered and worse, he fell to visiting less often, then sporadically, and finally, her telephone calls rang unanswered. She had not seen or heard from Richard in five or six weeks.

G'vieve is able to make her body stop shaking, stanches the flow of her tears. "It was important," she says, "for me to apologize." She has no idea why, except that righting the wrong of that night perhaps is the first step of righting the wrong of all the nights and days since. Esther has paused with her coin, an event almost without precedent. G'vieve has her attention, and it is an attention of solace or sympathy or some sort of good, nice feeling. Its exact name is unknown to her. Still, she is capable only, at this juncture, of staring at the pregnant woman, searching for words.

"Won't you come away and talk to me?" G'vieve says.
Esther nods and rises from the chair. She stoops to retrieve her purse, collects it, and follows G'vieve to a booth. In no time, there is coffee steaming before them. Their conversation is natural and easy, a pleasing surprise for both. The coffee sobers G'vieve a bit. They are the same age. Esther thinks G'vieve is beautiful. And Esther, despite the hundred pounds she has on G'vieve, is pretty as well – or seems so, to G'vieve, when she studies Esther's face. They share their names. Esther is named for a queen who saved her people – that's what her mother and father, who are long dead, told her. G'vieve's full given name is Genevieve, but her sisters shortened it when they were all small and fatherless, and it stuck. They allow each other the privilege of secrets and desires and dreams, Esther to sing, G'vieve to be needed.

The oddest, most lovely moment of her life: When they part, Esther kisses her on her bare, soft lips. Not a kiss intended for passion, but nevertheless, her body is electrified, and the baby's as well. Voltage caroms off her soul.

What's more, Esther is with her, singing softly *Leavin' On Your Mind* and *Back in Baby's Arms* when she reaches full dilation. G'vieve

20

insists the doctors and nurses allow her in the birthing room. Hours afterward, the first thing her son will hear are the lucid bells of Esther's voice, and his birth-squalls will rise and merge with her, and G'vieve's laughter of relief and joy will conjoin their music, and the chambers of their hearts will be the chambers of one heart, and their song will be as beautiful as anything on the earth's face since its beginning.

The longest bus G'vieve can imagine takes Esther away. There is the diesel roar of its departure, a great grayish-black cloud that belches from it, in the full light of a clear mid-day, and tiny Andrew is swaddled in a carrier on the sidewalk at her feet as the bus recedes to a vanishing point down the highway on the thunderhead-topped horizon. NASHVILLE read the destination on the front, atop the vast windshield.

"I love you," Esther had said. She embraced G'vieve, Andrew in his striped T-shirt and jumper shorts at their skirts, looking around at all the giant things.

"Oh sweetheart," G'vieve said. "I know you'll knock 'em dead." A Negro man, wearing a blue uniform, loaded suitcases into the bus's undercarriage.

"Ma'am," he said, momentarily interrupting their goodbyes, "May I take your case, there?" He pointed at her luggage. Andrew gabbled at the air.

"Of course, thank you," Esther said. They all laughed at Andrew, who looked up to take into himself the sounds of their joy. He could not know of the sadness underpinning it. G'vieve lifted him out of the carrier with a gentle swoop, pretended he was an airplane, made engine sounds for his delight. The porter took the suitcase away.

"Be safe," G'vieve said.

"Be good." Esther embraced her again, the baby between them. Andrew's baby scent rose. Please say it, Esther thought. The part about love.

And now, as the bus disappears toward the stormclouds, G'vieve says it: "I love you."

That the wipers could not keep clear the bus's massive windshield in a merciless rainstorm a hundred and twelve miles up the highway, G'vieve could not have known. That the driver would realize, too late, that he had exceeded in speed the safe envelope of the bus's operation, she could never have predicted. It could not be, in any guesswork her imagination could have produced, that its tires lost contact with the asphalt and it would swerve, then spin lengthwise, trading front for back, catapulting several occupants from their seats. That Esther would never get her audition.

"I love you." All she said, too long after the words could do any good, but hoping they would fly from the chambers of her heart like birds to catch the vanishing bus.

March 5, 1963.

A taxi and takeoff, Kansas City, Missouri, in the exhaust. The wall of a storm. A blind fall onto the Tennessee countryside, the huge energy impact of a small airplane near Highway 70 just west of Camden. A hollow known to locals as Fatty Bottom, along the line of a heavily wooded ridge. A small and large body come together, and make a memory of that voice, that perfect clarity, the grief of bells now made plain and irrefutable.

Hundreds of miles away, even today, an inscription on Virginia H. "Patsy Cline" Dick's headstone: "Death cannot kill what never dies – love."

Two sweeping sorrows, and we are only beginning.

As Many Hands As God

He used to enjoy the feel of her hands on him. Now he regards that same touch as cloying – a grasping, confining thing – and at the same time believes he is unworthy of it.

"Orange," she whispers, using, as she nearly always does, his last name, the name of his business, "you pull away, baby."

"I can't explain it," he says, placing safe space between them. He looks at his own hands, the backs of them. Spreads his fingers, supposing the wrong lies in them, that they have fashioned nothing but wrong things. That he has made manifest careless decisions with them. Weighing this against his fatigue, kernels of resentment tumble there, clot in the raised veins he stares at. They breed malignancy in the fifty-four bones of his hands. Byron Orange clutches them tightly into fists and takes another step away from her.

"Orange?" she asks. The sound of his name rattles like the sound of all names that have been lost. It covers expanding air between them, but snuffs out when it reaches his ears. In the street outside, the percussive pass of something large and diesel powered. Annie has made him a lunch and packed it in a stainless steel lunchbox. Its lid cradles a thermos of black coffee. In cellophane bags are a tuna sandwich, a dill pickle, and corn chips. There is a small paper napkin folded once. She turns to lift the lunch from the counter, offers her gift of service from the side so he cannot see she has started crying. She feels him take the lunchbox, the absence of weight in her hand. There is the screen door's sound, and the firing of his engine outside in the dark.

Orange turned his tar truck over on a slick winter morning. A veil of rain that was almost ice had been pissing down for several hours – he recalled hearing all night fat drops on the roof as sleep failed him. There had been no opportunity to react, to steer out of the slide and ensuing catastrophe. The driver of an auto so small and low as to be undetectable as it revved up alongside had accelerated, slid forward into his lane, and had lost control. The vehicle spun once in front of him and, without any volition, Orange's hands spun his own wheel. In all of his life he had never been so hopeless as when his tar truck lifted itself onto two wheels, paused there while momentum and the center of gravity consulted physical laws, and shrieked onto its side. The windows – all safety glass – broke in a thousand ways but held their shape.

Belted in, he drew a short breath and held it. He was nearest the pavement, that is, the truck had gone over on the driver's side. Through the shattered window he could see lights of various colors, but they were fractalized in the facets of the webbed glass. He let out his breath. Took stake of himself – was he badly hurt anywhere? – and discovered that no, he was fine. His blood pumped in his head. He saw that the lunchbox had come open, the modest lunch strewn along his thigh. The thermos lay next to his head on broken glass. It would be broken inside, shards and coffee. It occurred to him to worry about a fire, and he released the buckle of his safety belt. Awkwardly, he extricated himself. The sandwich in its bag fell to his feet. Glass crunched under his work boots as he stood on the driver's side window. The bench seat to one side of him, the shattered windshield to the other, he was put in mind of the dimensions of an odd closet or phone booth. He lifted his boot into a crook of the steering column, stepped further onto the gear lever and, crouching midway on his climb out, lifted the heavy passenger-side door open as if he were emerging through the hatch of a submarine. He grasped the jamb, holding the door – which wanted to close again – open with the top of his head. His bare fingers clutched for anything that might serve as a handhold, but discovered only slippery road grit. Nevertheless, he pulled himself out and let the hatch shut next to him. He looked around in pre-dawn, the absence of light.

The agent of this disaster, the driver of the small car, had apparently regained control and sped off. Perhaps he or she hadn't even been aware of the accident. It is possible, Orange thought, that the driver, having recovered a seemingly hopeless predicament, had simply continued on – adrenaline-charged, to be sure, and more cautiously as rain continued to fall. But oblivious to Orange's sad condition.

Orange, at first, did not discern the odor of leaking tar. Like a man who works as a chef and can no longer smell cuisine, or a sailor on a trawler no longer sensitive to spilled guts and fish oil, Orange was immune to the aroma of roof tar. He saw, instead, great billows of steam rising. In the sweep of headlamps passing across the highway barrier in the opposite direction, he saw, at the tank's orifice, tar spilling forth. It dropped onto the pavement and spread in a pool so black as to open a massive hole in the earth. Cars had begun to queue behind him, and he realized the attitude of his broken, bubbling truck blocked the way totally. He sat atop the wreck for a few moments longer. He watched his own breath make steam in the cold air. He noted that many of the blocked cars executed tight three-point turns and attempted to drive against the flow, seeking another turnoff. He imagined their drivers taking personal umbrage, incensed that some fool had shut off their route to work and thus inconvenienced their morning commute. They would be on cellular phones now, braying to answering machines or voice mail, or workmates who had arrived early and waited for them in their offices, about the idiot who had spilled over his tar truck and made impassable their street. Dumb Ass. Dipshit. Motherfucker. Orange imagined all these words – new names for him, synonyms for Byron Orange – spilling from their lips, carried on digital pulses through the atmosphere which still dropped rain, rain.

Down the clogged road he saw the lights of a police cruiser. Its siren called a single, piercing glissando at intervals to clear the way before. The oscillating blue from atop the car made Orange think of dazzling, brilliant gemstones he would never, ever buy Annie. Not now. The cop pulled up cautiously, braking several yards from Orange just at the pool's frontier. Without warning, the searchlamp mounted on the cruiser's quarter panel blazed. Orange squinted into the candlepower, the light of an approaching locomotive that would soon grind him. The amplified voice that came from the light was a woman's.

"Are you all right?" she asked.

"Yes," he shouted, and nodded in an exaggerated manner so the policewoman could see from across the distance.

"Stay where you are," she commanded.

The amplification rendered the intent behind her command

impossible to discern. Was she angry, Orange wondered. Would he be ticketed? He shielded his eyes from the light with one hand. His fingers were growing numb and cold breeze chilled him despite his parka.

The policewoman and her partner – a male – emerged from the car and made an assessment. They held a brief conference. The policeman stepped to the rear of the car and opened the trunk. The policewoman skirted the tar pool and arrived smartly aside the cab. She looked up and trained a flashlight on him.

"Sir," she said, "we got a real mess on our hands here."

"Yes."

"We're going to have to get you down and talk about it."

"I can get down O.K."

She nodded, then gestured at the tar. "We're probably going to have to call for a HazMat cleanup."

"Looks that way." He hadn't meant it to sound flippant.

"Well," she said, and paused.

Dawn evolved, slowly, about them, so that a dull half-light informed her features. Not especially attractive, Orange thought. The corners of her mouth turned down in a way that seemed like a frown, even as she looked around. He saw – of course – that she carried a weapon. Two weapons, a baton and a pistol, at her belt. He heard her speak again.

"Yes?" he asked.

"I said come on down then."

Orange evaluated descent routes. Then, instead, he decided to leap. It was seven feet – at most maybe eight. His boots hit the pavement first, as planned. His body, however, unwieldy and frigid from sitting cross-legged atop the cab, folded onto itself and he went over on one side.

"Are you all right, sir?" Her frown hovered over him. He scrambled to his feet, not answering.

"What happened here, sir?" she asked, but before he began an explanation, she added, as if in afterthought, "Do you have a license I could look at?"

He fished for his wallet and watched the policeman set orange cones around the spill. Then the male cop stepped to the first, stalled car and gave the driver instructions. Down the way, Orange could see the lights of a second police cruiser. He looked at the tar pool again. The bubbling from the tank's cap had slowed to a torpid ooze. He wished for everything, for all of this, that he could bend down, form his freezing hands into a ladle, and scoop the tar pool – handful by handful – back into its place.

Also, his business was failing. This fact he kept from Annie, instead growing more anxious with each frivolous purchase she made. He would fall silent and petulant when she arrived from the grocer with flowers or an obscure single-purpose kitchen implement. Of what use is a melon-ball scoop in a household of hidden crisis? The capital from his father-in-law was consumed. Numbers with parentheses around them blemished, in far too many places, his statement of earnings. His balance sheet carried a weight of short- and long-term debt that would stagger him when he paused to consider it. Free cash flow was a problem in that meeting payroll – his own and that of his two assistants – was always an unsure thing. Orange Tar Roofing Incorporated was a firm on a precipice. In the canyon below waited a rockslide of bankruptcy, or worse. And this Orange hid from his wife.

Byron Orange labored over the books late at night, as if his work ethic or power of will would change the facts. His father-in-law, a brilliant businessman, had encouraged Orange to take evening classes in business management, so that his decisions regarding tar roofing would be fiscally informed. "Understand the numbers," Annie's father advised. Then the distinguished, successful man offered a slogan: "The data will set you free." His father-in-law grinned, as if this bumper-sticker, fortune-cookie scrip were the sum total of all the ages' wisdom. The man clapped Orange on the back and shook his son-in-law's hand vigorously. Then he kissed his daughter – standing in their presence as regarded and silent as a coat rack – on the forehead, and departed Orange's home office for a Rotary meeting.

Orange thought of this now: *The data will set you free.* He looked, again, at his ledgers and the numbers blurred into Cyrillic forms. The columns merged in gray, cascaded onto their plinths. The balustrades of bookkeeping snapped under the weight of his accident, the spilled tar, the fines. "Beat the data and it will confess," he muttered, and it was like blasphemy. He closed the ledger, opened the top drawer of his desk and placed it, with the calculator whose keys his fingers had been poking half-hearted, inside. He closed the drawer and laid his hands on the desktop and studied them. He thought of killers' hands, how evidence of skin or fiber is retrieved from under fingernails and a story of homicide is built around these unlikely things. Under his fingernails was packed roof tar. He folded his arms and laid his head on them.

Byron Orange dreamed that he was a god. He was not the Christian god, the Sistine hand-extended god, the god who's got the whole world in His hands. Not the god whose hands wipe away every tear at the End of the Age. Rather, he was one of the gods of India or Pakistan or Vietnam, or somewhere where women go wrapped in dyed sheets and are veiled and do not carry sidearms or batons or write citations. He was a variegated god whose arms sprung from his back where wingroots would have blossomed had he dreamed, instead, that he was an angel. There were many arms and, at the ends of them, many hands. He was a god who rode on the backs of henna-dotted elephants. There was incredible, elaborate, articulate design that articulated his deity, and his dozens of hands, scores, no, hundreds of hands, were the agency of his omnipotence. He was marveling, in the dream, at these hands and the synchrony and beauty and utility of all their works. Some of the hands built wonders, others sustained civilizations. A group of them wrote out profundities, and he marveled at how the balletic collaboration of muscles and tendons formed symbols on thick sheaves of papyrus. Flexors bent his fingers. Extensors straightened the digits. He executed, on pages, intricacies, machinations, whole epics.

But the dream shifted and suddenly there were stumps fanned out – the ends of the wrists now flung toward the world and the universe, gnarled and blackened things like burnt hands or the hands of lepers: carpus, metacarpus, phalanges dissolved into ash. Everything they had held or fashioned collapsed. And the entropy was absolute.

God must have many hands, he thought upon waking, if he is capable – as the Bible asserts – of numbering each hair on each head of each human being.

It was excruciating when he told her. All of it spilled out of him in a rush, as tar will from an upset tank, hot and reeking and black and slippery. Annie wanted to put her arms around him, to sit on the sofa and cradle Orange's head as he confessed, but he remained a safe, sullen distance from her.

"Here's how it is," he began. "I can't keep it together."

Annie was silent, only her eyes pleaded for elaboration.

"The truck," he started again.

"It wasn't your fault," she blurted.

"No – that's not it. I know that. The thing is, I can't buy a new one." His voice rose in pitch. "I can't make it happen." He held his palms up as supplicants do.

"Please," she said. "Talk with me. Help me understand. I want to understand."

He told her about the accident fines, the failing business, his embarrassment with regard to her father. He admitted that he must file for protection from his creditors. That he had let his assistants go, that Orange Tar Roofing Incorporated lay in shambles. He would not look at her as he confessed these things.

His wife stood silent for some time. Then she crossed the room and sat down on the opposite end of the sofa from him. There was not a trace of fear or defeat or brokenness in her manner, but, rather, an obstinate resolve.

"First of all, my father can go to hell," Annie said. It surprised him, the way she spat it, the defiance that it came enveloped in. "And I don't give a damn about the business," she added. He looked up into her eyes and saw that she was earnest, that these declarations were true and zealous and emanated from the core of her.

"What I do give a damn about is my husband. That is what I care about. You, our marriage. Us. It's falling apart, Orange."

Byron Orange's guts split in half and he felt raw heat rushing to his face and head and neck. "You don't understand," he snarled. He bolted up off the couch and stood pointing at Annie. "You don't know the first thing about it. I'm a complete fuck-up, totally. There's nothing that won't turn to shit if I touch it. You can't just sit there and tell me you don't believe this, that you don't know this about me."

While Orange raged, she sat with her fingers laced in her lap. His invective slammed into her. Some of what he shouted – no matter how determined she was to keep reason and calmness in her own soul and demeanor – raised wounds on her flesh. His rage bloomed and roiled like an atomic cloud, but it wasn't really him shouting now: the words derived from his hopeless anger. Even so, some of what he said bit hard. But she let him continue until he was spent. Their living room was quiet except for the sound of an auto passing outside.

Then she stood and said, "Come here."

But Orange would not move. He stood with his arms folded across his chest, recalcitrant.

"Come here, Byron, right now." And this time, she let neediness creep into her command. She saw that he appeared uncertain, breached. The use of his given name. "Please, baby." His chest rose and fell as he panted – his arms fell to his sides and his shoulders dropped with them. Still, he did not come. She must cross the room to him. There was nothing left to do. The only possibility of his redemption was in the notion that she might make a final attempt. It was unfair – it *is* unfair, she thought. *I have been with you every step of the way, through all of it, yet you reject me.* Annie wanted to strike him, to beat his face in, and she wanted to hold him and draw her husband close to salve his defeat. To cross, for good, the space that separated them. This she did, took a step and another, and arrived close to him. Annie lifted her arms to gather Orange, and he lifted his own reflexively to push her away. But she had anticipated this and pushed his arms back down, and then drew him to her so that their bodies came together as they used to, when they slow-danced in high-school and later, early in their union, at the American Legion hall. "Don't push me away anymore," she whispered. "Ever again, no. Don't do it. Don't lose me. Don't lose me."

And she felt all the springs in his body uncoil, tension unbinding in the hard meat and sinew of him. It flowed out of his feet onto the carpet. Annie's hand cupped the nape of his neck and pulled his face onto her neck. "Say something, Orange. Whisper it."

"I love you," he said. "I'm sorry."

They danced with no music.

For the second time this night, Annie and Byron are making love while raindrops tap lightly on their rooftop.

Earlier – for the first time in months – they had indulged a frantic, urgent coupling. The starvation and near death of intimacy between them had produced the need to feast. There was no other way, at first, for them to sate themselves and consummate reconciliation. The bedlamps had remained on illuminating their forms in collision.

Now they move slowly, in great, deep pleasure. They have killed the lamps, abandoning light for gentle darkness. Their flesh cycles as he moves in her. He kisses every part of her neck and mouth and ears, and he tastes her sweat and moves to suck lightly all the skin of her breasts. She wraps her legs around his buttocks, crosses and locks her ankles. She finds his right hand and takes his fingertips in her mouth. She grips his fingers between her lips and moves her tongue across them.

The sheets under them are damp and hold in their heat. The scents of sex and her perfume rise and commingle. Annie's back arches and her hips rise to him. Her hands clench his biceps. Although it is dark, their eyes are locked, and they each see that far at the core of them is love that forever eschews abandonment of any sort. At precisely the same moment they come together, and it seems that they are washed by a high tide that bashes the shoreline, again and again, with foamy, delicious waves. When the waves subside, she finds that Orange is still hard and moving, again. She is delighted and eager, and accepts him there – in this and in all ways – with joy.

31

Later, in the moments before fatigue settles down and sleep may soon come, they still touch one another. It is as if their hands refuse to cease caressing, having remained aloof and immobile and unpracticed for so long. Orange's hands stroke her skin. Annie's fingertips flit across his body like moths. Orange closes his eyes.

His wife's hands cover him like a blanket.

Babe in Arms: A Still Life

Manprasad Lakshmanan, Bangladeshi-American, sits in a hard pew and stares through dry eyes at a marble urn. He can scarcely appreciate the eulogizer's words; his minister's voice is like the far buzzing of an insect. Deepali, Manprasad's wife, sits on his left, face set as a president on the obverse of an American coin. A minor Thursday breeze is flowing through the open windows of the church – Manprasad senses its caress on his cheek. He refuses to weep. His throat is clenched. *I believed in your Son; why have you taken MINE?*

It wasn't that Lokprakash had neglected a life jacket. No, the coroner had been clear on that in an unnecessary way that indicated approval. As if in having taken at least this precaution, his son had mitigated any condemnation as regards foolishness. The boy had simply been swept by current, his canoe inverted in rapid water, into a stone. A random death. Manprasad broods over this – that a riverstone, laid centuries in its bed, struck at that moment his son, and stove in his twelve-year-old head. The coroner had described this as head trauma. The bruise was raw, swelled, the color of eggplant skin. Just at the juncture of Lokprakash's hairline, at that familiar spot where strands rose into a part from his widow's peak. Manprasad imagines the happy scruffy feeling on his fingertips as he'd tousle his son's head – so many, many times. Touch had always been important in their communication, his touch on his son, his son's touch on him. There is only a phantom ache there, now, in his grasp.

He was furious with Deepali this morning. Unkind to her on this, the day of her child's memorial. When the couple had returned from the morgue Sunday afternoon, Manprasad had closed the door to Lokprakash's room. The boy's bed lay unmade, Oakland Raiders sheets roughed, pillowcase awry. His son's basketball shorts remained wadded where the boy had left them, at the room's center. But Deepali had opened the room this morning, gathered the bedclothes, the shorts, completed a final laundering. Manprasad had wanted this task for himself, to hold the cloth in his hands and drink in, a last time, Lokprakash's scent. His wife shrank from him as he raved, but could not cry. Deepali, stoic, simply left the hallway where Manprasad shouted his disappointment, steeped a cup of tea. Moments later, appreciating the awfulness of his behavior, Manprasad sought a reconciling embrace. Deepali hung on his arms as limp as a robe.

In their darkened home over the week, Manprasad had found himself anticipating during still moments – and they were all still – the bounding of Lokprakash's feet across carpet, the lilt of his voice. Its timbre had lately been evolving toward that of a young man's, deepening in unexpected squeaks and pops. Manprasad would have admonished him gently for the unmade bed, the dirty laundry abandoned in his room rather than the hamper. But instead of his son's words, the telephone would violate the silence. The parents of his child's friends would express condolences, offer help with small tasks, clarify details on the memorial service. Despite the exoticness of his skin among white children, Lokprakash had attracted many friendships.

As the minister continues, Manprasad reviews, again, the confluence of circumstances that resulted in Lokprakash's death. True to his vocation, he parses through them algebraically, as if they are elements of a mathematical problem. He sits uncomfortable, frustrated there remain none of God's algorithms to apply, to derive a solution. All denominators and divisors result in Lokprakash's wet appointment with a stone. Manprasad is confounded that God, who so perfectly ordered the universe with patterns and symmetry and purpose, has committed such a colossal blunder, has taken an interregnum from precision, in his son's demise.

Spuriously, Manprasad recalls his migration from Dhaka – 7,700 miles and a third of a sphere distant – Deepali pregnant with Lokprakash. He was a gifted engineer in his twenties, and Bangladesh required gifted engineers. But to be affiliated ethnically with the Hindu minority, and even further divided from his family in his conversion to the true faith – this had been overwhelming. He'd sought employment in the United States, found it, flown to Delhi then Tokyo and, finally, San Francisco with his second-trimester wife, planted them in Palo Alto. Lokprakash's birth had been a validation of their blessings, verification that God and his son Jesus Christ smiled on them from Heaven and approved.

But now he is struggling with a blasphemy – that Jehovah and Shiva are not all that different. Creators, yes, but destroyers as well.

The urn in which Lokprakash's remains rest is of marble. Its shape reminds Manprasad of a vase his grandmother displayed, enmantled in her small apartments in Chittagong. The marble's visual texture is like a network of veins. Sienna arteries on tan medium. *A riverstone to the head!* Manprasad visits alternate sets of circumstances, unfoldings of events that culminate not in this abomination, not in Lokprakash's ashes, but in his unremarkable return from the canoeing. His son is soaked to the skin, hungry, but flushed with his recreation. Deepali feeds him a largish supper. The condition of his room is addressed. Or, at the outset, Manprasad and Deepali hear of the proposed Sunday of canoeing and refuse to let their son participate. There are other, more important, objectives with which to fill a Sunday after church. Any one of them could have sufficed. What if Lokprakash had never met Trent Evans in the sixth grade, or what if he met him but never developed a companionship? Or if the canoes had been launched a minute earlier or later, would that have perturbated the outcome? Would the flow of current differ so over the ordered course of moments?

Manprasad is determined not to weep. His brain has sent this stricture to the nerves that stimulate tear ducts at the corners of his eyes. They are in rebellion, and tears are there, just below the lids. They may be a blink from spilling over. But so far he is the master. The tightness in his throat feels material, like he has improperly swallowed a large, dry bite. The minister continues. Manprasad is aware that the smallish church is filled to overflowing, that some mourners and those connected with mourners must stand in the narthex. He is aware that the Evans' are in attendance – Bill Evans, Trent's father, had proffered a consoling hug as people were assembling. And although Manprasad indicts no one in the accident that claimed Lokprakash, he is unwilling and unready for contact of this sort.

There is a moment where he considers a bargain with God: *If you bring my son to life again I will serve you perfectly.* I will be a better husband, father, friend. I will be kinder. I will give all my money to the church. I

35

will, I will… But in the same breath he knows that this kind of struggling faith, the kind that teeters on a precipice, will not be rewarded. His second bargain with God goes thus: *If I curse you, you will accept it deservedly, and it will have no bearing on my salvation. None whatsoever.*

And in the moment Manprasad considers the nature of his curse – whether he will offer it in prayer or whether he will stand erect during the eulogizer's verbal ministrations and proclaim it – there is a materialization at the corner of his right eye, in the church's single, center aisle. A small hand is laid upon his shoulder.

Mrs. Wilmott stands above the pew, unconcerned about the inquisitive eyes of those in attendance. The minister pauses in his remarks – Mrs. Wilmott, who is young, in her early twenties, cradles her sleeping baby Millicent Anna Wilmott. With a soft intentness, she offers Millicent into Manprasad's arms. He is unsure of what to do, but she has engineered this gesture so that he has no option but to accept the child. The infant, undisturbed by the exchange, breathes tiny aspirations as he supports her head. His eyes wander the new terrain of her delicate face as Mrs. Wilmott returns to her husband a few pews back. Their minister continues.

The scent that rises from Millicent calls Manprasad to a God from whom he is shrinking. Talc and lotions, freshly laundered blankets – these are odors that envelop Manprasad in a brief daydream of Lokprakash's infancy. The baby's breathing, his hearing of it, is like a lens – those things near are in clear focus, those things far are happening away from him. There is only Millicent's face and all its meaning.

Her eyes, for instance. Lidded in her nap, he sees them move gently as if under a cover of vellum. The membranes of her lids are so thin, Manprasad may study the network of veins and arteries that branches within them. They are like filaments with which he may stitch together the shards of his heart.

There is the flawlessness of Millicent's forehead, blond curls latent against her Caucasian skin. The infinitesimal symmetry of her miniature ears. Tiny lips, pursed as flowerpetals. Her nose, turned up at the end with nostrils no larger than decimals. Manprasad brings his right hand along her stomach, over soft cotton, across her chest and chin to feel her exhalations. They are warm and dry against his palm, miniscule twin air-jets that validate life and promise.

Millicent opens her eyes. This sudden unveiling startles Manprasad, who shifts his buttocks on the pew and in so doing, jostles the infant into alertness. There is a communion that follows, eye on eye, his brown, hers a life-deep blue that may change, as infants' eyes customarily do. But for now they are rich, communicative. *There is life,* she vows. *There is life.*

Manprasad weeps.

He weeps clutching her to him, to his chest, to his lungs, his heart, his organs. To his marrow he brings Millicent and drinks of her promise. Tears fall from his eyes like mountain cataracts drop to the sea and are never refused. He looks at Lokprakash's urn no more, but steals a gaze at the ceiling where angels of succor muster. A mote of faith, seed-sized, may have returned to dwell and grow again in Manprasad's crushed heart. Millicent Anna Wilmott perhaps has fulfilled, even now, her short life's purpose.

Deepali flutters his thigh with her hand, seeks his fingers that cup Millicent's head, laces her hand around his, around her skull. Manprasad glances at her, sees she too has released, finally, tears.

The eulogizer concludes his business. Manprasad unknots his grief from around a core of hope. He hugs the child to the two of them, slowly rocking.

Under Cover of Snow

     A mass of unknown constitution in her left breast, and Vanessa stares from the dining-room window through rainfall into the backyard. She hasn't told Harold about this. In thirty-eight years of marriage, the lump isn't the first secret she has kept from him. But it may be the most significant. Her lips are a thin line as doubt metastasizes in her.

     The ticking of the clock above their table. The patter of drops on the skylight. The sighs and settlings of their house. Sounds that provide underpinning as Vanessa thinks one thing: It's malignant and will kill me; then another: It's surely benign. All this worry is for nothing. Unproductive. She glances from the soaked back yard to the clock. Harold will be back in a few minutes. With him will be her granddaughter Cassandra, and Cassie's new husband, Paul, of whom they know nothing. Except that Paul is twenty-two and Cassie nineteen, and that they met at school, and that they were married by a justice of the peace before informing anyone. "The Lees," they are called. Paul and Cassandra Lee. Mr. And Mrs. Paul Lee. Even so, Vanessa thinks, the season for forgiveness is upon us. She believes she is ready, already, to forgive her one grandchild's thoughtlessness, this reckless act. Nineteen years old!

     She glances through the alcove at her and Harold's Christmas tree. They have left the lights off today, and it looks paltry underneath with just one present remaining, a set of table dishes for Cassie and Paul. "They are starting their new home," Vanessa had told her husband. "They will appreciate practical things." Harold had squinted, processing this, then suggested tools – a hammer, screwdriver set, and so forth. Vanessa overruled her husband, put the stoneware on their credit card.

     Now she hopes the telephone will ring before they return. The nice technician at the mammography center had supposed results might be available as soon as twenty-four hours. An image of the massive white machine recurs to her, and she shudders anew thinking of the plastic paddles closing on her breasts. Squeezing the tissue flat so a strange pain had radiated from her chest across her shoulders and arms, down into her belly. All the way into her back. Diagnostic mammography, the technician had explained. Courteous words had spilled from her mouth, words intended to calm and explain. Vanessa recalled a description of how the process is performed, the low-level x-rays, what they look for on the films. The minor reassurances that two-thirds of these lumps turn out benign. That they could be masses of another, unworrisome sort: harmless cysts, other "anomalies," as the technician had put it. *Blah blah blah.* All she could think of as the paddles squeezed was how Harold had enjoyed nothing so much as the first time he saw them. She had tried to abrogate the pain with thoughts of his first handling of them, his fingertips, his greedy mouth. The wonderful, delicious impatience of him. It had worked for a moment, these reflections on the simplicity of her husband.

Vanessa turns from the tree to stare outside again. Imagines that her breast hurts. Wonders what the mass will look like on the films. The rainfall has abated, and she can see that the outdoor thermometer mounted on the window frame reads in the mid-thirties. The weather report had speculated about snow. For now, fog has mustered in the back yard – she can still see the fence, but the back of their neighbor's house behind them, sixty yards away, is almost obscured.

Her teakettle summons its whistle. It begins as a bare murmur, which only just registers, then climbs insistently so Vanessa slides off the chair at the window and scrambles to the stovetop to stop it. Pours boiling water into a mug with a teabag. Watches the tea dye the water, slowly but inexorably, darkness overcoming light.

Please ring, she thinks, but the damned phone will not.

On her counter, the half mug of tea has gone tepid. The teabag's paper and string are glued to the mug's wall. Vanessa realizes small snowflakes have started falling. Then there are the muffled sounds of Harold's arrival with the kids, car doors opening and closing outside.

As Vanessa rises the front door is thrown open. "Grandma?" Cassandra's voice reminds her of the bell-choir at Advent Service. "Are you downstairs?"

Vanessa crosses through the alcove between the dining- and

39

living rooms, and there is her lovely grandchild, Cassie, down-jacketed, slipping her shoes off already and simultaneously unwinding a plaid scarf, shaking her head so her ponytail flaps behind her. The child's cheeks are red from the cold outside, or perhaps flushed from the heater in Harold's car. Cassie's lips form a joyful O the color of a rose. She leaps into Vanessa's embrace and folds her small body into her grandmother's. Vanessa, beneath her own skin, feels like bursting forth. The scent of her grand-daughter rises, herbal, not floral – the soap she is using – as Cassie clings to her. "Grandma," Cassandra whispers. "I'm so, so happy to see you." Outside, behind Cassie, Harold and the new grandson are wrestling luggage. Vanessa can hear their masculine sounds. How clumsy and oafish men are she thinks, disengages the hug, examines her pretty granddaughter with her hands on Cassie's upper arms. "You are so lovely," she says. Cassie's smile is electric, brown eyes twinkling below a conservative application of bluish shadow. She looks untouched and clean. "How was your flight?"

Cassie explains that it was fine, bumpy at the end, but the captain had come on and warned them it might be. "Have you eaten?" Vanessa asks. Cassie makes an absent reference to airline breakfast, but it's clear she wants to tell her grandmother something else, and finally does. It comes as only two words: "My husband." Cassie points with a thumb back over her shoulder. Vanessa can see moistness at the corners of her granddaughter's eyes. "I want you to meet Paul. He's helping Grandpa. I mean, they're helping each other." Cassie giggles as Vanessa dabs from her grandchild's cheek a joyful tear that has brimmed and spilled.

"Yes," is all Vanessa can manage as she returns the tissue to her pocket, and follows her granddaughter to the still-open door.

The flakes have fattened and the new snowfall is dense. They already are sticking. Everything looks white and close. Harold's feet make an odd, flat sound as he shuffles up the steps. There is a man at his elbow providing support. Only fifty-nine, Harold's arthritis has begun the process of enfeeblement far sooner than is fair. The luggage is resting behind them on the walk. Vanessa waits for the man to look up, but he is intent on Harold's shoes. She hears him ask, "Are you doing O.K.?" Harold's deep reedy voice, like the deep note of a clarinet, "Sure, thanks."

40

Cassie comes to her side, laces her fingers with her grandmother's so that they are holding hands. The fog has lifted a little. Vanessa can see the man has black hair, cut close as a military fellow might wear. Beyond them, she sees where Harold's tires have left trails up the driveway, but even these are filling quickly with white.

The husbands crest the top step, and Harold looks up. Vanessa loves how his ears stick out, one more than the other. The graying hair that swirls and is combed close. The sideburns he refuses to abandon despite their sparseness. His ruddy complexion and warm hazel eyes behind thick lenses. Those fat brows that almost meet. Her heart swells with affection for this simple man, a year younger than she. The man next to him now looks up as well.

"Grandma, this is my husband Paul," she hears. But something is wrong. She notes Paul's flat nose, high cheeks. The color of his skin is not the healthy pink of her people. It is paler, and somehow – she is searching for the name of this color. The epicanthic folds of his eyes show his heritage is from the East. He's Chinese or Japanese or Siamese, whatever. She cannot believe this. She is standing there with her mouth open, knows it, cannot bring herself to close it. It must appear that she is gawping, but the boy (for that's what he is, really, after all, just a boy) has extended a hand the color of jaundice, as men will do, no matter whether the situation calls for this. He wants her to take his hand. For a small segment of a second, she imagines this, to touch his yellow flesh. And of course she must, what else could she do standing there in her doorway with her arthritic husband and her granddaughter, and cold leaching into the house, all of them awkwardly on the stoop? She presses her lips together. And takes his hand, but can manage only to croak, "It's so nice to meet you." Her throat feels like she has dropped her tea-mug on the kitchen floor, swept up the ceramic shards, and eaten them warm.

She remembers she most certainly probably has cancer. Her breast throbs and she remembers that she is waiting for the telephone to ring. Harold comes inside. Paul descends the steps Asiatically, Vanessa clearly sees it now: They walk a different way, carry their shoulders oddly. "You want me to help?" Cassie's bell-voice rings next to her grandmother's ear, but Paul waves her off. There, in the movement of his hand Vanessa sees a curt dismissal: Oriental men are like that are they not? Dismissive of their wives. They believe females are unimportant, practical for the breeding of sons. Paul humps the suitcases back up the steps and Vanessa must back away as he draws close. Cassie reaches out to take one of the bags, pauses, and then steps around her husband to close the door. Paul deposits the luggage on the carpet just inside the door. He notes the carpet is light in color, glances at his wife's feet. Stoops to untie his laces. Cassandra Lee has closed the door, the hasp clicking, and they are all inside.

Vanessa and Harold are in bed, tucked underneath the electric blanket, but she refuses to accept the refuge of its warmth. She left two messages at the clinic – neither call was returned. The snow outside is eight inches deep, and the storm has shown no sign of letting up. Cassie and her husband are settled in the guest room downstairs. Even so, Vanessa whispers her indignation.

"But Harold, he's Chinese."

"Korean."

She asks what the difference is. He is not able to say, but takes her hand. Of course, he cannot intertwine his arthritic fingers in hers. That would hurt too much. So he simply cups her hand, draws it to his chest. She feels the flannel of his pajamas, the softness on her aging skin.

"How could she have done this?" Vanessa asks this when she really wants to tell Harold about the lump. "Married this foreign man, brought him here. How could she not have told us?"

"Paul is as American as you or me. He was born here, his mom and dad were born here, probably his grandma and granddad. Who knows? I think he's a nice kid."

"And that's just what they are, kids. Both of them." Vanessa's whisper has gone hoarse and urgent. Why is he suddenly siding against her? "It's crazy."

She retracts her hand from his weak grasp, turns on her side, back to him. Harold moves slowly to spoon behind her. Drapes his arm over her chest and tucks his hand around the bodice of her nightgown into her cleavage. She instantly moves so that his hand slides away. She will not have him touching her breasts, not now, contaminated as they are. What if he felt the lump? But he would have no idea what he touched. No comprehension of the edge she staggered on. At once weariness colonized her. An equation multiplying her unease over the unreturned calls by the energy she'd invested in preparing their home for Cassie and the new husband's arrival – the product of that made her arms and legs and neck heavy, immovable, like lead. All the vacuuming and dusting, baking, making up the guest bed, cleaning the toilets and sinks, ironing the tablecloth. And the damned clinic that would not call to tell her it was O.K., that everything would be O.K. This betrayal by the consoling, friendly technician. Twenty-four hours. So much for that.

"No one will tell me anything." Vanessa's whisper is miserable.

"Our granddaughter loves him." Harold's voice is deep and gentle. "He treats her nice. I like him. I don't care if he's Korean."

Harold settles back on the sheets and soon is breathing evenly. Vanessa is awake until early in the morning, imagining corruption at the core of her, a black death-bringing bloom. At 1:24 by the soft-green colors of their digital clock, she reaches to reset the alarm from their customary 6:30 to 7. She lies back and hears the house crack under the weight of the snow, shift in its foundation, contract in its cold joints. When she finally crosses the threshold of sleep, it is only after she has considered scores of times how she might tell Harold, whether the mass is malignant or benign, that two-thirds of women beat this, that Cassie has surely had sex with him, that her child-granddaughter has opened her legs and surrendered to the intrusion of Paul's strange penis.

When the alarm beeps them from sleep, Vanessa rises and uses the toilet. After she is finished, she stands, flushes, washes her hands, and brushes her teeth. All she can see in the mirror is age. Her cheeks used to be creamy and soft, now they sag and are matrixed with furrows. Creases pull the sallow skin from the corners of her eyes. Those eyes used to look out at the world enlivened, grayish-green, with minuscule flecks of brilliant blue in the irises. Now there is dullness. Her hair has gone irrevocably gray. She remembers that she has a cancerous mass, or may have, in her left breast. She remembers that she has taken into her house a Korean man who is her granddaughter's husband.

As she spits out the paste and rinses, Harold appears in the doorframe. Eyeglasses in hand, he wipes sleep from his eyes with inflamed, knotted fingers, and moves like a man of glass. Bent too much, he will simply snap in half – that's how he seems. Frozen, like outside.

"Baby," he says. "Come see."

"What?" She already is irritated with him.

"Outside." He points and grimaces with the movement. "The snow. It must be a couple of feet deep."

She follows him to their bedroom window. She sees in the pane where he has rubbed away the condensation to see outside. He rubs there again with his pajama sleeve to re-clear it. She stoops to discover that the pre-dawn world is white and misshapen, and that snow is still falling lightly. The shrubs across the front yard are like rising bread loaves – the car in the driveway is completely obscured. Everything is a muted gray-blue in the semi-darkness. It exactly replicates the texture and hue of the eyes she just witnessed in the mirror.

"Harold, dear."

He answers yes.

"Sweetie, I have something to say."

And even as the two stare into the covered morning, she alters her disclosure. It becomes so different from the disclosure she had intended that the words simply spill from her, without any pre-thought as to their formation. They are a banality, not meant, but uttered nonetheless, and taken as truth by her uncomplicated husband.

"I'm going to try, Harold."

"Try?"

"That boy. Cassie's husband."

"Paul."

"Yes, him. For Cassie's sake, I will definitely try."

She wonders whether it's possible the clinic may call today. Sometimes they might be open on Saturdays. They will have her come in and interpret the films. There will be testing that will hurt. An extraction of some portion of the matter. A biopsy and chemo. Or maybe it's already too late. She realizes that with the snowfall there is no hope of this. Even if they regularly opened on weekends, no one in her right mind would drive on these slippery streets.

She turns from the window, dons a robe, and descends the stairs to put on coffee.

When she reaches the landing, she sees that Paul is reading in the living room. He has turned on the tree-lights – they dance and sparkle. On the end of the couch in lamplight, he looks from his pages as her footfall creaks on the bottom step.

"Good morning," he says. He lays down his book on the cushion beside him. Beyond, in the window, snow falls past his strangely configured head. He motions toward the tree. "I hope you don't mind. It's so pretty, all the lights."

"Of course not," Vanessa says.

"Thanks."

"Where's Cassie?"

"Beauty sleep," Paul says, "although she doesn't need much for that purpose."

Vanessa is warmed by this charming afterthought. She allows the slightest smile.

"I'll just start some coffee," she says, turns to the kitchen. Paul returns to his reading. As she walks through the alcove and flicks the light switch, Vanessa thinks again of the mass and her smile falls like a vase knocked from a mantle. It crashes on the linoleum in a million pieces and she cannot imagine how it might be mended.

They have finished a massive breakfast of bacon, scrambled eggs, orange juice, biscuits with gravy. Cassie is clearing the table, bringing the dishes to Vanessa at the sink. The men have stomped through the snow in the back yard to Harold's shop, a structure a few yards off the back porch. Smoke curls from the shop's tin-pipe chimney, which sprouts at an angle from the plywood side of the shack. Against

45

this wall has been stacked alder and birch, lengths of wood for the fireplace. Harold had paid some high-school boys at the church to drive the wood over and place it neatly there.

Vanessa is pondering the trail left by their passage through the snow-drifted back yard. There is a canyon in the shape of their steps. Paul had offered to help with the clean-up, but Cassie shooed him away. "Go with Grandpa," she had said. "You guys can putter around in the shop. We'll get this."

So now she is alone with her granddaughter, and wants to confess her fears. But she pauses, reflecting on the appropriateness of this. Should a sixty-year-old woman burden her loved ones with news that may be frightening, but may turn out to be nothing? Vanessa cannot decide, and as her submerged hands swirl the dishrag in silky water, she opts for gentle silence. Cassie has brought the last of the breakfast dishes. Vanessa pauses in the water, then bends to a drawer. She withdraws a dishtowel from it, passes it to Cassie, who starts drying the rinsed dishes. There is the unmistakable smell of bacon, although the two have become accustomed to it, so that it is there only as a faint suggestion. The coffee maker gurgles as its pump finishes brewing a third pot.

"Paul is a big surprise," Vanessa says, suddenly. She has stopped scrubbing the dish in her hands.

"I know. And I'm sorry. We didn't mean to surprise everyone. We weren't thinking about that. We just did it." Vanessa resumes with the dish. "Do you like him?" Cassie asks.

"If he makes you happy."

"We make each other happy, Grandma."

"Yes, like your grandfather and I." But Vanessa is biting off the words as she says them. They come automatically, as if they flow from the script of what one is supposed to say in situations such as this. She wants to tell her granddaughter about the lump in her breast, and she wants to tell her that she doesn't fully approve of her interracial marriage – for that's just what this is, she thinks. Interracial. It's no different than a black man and a white woman marrying. Two races, two types of people. And the children are the ones who are hurt. The way folks stare at them in the shopping mall, little brown ones. A white mommy pushing

46

the stroller, a black daddy stepping alongside. People just don't think about these things. She has nothing against Blacks, or Mexicans or Arabs or Chinese. It's just the repercussions of combining them that worries her.

"Not that I worry about this," Vanessa says, "but how do you manage the fact that he is so different from you?"

Cassie places the dish she is drying on the counter. "Korean-American, you mean," she says. "Or do you mean unbelievably handsome? Perhaps what you meant is that he is incredibly tender and thoughtful. Or that he, at twenty-two," her voice rises, "is already a hundred times the man my father was."

Vanessa blanches at the mention of her son. Cassie's words have the affect of a slap, and rock her grandmother back on her heels. Trent and Cassie's mother, Susan, had died when Cassie was two. Her father was drunk. He drove their car, with Susan in the passenger seat, into the stout trunk of a hundred-year-old apple tree on the corner of Blanchard Avenue and Wilson Street, just seven blocks from here, at more than sixty miles per hour the police reckoned. Both were launched through the windshield. Both died at the scene. They had been returning from bowling. Her father was twenty-two years old, Paul's age. Cassie had been staying with her grandparents, Trent and Susan on the way to collect their daughter.

And then Harold and Vanessa had raised her.

"That isn't fair, Cassandra." It has been years since Cassie has raised this point. It must have been as long ago as when she was a high-school freshman. God, how they had fought then.

"My father killed my mother. He would have picked me up and drove me home too, drunk as a pig. He thought that little of her, and of me."

"Your father loved you. You should have seen him when he played with you. He adored you."

"He was a drunk, Grandma. That's simply a fact."

"He had a problem, honey. And no one could help him. We didn't know what to do." Vanessa's hands splay before her. It appears that Cassie will say more, that this might further escalate, but suddenly

47

color drains from her cheeks and the tears come.

"Oh, Grandma," she weeps. "Oh, God. Please. I'm so sorry."

Vanessa collects her, enfolds her in warm grandmother arms, arms that served as mother's arms for so many years.

"I'm sorry, too, sweetheart," Vanessa says. "We have to love each other."

Cassie pulls back from her grandmother's embrace and says, "Yes, and that's why I picked Paul, Grandma." She wipes her own tears away this time with the dish towel in her hand. "I love him like magic."

And Vanessa realizes that she cannot deny her granddaughter this. That there is nothing that can be said in the face of this careless passion. So she takes a safe, neutral route, and attempts to demonstrate interest. To flee from the agonizing memory that forms the foundation of her thoughts about her son.

"What does he do?" she says. "I mean, what is he studying?"

"He's in the English Department. In the graduate program. He wants to be a writer."

Vanessa doesn't have a response for a moment. After all, what can be said about this? Should she ask her granddaughter whether Cassie plans to support him while he toils cerebrally to forge a masterpiece of words? Cassie's studying nursing. What's that pay? Virtually nothing, a pittance, sticks. Vanessa had hoped for an engineer for her granddaughter, or an architect, some sort of professional. But a writer, for God's sake. With Cassie's latest revelation, Vanessa is never so close as now to revealing the problem pin-pricking the back of her mind: that there is no damned phone call coming today yet the mass may be growing larger and more malevolent by the minute. It's almost as if revealing the potential for cancer might drain a sympathy so deep and wide from Cassie that she would altogether abandon this notion of marriage, annul this huge mistake. That she would run from this foreign man back to her grandmother's arms.

But at the last possible moment, while the clock above the dining room table ticks and the soap bubbles in the sink disperse, Vanessa looks again out the window at the trail the men have trodden to the shop. The snow has covered everything ugly about the backyard: the moss in the too-long grass that Harold has been unable to mow, the weeds growing tall next to the fence, the mud trail her husband has worn dragging his aching feet to commune with his tools and gadgets. Now it is pure white. And flakes have begun again, modest now, floating down like tiny feathers.

"Can he make a go of that?" she asks.

"You should read him, Grandma. His poems are stunning. He's won several awards, published in some magazines. When you read his stories you'll be mesmerized."

"So he's talented, then?"

"I'd say so, yes. Most people who know about these things think so."

"Are these people ready to pay him a working wage for their admiration?"

"He makes money – he cooks and waits tables, he makes a little as a T.A. He might be able to get a position at the college, or *a* college, somewhere."

"And you would go with him, you would find a hospital wherever he went?"

"I'd have to, Grandma. I'm pregnant with our child."

On Saturday evening, the front passes. The snow ends and in its wake is left stars. The television says that the airport is closed; airplanes grounded there are stranded. Paul takes this news with grace – it means he will miss shifts at the deli, and that his first classes of the new semester are at risk.

The four are in the living room with the tree lights again. Paul has described his family, who live in Boston. His father, for whom he clearly possesses immense respect, is a dentist. His mother keeps their home, and he worships her. They have not met Cassie, but are eager to when they journey to the school in the coming spring.

It turns out that when Vanessa discovered him reading that morning, he was actually proofing galleys for a thing he calls a "chapbook." It is his own work, soon forthcoming from the university's press. He entertains them by reading from it. Although Vanessa and Harold know nothing about poetry, what they hear is pleasing, rhythmic, melodic. The tree-lights are merry, teacups are warm. Paul finishes and Cassandra leads the clapping. Harold asks about siblings, and Paul tells them about a sister who is a painter and gallery proprietress in Myrtle Beach, South Carolina.

Vanessa's smile is a forced march. It's not that she isn't enjoying herself – she actually is, somewhat, and given the circumstances, probably this is the best she could anticipate. But carried on the back of her thoughts is the problem of her breast, and it emerges enhorned from time to time, always there, a reminder. For a moment while Paul had been reading, her mind drifted morbidly: who would take care of Harold?

Would he keep her ashes or have them placed in a vault? How many months or weeks did she have? Years? And this waiting was more than a person should be expected to endure. She knew, now, with no call on Saturday, that there was no hope for one on Sunday. And with all the snow and no sign of it melting, Monday seemed in question also. If it was serious enough to keep the airport down, this surely meant travel on the streets was impossible. To drive these thoughts away, she thought of her great-grandchild, forming there three feet away in Cassie's womb. This mixed child who, despite its variegation, would bind them together forever, with no possible door out. She and a pair of middle-aged Bostonian Koreans linked for all time by the happenstance of Cassie's and Paul's passion. A grandchild in common with them, a pair she could only imagine as the composite of all Asian people she had ever seen in newspaper pictures or on television, a husband and wife whom she had never met but now has a curious desire to do so. In Boston, she now has in-laws. People with whom, before now, she had nothing in common but the requirement to breathe air.

They were talking about the baby. Harold had asked something corny, something like, "What's the date of the blessed event?"

"The end of August," Cassie says. "Right in the middle of summer." The same time of year she carried Trent, Vanessa recalls. The same time of the year he died with Cassie's mother. Maybe the same time of year she, herself, will die.

"Do you know the sex?" Harold asks.

"Harold, for crying out loud!" Vanessa shouts.

Her husband appears startled behind his glasses. His bushy eyebrows rise in surprise, and his knotted fingers leap up in front of his chest as if to ward her off.

"I'm just wondering," he says. "They can tell that these days, you know?"

Cassie is laughing, those bells again. Vanessa calms quickly, chalking up her husband's nosiness to his silly demeanor. He has no idea what to make of a pregnancy, she thinks. Even in his own granddaughter. Probably can't even remember how it happens.

"We don't know," Paul admits, as if not knowing in modern times is an oddity.

"We don't want to know before," his wife adds.

But from Paul, "I hope it's a girl."

Vanessa awakes and there is light at the curtains. Harold is snoring softly beside her. She checks the clock but there is no display.

Sunday morning has brought with it a power outage. Somewhere, in the night, snow on power lines that had thawed yesterday froze again, and the weight was more than the line could manage. This all comes to her as she rises and notes the chill in the house, and remembers at once there is a mass of unknown constitution in her left breast. She feels of it to make certain it is still there. That there has been no miracle of spontaneous healing during the night. The electric heat is off. Her breath makes a cloud as she exhales.

She hears the percussive thump of wood-chopping from the back yard. She walks slowly to the bathroom window, curious. Outside, Paul is splitting the segments of alder and birch. He stops for a moment and sips from a cup. She hears Cassie's voice, muffled through the flooring of the house, call to him. She asks whether he wants more to drink.

"Thanks, not just yet," he says, and hoists the ax again. It crashes against the log, which cleaves neatly with the impact. As Vanessa attends to her teeth and watches, he splits another, then another.

She sits on the toilet to urinate. Rises again to watch Paul's labors. There is a substantial stack of split wood next to him. He is moored there, knee-deep in snow, and it clings to his pant legs. He has removed his jacket, slung it across the woodpile. He pauses again to drink. Then he bends to collect the split wood, carries it toward the house and disappears through the door downstairs.

By the time she is dressed and has wakened Harold, she can hear the far crackle of pitch from the fireplace downstairs. Harold is stretching at the bedside, commenting on how cold it seems.

"The power's failed," she says. "Paul and Cassie are making a fire, though." The loss of power will be a nuisance for her all day – it will be impossible to cook, and if it lasts too long they will have to pack out contents of the freezer into the backyard. As well, the refrigerator might have to be emptied. But Harold greets the notion of a power outage like a little boy. Vanessa has never seen him, at least not recently, bound down the stairs with such flexibility.

They breakfast on bread and peanut butter and jam. Harold has dug out an old camping pot, and they heat water for instant coffee in it at the edge of the coals in the fireplace. Cassie wonders whether the telephones are out as well, lifts the receiver to hear the familiar tone and notes brightly that they can call the airline for an update on flights. There's no way for Harold to drive them there until the streets thaw, but at least they will have an idea when might expect to fly out – tomorrow, or perhaps the next day. And Paul can call to leave a message at the deli, as well as with the English Department.

Later, they all move stuff from the freezer outside. By the time they're finished, Harold is trembling and aching so bad he can barely walk. Cassie takes him into the house and settles him on the couch. Paul re-kindles the coals, adding the last segments of the wood he split earlier. Soon there is some heat in the room, enough to take the edge off of Harold's pain.

"I'm going to get more wood," Paul announces. "Depending on how long this lasts, we may need a lot."

"I'll help you," Cassie says, leaving her grandfather's side to retrieve a coat from the closet.

"Stay with Harold," Paul says. "I'll be fine."

And Vanessa, in that moment, makes a decision. She will go help Paul. She will reach out in opposition to all that is intuitive and familiar to her, to her new grandson.

"I'll go with you, Paul," she says. "Two can get the job done twice as fast," she adds, as if an expression of mathematic principles were the explanation for her sudden will to engage.

"Are you sure?"

"You bet."

The pair disappears out the back door, leaving Harold and Cassie to the fire.

Outside, a frigid breeze has come up. The sky, blue this morning, has now collected a dull, high cloud cover. Vanessa wonders whether this will mean more snow, has never understood how to read clouds. "We may be in for it," she says, looking up still.

"Could be," Paul says. "I wouldn't mind, though. You folks are real nice people. I'm happy to be here with you. I can see why Cassie is such a terrific person."

Vanessa struggles with the veracity of this string of compliments. Is he saying this to earn favor? But she dismisses this, believes what she hears.

There is an honesty and earnestness about him. He is uncomplicated in a way that reminds her of Harold as a young man starting out. Her mind searches for the word, then happens upon it: integrity. She believes there is integrity in Paul, in this young man who has come to be her grandson-in-law, her son-in-law. He is a man to whom she may safely confess. The time is now.

"Paul, may I tell you something?" she asks. "Something private?"

"Of course," her grandson says. He is poised above the splitting log, placing a length of birch thereon, finding the ax handle's fulcrum, sensing its balance. Ready to use the tool.

She looks directly into his eyes. She sees that they are brown, that their alien folds do not obscure this fact. He looks friendly, interested, trustworthy.

53

"Harold doesn't know this, neither does Cassandra."

His brows rise in minor surprise, but he waits for her to speak again. The ax head descends slowly to rest on his boot.

"I am waiting to find out if I have cancer," she says. "I was supposed to know Friday, but they never called."

"Where?" Paul says.

Tears fall from her eyes as she points at her breast.

"I've been so unkind," she says. "I'm so sorry."

Paul abandons the ax. Its handle clacks against the chopping block. He embraces his grandmother-in-law. This gesture is so unexpected that Vanessa scarcely has time to see it coming, much less make any sort of interpretation. He is simply there, and she is in his arms. For a second, she hugs her own father. With her eyes closed, she can see his face. And then she remembers this is her grandson-in-law, but for that exquisite second, just then... She melts into Paul's arms and breathes of him, and his smell is familiar and the same as Harold's. The smell of every honest, good man. His arms have gathered her in exactly the way her father did so many years ago, the same way her husband does today. She can even feel his heartbeat, she thinks, the pumping of an oxen, mannish vessel. Vanessa clings to Paul, buries her wet cheeks in his collar.

Slowly, he lifts her away, and she thinks, *No, don't let this end, it's so cold*, but he fixes her with a gaze that is authoritative and loving and concerned, yet unified.

"This happened to my mother," he says.

"Your mother?"

"Her name is Patricia. She lives in Boston."

"In Boston."

"She *lives* in Boston. She beat it. You may also."

Vanessa's core of fear begins to soften. She can almost feel the mass dissolve and drain away – though she knows this is not the case – what she feels emanate from Paul on the wings of his own disclosure is relief on the order of a favorable call from the clinic. His mother once, like she, had a mass in her breast. Patricia is her name. There is a woman in Boston named Patricia Lee who beat this. Vanessa trembles

54

with the possibilities.

But there still is the countenance of deep concern on Paul's face. Its strange contours, which have suddenly taken on a familiarity she cannot explain, are twisted into a frown.

"We gathered around her," he says. "We supported her. We prayed unceasingly for her and showered her with love, as if every moment with her were our last together. And she beat it."

"It hasn't come back?"

Paul shakes his head. "But you miss my point," he says. "Her family knew. You may not make it if yours doesn't. How can you steal from them the right to intercede, to mitigate this? How can you rob from them the opportunity to heap comfort on you?"

He makes absolute sense, this Korean-American man in her snow-covered back yard. Above the drifts, the ax handle lying at his boots, the wood arrayed at his back, Harold's goofy stovepipe canted at its ridiculous angle behind his black-haired head. This bringer of good news, the father of her great-grandchild, stares confidently back at her. She says his name once, "Paul." It tastes like honey, and freedom.

"You need to tell them, Vanessa."

She shakes her head – what he suggests would be impossible. To trouble them without knowing. To tell them of what she fears: that she no longer is whole. That she is, somehow, less of a woman. Infirm, sick, embarrassing. That she may lose a breast and that Harold will retreat from what remains, fleeing her disfiguration. That Cassie would see her own breasts in a mirror and face her future staggering under the weight of this ghastly promise. These things, Vanessa thinks, are worse than death.

"Yes," Paul is saying. "You must."

"I can't."

"You can. Please believe me when I say it is very urgent."

And she realizes that yes, she agrees, it is. She nods, the freezing world around her quiet and still. The peace that comes from a place not one person understands descends on her like a small bird.

"Come back inside," Paul says. He holds out his hand to her, his strange yellow hand, and beckons. "I'll help you in. We'll tell them together."

The Confession of Titus

My name is Titus, and I have this advice: never have anything to do with your wife's former girlfriends. I mean nothing. This is not for you. If she introduces you to one you will want to be charming. You'll think this will make your wife proud. Have none of it. Resist the temptation to be cool. This will be harder than you think. But you've got to act like an idiot, or better yet, an asshole. Believe me, it's better in the long run. What the hell was that all about, your wife may ask afterward. It's possible she will be very annoyed with you. Just tell her sorry, you weren't feeling good.

MeShelle introduced me to one of her high-school girlfriends down at the ballfields at one of Nelson's mid-season games. Nelson is seven, but plays a year ahead of most of the boys his age – in the coach-pitch league. I guess most dads don't have time any more to throw the ball with their boys or help them learn their way around a bat. But I did, so like I say, Nelson is advanced in skills. He played on a team sponsored by the American Legion Post 117, which is on his T-shirt on the front, and his number is 11, on the back. His team is called the Jaguars, and he likes that – Nelson likes animals, especially sleek, exotic ones like big cats and so forth. A lot of African animals, and I guess that makes me happy. Nelson was the only black kid on his team. It didn't seem to be a big deal to him but it sure made me feel funny with the rest of the parents. Add to that the fact that MeShelle was gone an awful lot – usually six to nine day stints in the air – and I was feeling pretty alone in those bleachers.

Anyway, MeShelle did happen to be home during this one game mid-way through the season. While the boys were warming up their gloves and she was talking with some of the mothers, she looked up over the diamond at the other team's huddle of parents. It seemed like she recognized someone. And then she was sure of it, and said, "Honey, I see somebody I know. I'm going over there to talk to her for a minute." She asked if I would be all right where I was. Of course, I said.

It was a bright April Saturday morning, unusual – it mostly rains like hell hereabouts that time of year. As MeShelle walked away, I appreciated her shape and the fact that she was here that weekend and not her usual – in the air between San Francisco and Australia, or Los Angeles and Hawaii. My little world traveler, I used to joke with her. I've been out of the county maybe nine, ten times in my lifetime. Out of the state only once, when we took Nelson to Disneyland last spring. People ask me what does my wife do, I say she's a flight attendant with United. She says no matter what they call it, it's really a stewardess, which is what they've always been called. She's good at it, or they wouldn't put her on flights to other countries – Australia, and like that. Anyway, I saw her meet up just a little past the backstop with another black mother, I mean, I was guessing it was a mother. I watched them do this women's hugging thing, and then talk for a while. Then I turned to watch Nelson and this other boy throwing the ball.

Next thing I knew MeShelle was there with her friend. She'd dragged this lady all the way across the diamond to meet me.

"Titus, honey, I want you to meet someone," she said. "This is Lisa."

I told Lisa I was pleased to meet her, and I was.

"Lisa and I were girlfriends in high school," MeShelle continued, "and it's just amazing, but we haven't seen each other for" – she turned to Lisa to confirm the timespan because they must have discussed it across the diamond – "ten, eleven years." They kept talking, mostly to each other, and once in a while I would understand they were asking me a question and trying to involve me in their conversation. At some point MeShelle told her I was a cabinet maker, that I was sought by general contractors all around the region for my finish work. I said nothing much about this, just smiled. Somewhere along the way I gathered her son's name was Patrick and that he didn't have a daddy. Lisa was a single lady, I mean. The dude was no longer in the picture. They got divorced I guessed, although I never heard that for sure – I was trying to still watch Nelson. At the same time, I was trying to seem cool and make MeShelle proud of me. I should have known that wasn't necessary, but you know,

57

I believe this is the sort of thing all men do. I will tell you this: this Lisa woman was a lovely lady. Enough so that part of my being cool was simply trying not to let this old girlfriend of my wife's see that I had already assessed her shape and found it pleasing, as well as her eyes and lips. Now MeShelle is very foxy, there is no doubt about it, and no complaints from me in that department. Especially since I think of myself as about as ugly as a dirt sack. But her friend was a knock-out. I wouldn't say brown sugar, because she was darker than that. Lisa had skin like an African, and it was a sunny morning: while I was busy trying to look and act cool, part of me was watching her ebony arms and legs suck up sunshine. Her son's team's name was the Tigers and Ace Hardware was their sponsor. I do remember that also.

After a while the game was about to get under way and the two women separated. "Good luck," Lisa said, and of course she meant for Nelson and the Jaguars, but I had this feeling there was more to it than that. Maybe I imagined it, but I thought she was saying this more to me than to MeShelle. At least I know it was me she was looking at, because I thought about her eyes and the way they looked directly at me that moment for several days afterward. Driving MeShelle to the airport I was thinking of Lisa's eyes. When MeShelle kissed my cheek and trundled down Passenger Loading with her tiny roller suitcase, I checked Nelson in the rearview and thought of Lisa's eyes. And other parts of her, I suppose.

It was the third week of May before the schedule cycled around and the Jaguars played the Tigers a second time. MeShelle was on a trip and I was playing Mr. Mom again. We got to the ballfields a little early that afternoon and I was in a foul mood – I had been grousing in my head the entire way from the house about our minivan.

I had wanted a small pick-up or a Jeep, but MeShelle wanted this goofy van thing. My point was that we had only Nelson, and I needed better space for my lumber and tools during the week while she was away. But she pointed out that the seats folded down and made a lot of cargo space. I was trying to be cute and told her I thought she was thinking less about cargo space and more about filling the extra seats with babies. She laughed, and said I might be right. And I guess I gave in on the strength of that argument, or maybe just because she makes three times the money I do, because if the truth were known, I'm not all that great of a cabinet maker. Anyway, I would tease her about this minivan. I joked around with her that I felt like a white man driving it. It seemed like a white folks' car. MeShelle didn't appreciate the humor in that, so I thought the hell with and shut my mouth. Still, every time she was gone and I had to drive the damned thing around, it bugged me. I imagined me and Nelson, the two boys, in a big, red truck with four-wheel drive and lots of payload. A year and a half later, and I still hadn't let it go.

Anyway, we piled out of the minivan and started throwing the ball back and forth. I didn't even realize, at this point, that Nelson's team would be playing the Tigers that morning. Even if I had, I doubt whether I would have made the connection. That playing the Tigers meant seeing little Patrick's mommy again, I mean. It just didn't occur to me, so I was surprised when I heard Lisa's greeting. I turned toward her voice and it hit me at the same time, that we were playing the Tigers and MeShelle's high-school friend could be there, and Nelson's throw hit me in the chest. The ball plopped in the grass at my feet and I rubbed where it had hit me and waved back. She came over holding Patrick by the hand, and I was tongue-tied in no small way. She liked to talk a lot, I remembered. It was clear right away that this fact about her had not changed. I caught about half of what she said, I guess, mostly just trying to keep up. Where was MeShelle, she asked and when I told her, then it was, how was I making out with Nelson, MeShelle being out of town and so forth. Most of this conversation had her talking and me gawking. Although I hope it wasn't too obvious – that in general, I mean, I am not too obvious about these kinds of things. But I'm afraid it probably was, considering what happened later. She was just so fine, I know there's no excuse for it. I'm not asking for one. She had on an orange shirt with white buttons up the front and no sleeves and a pair of men's blue jeans that fit exactly. Her feet were in leather sandals. She had her hair done straight and gathered in a ponytail. Her eyes were the color of chocolate. Her lips were moist and had a natural-colored lipstick on them. I barely tore my eyes off

59

them when the coaches gathered the boys.

Ice cream with Nelson and Patrick after the game was her idea, not mine. I want to get that straight. We drove separately to the Baskin-Robbins up on East Hill and entered the cool restaurant with dry throats and the promise of sweetness on our tongues. The boys took forever to decide what flavors they would like, then it was waffle cone or regular, all decisions to be made. Nelson settled on a scoop of blueberry ice – it was more a frozen yogurt than ice cream, but still the sort of thing where a lot of it would end up down the front of the Jaguars T-shirt. Patrick took Rocky Road. I wanted a scoop of chocolate-cherry in a dish. Lisa wanted a Diet Coke only, and I teased her for it.

"I have to watch my diet," she said.

And out of my mouth popped: "I don't see that as a problem." She could have taken it any number of ways, which was the spirit in which it was offered. She could have thought I just meant, O.K., all the boys will have ice cream and the girl will have a soda. Or she could have thought what I actually did mean: that she looked so fine and desirable that I couldn't imagine a few calories would have made any difference. I had meant it to come out vague on purpose, so if it backfired I could spread my hands and ask, "What? What'd I say?" You know what I'm talking about – as if I was innocent. As far as I could tell though, my comment did not backfire. Instead, it clearly pleased her.

We chatted for a while between the big glass panes and the colors of the ice-cream tubs, and Nelson and Patrick were goofing around with straws and napkin holders. They got up to go look at the ice-cream cakes and flip through the books you could order them from. Lisa sipped her Diet Coke – I didn't quite remember ever watching MeShelle use a straw in that way. I noticed how she held the straw, between her index finger and thumb, and that she wore a silver thumb ring. I found this sexy, this ring. About three spoonfuls away from the last of my chocolate-cherry I dribbled some down my shirt. I looked up and around, exaggerating surprise, and joked, "What ... how did that happen? I don't know how that happened!" Lisa giggled. Before I knew it she was gently blotting the stain from my chest with a paper napkin. And there was a lot of something in the tiny pressure from her fingertips, of this I am sure.

Then the boys clambered over. They had cooked up, between them, a sleepover. This annoyed me for a moment – I had instructed Nelson many times to discuss staying the night, or inviting someone to stay the night at our house, with me, before asking the other boy. It just made it easier when I had to say no, which was most of the time. And here he had done it again, knowing perfectly well that it was against the rules. Still, the boys had this heartbreakingly hopeful look on their faces. They looked so young and strong and happy with ice cream smearing their mouths and shirtfronts. It was a good thing, I thought, their small blossoming friendship. My son had only white friends in the neighborhood. I didn't know how far away Lisa and her son lived, but I liked this. Seeing them together. I asked her what she thought. It was fine with her, although she would have to go home and get Patrick a change of clothing and his sleeping bag. I gave her directions to me and MeShelle's house, wrote them on another napkin with the assistant manager's pen.

Ten minutes later Nelson and I arrived at home and I checked our message machine. No call from MeShelle. I told him to go change his Jaguar shirt and stuff it in the dirty clothes. Then I suggested he might want to straighten up his room a little before Patrick arrived. About twenty minutes later our doorbell rang. Lisa and Patrick were on our doorstep, Patrick hugging this huge green sleeping bag nearly as big as himself. I opened the screen door and ushered them in. "Nelson's down the hall," I said, pointing the way for Patrick. He scampered down the carpet and disappeared in Nelson's bedroom door. I waved at the echo of him. "Nice seeing you," I said, and turned to his mother. I intended to ask about arrangements for returning her son the following morning, I swear, but what I asked Lisa was whether she wanted something cold to drink.

"A beer?" she asked. I knew I had seven or eight long necks in the fridge, so I invited her into the kitchen. I grabbed two beers from the refrigerator shelf and twisted the tops. I asked her if she wanted a glass, which she declined. She was looking around the kitchen, looking for MeShelle's signature I guess, of which there was very little. It was a man's kitchen, with a few more plates in the sink than I would have liked at that moment. She looked out the small window above the mess into our back yard. She tilted the long neck a couple of times, took drinks. I couldn't take my eyes off her lips at the bottle's rim.

"It's so hot out," she said. She was right. Seventy degrees is hot, around here, in May. "Nice and cool in here though." She turned and took a step toward me and paused. But it was I who took the final two steps to her. I have to admit that. I took the bottle from her hand and set it on our counter. I put my arms around the space of her waist, and my fingertips came to rest barely on them.

"What is going on here?" I asked.

"I don't know," Lisa said. I looked at her longer. "Do you want to kiss me?" she asked.

I shook my head yes. There was a tiny bit of moisture above her upper lip, beer or sweat. She moved her face closer to mine and I did, I kissed her. The taste of the fresh beer on her mouth, and her lipstick and the salt of her rushed onto me. She was wearing a scent that rose and filled my nostrils. The inside of her mouth tasted good, and cool and warm at the same time. My hands slid up the side of her waist to the soft place just below her arms and slid forward. One of her hands was hot on my neck, I don't know where the other one was. She made a small sound and I realized that our bodies were together, the full length of them. I wondered whether she could feel that I had grown hard. I backed up, disengaged. My fingertips came away from the sides of her breasts.

"The boys," I said.

"Are you kidding?" she asked. "If Nelson is anything like my Patrick, there's nothing that could pull them away from their Nintendo." She smiled as if she were making a joke. But her eyes were saying come on. I glanced around the kitchen doorway down the hall and heard video-game sounds. I stepped back into the kitchen. The kitchen was separated from the hallway by one of those doors that slides between the walls, and I pulled it shut. I clicked the lock.

When I turned around Lisa was undoing the top buttons of her orange shirt. Her thumb ring flashed in light from the window. She pulled her collar open and showed the front of her bra. She told me to come open it. "Here," she said, and I understood the clasp was on the front. My fingers were trembling, but I popped the hasp O.K. and approved of what I saw. Her breasts were like my second and third helpings of chocolate-cherry ice cream in one day and I wanted another taste.

After a while I lifted her onto the counter, pulled those blue jeans off long ebony legs. Her underpants fell at my feet.

"I love my wife," I said.

"Of course you do, Titus," Lisa said. "But your wife is not here right now. So love me."

God help me, I did.

Everyone knows the feelings and sounds and smells and tastes of sex. I won't go into them here. We finished in the kitchen then made the boys some popcorn. They started watching a movie on The Disney Channel and I took Lisa into our bedroom. We did it two or three more times. She said she was getting sore so I put my mouth on her instead. Then I was ready again. When I got tired, she was patient. And vice versa. I do not believe the boys were any the wiser, in fact I'm sure of it because when Lisa woke Patrick the next morning he asked why she was still wearing her orange shirt. It was naturally odd to him because she would have gone home, right? It could not have entered either his or Nelson's mind that she had a sleepover as well.

The first thing I should have done was put the same sheets back on our bed. I had to wash them – they smelled of Lisa over every square inch. I had to wash the pillows and pillow slips and the blanket – she was everywhere! But I only thought of putting the same sheets back on as MeShelle, Nelson and I walked through the front door four days later after I picked her up at the airport. She was seriously jetlagged, having flown across the Pacific Ocean for fourteen hours, then a two-hour layover in San Francisco, and another hour and a half flight back home. She said she was going right to bed for a while. Would she notice? I never changed the sheets while she was gone. I can't imagine a man who would.

In fact, it was almost three weeks before she asked me about the sleepover. She wondered why I hadn't mentioned it. It was Lisa who did, at the league's awards banquet. Nelson and Patrick had exchanged phone calls during the three weeks, but had not seen each other. Nor had I seen Lisa, of course. Until the evening of the awards ceremonies, I wanted the whole thing to just go away. I wanted to pretend it never happened. I loved my wife. I had told Lisa this, and still she opened herself up onto me. I never expected to break by wedding vow, I swear. I fully anticipated going through my entire marriage absolutely faithful to MeShelle.

As my wife talked with my lover, I watched the two of them. I wondered whether there were any signals that would pass between them. Whether there was a sort of unwitting communication women give off in the presence of each other. I don't know about this kind of thing, but I've heard of it. Like when a bunch of women who come to live together under one roof, all their periods start to happen at the same time. What a hell of a place that would be. So maybe something like that, I was thinking. I got myself into a sweat, panicking like that. What if Lisa just flat out told her? I didn't know why a woman would do a thing like that, but the more I thought about it, the more possible it seemed. I had spent three weeks trying to rip out of my mind the memory of Lisa's dark body swallowing me on our bed. Of her above me, her mouth on me, the tips of her breasts like tiny hard cola nuts. I was sorry, and not sorry. Glad I did it, and ashamed. And I was afraid.

My mom and daddy named me after one of the followers of Saint Paul, in the Bible. Paul was the disciple who got blinded by the light on the road to Damascus, and sinned no more. Titus was one of his main friends and a guy Paul really depended on as he preached the gospel of Jesus Christ across Greece and Turkey and Crete. Titus helped Saint Paul figure things out and coordinate things. He was a helpful fellow. Paul wrote a letter to Titus that's in the Bible. In it he warns Titus to be sure and tell the people of Crete that the Christian life is one of discipline. They are going to have to set down the bottle, stop being belligerent, stop resenting authority, and so forth, if they are going to follow the Lord. My parents told me all of this. I have not read this chapter for a while. I can't remember whether it says anything about committing adultery, but I know it says not to elsewhere in the Good Book. So this is another problem.

"Lisa!" I called, as we were all leaving. MeShelle was in the ladies' room, and I saw Lisa walking hand in hand with Patrick down the hall toward us. Nelson saw them too, and broke through the throng to greet his friend. "Lisa," I said again, when she got closer. I looked around, and toward the ladies' room door to see whether MeShelle was coming out yet.

"Hi Titus," she said. She was very warm and friendly, and she bent toward me and whispered in my ear, "Sugar."

"Lisa," I said for the third time. "You didn't ... I mean, you were, when you were talking to MeShelle, you didn't ..."

"Relax, Sugar," she said. "I would never, ever do a thing like that."

We heard MeShelle calling then, and I snapped to a different sort of attention. I was relieved on the one hand, that Lisa hadn't said anything, but still nervous.

"Hi Honey," I said. I realized it sounded ridiculously overeager, and hoped she didn't notice. Then I thought how funny it must be to Lisa, to stand here and watch me act like such an obvious jackass.

"She sure acts silly around you," MeShelle commented, a few minutes later, in the minivan.

"I don't know what you mean," I said, probably too quickly.

"I don't know. She just looks at you a lot. It's hard to say what I mean. She just watches you. I think she's sweet on you, Baby."

"Hush," I said, glancing at Nelson in the back seat so that she would see I was indicating her comments were not fit for his ears. "That's ridiculous."

"Why?" she asked.

"What do you mean why? I don't know why. It just is." I thought that I had better cool out. I wondered how I could get us onto another subject without being too obvious. I thought MeShelle knew it all at that point, that she was playing with me. I thought she would tell me at any moment that she was aware of what I had done. I thought she was going to say, I'm out of here, even with our sweet son in the back seat. Instead she said something totally different.

"Titus, Baby, you are a damned fine man. She hasn't got one. Probably run hers off." She paused for me to acknowledge this.

"I don't see how."

I can't believe I said it. I felt like crap. I deserved to.

I got this idea in my head: if it was possible for me to sleep with somebody else then maybe MeShelle had done it too. All those nights, you know, away from town. There's all those stories about stewardesses – flight attendants. It would be easy for her, much easier than for me. When a great-looking woman wants to do this, all she has to do is snap her fingers and a hundred guys will line up. Maybe she took her clothes off for one of her pilots on layover somewhere in Australia or Hawaii. Or some passenger who struck her fancy. Even another flight attendant – I guess, as you probably know, they have men.

She's told me dozens of times how lonely she gets when she's flying.

The more I thought about it the more convinced I became. She was full of love when she got back, there was no shortage of that. And the first time after Lisa was particularly fine. I guess this is because I closed my eyes and saw Lisa, and not MeShelle. I know that's a shitty thing to do, but I did it. And I started to think she might be seeing someone else in her mind when I was loving her. At various moments I would realize I was in bed with my wife. I would realize that I could start new, right then, at that moment. It could be like there was no history, and that my familiarity with MeShelle – what she felt like, what she liked, where she liked to be touched and kissed – was a new, fresh thing. Then she would move in a way that reminded me of Lisa. A picture of Lisa, the curves and moist places of her, would unfold again.

MeShelle got ready for her next trip, packing her little rolling suitcase. I sat in the chair in our bedroom with her, pretending just to want her company. But I was really taking a careful look at each item she put in the case. Like whether she was putting her really nice silk panties in there or just some old cotton ones. Her nice, lacy colored bras – black or red – or plain white. To be honest with you, it seemed like a pretty even mix. Almost as if she had just grabbed whatever was on top in her drawer. Almost, but I couldn't be absolutely sure. Besides, if she was on to me, that's the kind of thing she would have done with me sitting there watching, right?

Nelson and I dropped her off at the airport. We watched her walk down Passenger Loading, like a hundred times before. This time I watched the uniformed guys working curbside check-in. Their eyeballs slimed all over my wife as she walked past. I almost got out of the minivan, almost embarrassed her in front of all of them. Instead I rolled out into the slow second lane of exit traffic. But when I got up even with the first check-in guy, I hit the electric switch that rolls down the passenger-side window. "What you lookin' at, buddy?" I shouted. He looked up from a ticket he was checking. He seemed confused, then got a look on his face like I was nuts. He didn't know me, didn't even really know it was him who I was shouting at.

"Who was that?" Nelson asked. "Do you know him?"

I was surprised to get a call from Lisa. I didn't give her my number. Then I remembered that Patrick and Nelson had been calling each other – she probably got it from her boy. "You can't just call here," I said. "You never know when MeShelle is going to be home." She told me to settle down, that she wasn't calling to start anything. Patrick had been asking about Nelson, she said.

"Oh," I said. Was I a little disappointed? Yes. So I'm sorry to say I got a little bit nasty: "Well since you got the number why didn't you just have Patrick call and ask for him?"

She was silent on the other end of the line. Then she said, "Do you have a problem, Titus? Do we have a problem?"

"I don't know what you mean."

"Because if you have a problem," she continued, "I need to let you know that I don't. I enjoyed my evening with you, and I had not been handled that way in quite a few years. I appreciated what you did, and how you did it. But I just meant to have fun. I think you should look at it that way too. I'm not looking for that again with you."

I thought about this for a full minute. Then I said, "I think you better get Patrick on the phone. I'll go get Nelson." And I set the phone down on the counter and hollered down the hallway for my boy.

I asked Mrs. Candless, the lady who lives across the street, to watch Nelson. I was going to get MeShelle at the airport and I needed some time with her by myself. I explained this to Mrs. Candless, who got a goofy smile on her face and tried to wink at me.

I picked MeShelle up at curbside, jumping out to stow her suitcase in the back. She grabbed me hard. It seemed that way, anyway – she hugged me as if she knew something bad was about to happen. Maybe it was just my imagination, too. We got in the car. I pulled out into the exit lane and wound around the taxis and folks parked whichever way the hell they wanted to. We got out of the airport and I asked her the question I always ask: "How was the flight?" She said it was fine, and looked out her window.

"MeShelle," I said. "Honey, what I have to say I don't know how to say. It's been eating me up. I'm just going to say it." I paused and drew breath. "I was with somebody." She was very quiet. Finally, after I'd driven well more than a mile, she said, "Titus." Her voice barely came out of her and was small.

I waited for her to say something else, anything. I said, "I'm sorry," and reached for her hand. My fingertips touched her diamond, her wedding band. She jerked away like she'd gotten an electric shock.

"Don't say anything," she said. "Not one word."

After we got home and she went over to get Nelson, I stood in our kitchen with a beer. I looked at the countertop where I had screwed her friend. I wondered whether she knew it was with Lisa – maybe she thought it was some anonymous person. Christ – maybe she thought it was a hooker. Somehow, as confused and twisted up as I was at that moment, it almost seemed better to me if it came out that way. Because

68

maybe an old friend would hurt too much, if the hurt could be any greater.

She came into the kitchen and poured herself a glass of white wine. I saw that she was exhausted. Her eyes were red. The bones of her cheeks pushed up toward them and made dark hollows there. I thought about saying something, but remembered her command in the minivan. I swallowed more of the beer and waited. I didn't have to wait much longer, just until she finished the glass of wine and poured a second. Then she turned toward me and I saw her tears. They left two wet tracks down her cheeks, still lovely even in her exhaustion and sorrow. She tried to say something and only air came out. She took another sip of her wine.

"The hell of it is," she said quietly, for Nelson's sake, "there's not a fucking thing I can do, you know?" I stood there with one fist around the neck of a half-empty beer bottle and the other in my jeans pocket. I tried to look her in the eyes. "Don't you even think of looking at me!" she snarled. "You don't deserve to ..."

"MeShelle ..." I tried to interrupt. She held up a finger and I shut my mouth absolutely.

"I don't know who the whore is – I don't want to know, ever. Don't you think you feel so bad you've got to get it all off your chest. You keep it in there, Titus. You hold on to it, because I know you. I know it will feel like something you want to gag on and puke out – it's obvious. But you hold it in. I don't want to know. You are so fucking guilty – I know enough right now." She stopped to take another sip. "There's not a thing I can do about it," she repeated.

I set my beer on the counter and hung my head. I wanted to tell her that I had lost control. That I didn't know why. That it wasn't my fault, but it was. I wanted to tell her I didn't want it, that it just happened. That would have been another lie. I wanted to answer her questions about it, but it was clear she didn't have any. She didn't need or want any more information. I wanted to tell her I was sorry, and that was true. I asked God please to tell me the one thing to say and to tell me how to say it. But it wasn't necessary. She forgave me at that exact moment.

"I love you, Titus," she said. "With everything inside of me, everything that loves, I love you and Nelson." I looked at her again, and this time she let my eyes stay there. "What would I do anyway?" she asked. "I couldn't take Nelson away, could I? I mean how would I take care of him? I'd have to quit my job." Yes, I nodded. "So you've got me, there," she continued. "And I'm not through with our marriage, I want another baby. I want a sister or brother for Nelson. I want a baby with you," she said.

She made me cry, too, a big man like me. I didn't want to. I didn't think she would want to see me do that – I wasn't the one who had been betrayed here. But I hurt because she shamed me. Where I believed she would want to punish me, and wanted her to do it, she showed mercy. All the false thoughts that she might have cheated on me fled in that moment. I recognized them for what they were – more lies I told myself to justify what I had done.

"MeShelle," I said. "Thank you." I went to embrace her. She held up both of her hands, stopping me.

"Not. Yet," she said. "Not for a long time, Titus."

My wife left the kitchen, and I drained the last of the beer bottle. I tossed the empty in the waste basket under the sink.

Damming the Carbon

Donnie finally let her senses overtake her. Here was a sky so blue it must have been extracted from the core of an iceberg. Here were valley walls so steep and green that a civilization could have been founded, flourished and passed away within their boundaries. Here below her was a boulderscape of igneous stones, of broken barkless limbs, of the resolution to flow downhill of water and ground sand. A soundtrack of the rush of fluid through channel – around and over stone – filled the receptors of her ears. A pair of Cascade hawks paired in spiral plunge neared the river base fifty yards away and rose again in formation.

Midday sunlight laid like justice on the tops of Donnie's bare arms and neck, so that the surface of her skin was hot, and layers of muscle and tissue underneath were warm in the pleasant way that a nest is warm. A breeze blew down the valley from the glacier, moved her hair around, faded. She lifted her eyes to the star, put her hand up as a visor, saw the matter of light swirl and eddy in filaments of down on her wrist's surface.

Donnie and two hiking friends, Tyler and Audra, had already completed an eight-mile trek from the park gate – the northwest entrance that opened Mount Rainier from Carbonado and Wilkeson – to the terminus of the Carbon Glacier. Four miles to Ipsut Creek campground then four miles up a forest trail to the glacier's terminus, a dirty gray wall of moraine, scree, blackened shrubbery and ice. The trio had finished these legs of the hike by nine-thirty in the morning, ate trail mix and drank bottled water on the way, and had hiked three quarters of the way out by 12:45.

In past years, the hike to the ice face had been shorter. But a pair of impossibly savage winters had forced a rogue finger of the Carbon to seek old channels – which happened to roughly correspond with the asphalt road servicing northwest access to the park. The cumulative effect had been a series of washouts, bank failings, tree fellings and great, gasping sinkholes. Here amid western red cedars whose circumference at forest-floor level would be better than eighteen feet, whose trunks lifted greenery to a two-hundred foot canopy, whose root balls were the dimensions of good-sized locomotives, in whose bark faces could be seen a series of ever-changing glyphs – in a forest of these mighty giants, the simple insistent urgency of one raindrop too many had cavitated the landscape. To put a fine point on it, the road to Ipsut Creek campground and back was no longer passable by motorized vehicle.

The cratered trail made for a hell of a hike. As Donnie, Tyler, and Audra neared the halfway point on the return from the campground to the park gate, they had waned, like the exhausted approach of new moon, to silence. The Carbon River could be heard to their right, to the north, as white noise behind an occasional raven's honk, flycatcher's cree, or woodpecker's rapid ordnance.

Donnie was thinking about her job again, quietly, in desperation, even in the magnificence of nature – even here among this, this beauty – she couldn't shake it. Could never quite escape the notion that the electronic pager she wore, even now, might go off at any second.

Several months before – in March, she recalled as she walked – a recently laid-off subordinate over whom Donnie had had supervisory responsibility called her to threaten her life. Then there had been meetings with the human resources representative, with the company's hired-security officers, with her boss and her boss's boss. The threat had never actually materialized, that is, physically manifested itself. But the coiling, cawing anxiety of it – a possibility that seemed less and less implausible each day – and the knowledge the company where she had chosen supervision as a career was "right-sizing" made the threat real and ever-present.

Donnie recalled she had realized that one day she would die – finally really realized it – on Valentine's Day a few weeks before the incident with the ex-employee. It occurred to her in the same abrupt manner as would an accidental stroll through plate glass. As a teenager, she had seen a movie in which this hopped-up dope fiend girl walked through the sliding door of her parents' suburban home, completely oblivious to the lacerations and blood loss that resulted. This realization of Donnie's had been like that: on one side of the door she was immortal;

72

on the other side she was surprised to discover that one day she'd be toast.

It's not fair, Donnie had thought. A person should be able to inventory risk factors for death, and then avoid them. A person ups the ante a little, flirts with surprising, sudden, fulminant demise when one spends all of, say, his or her time at some Little Italy joint sucking white sauce and pasta from a sour fork. A person shouldn't be surprised that immortality doesn't eat in a place where the walls have to be scrubbed of blood, where spacklers have to come in to repair holes in the plaster. A person shooting smack or hanging around in meth labs is inches closer to The Dirt Nap with every passing moment. Maybe giving the finger to a Harley man could bring risk as well, or walking through East L.A. flashing gang signs indiscriminately. Those kinds of behaviors teased, mocked and invited death, Donnie had thought, but not just going about one's own damned business. Or doing one's job.

She had once heard, and wondered whether there was science to back it up or whether it was just a place-of-business myth, that if a person made it past 9 a.m. Monday morning they would live out the week. That is, that most heart attacks occurred from the stress of coming back to work from the relative succor of the weekend. If someone's ticker didn't blow by Monday, they could probably count on it for six more days.

Donnie discovered mortality on Valentine's Day 1998 when an acquaintance was fatally mangled in an automobile accident. This random event had the result of bursting Donnie's chrysalis before she was ready, of dashing vague hope borne of insubordination to the nature of things. Combined with the employee's death threat that shortly followed it, her acquaintance's death was the beginning of a long, cool slide that had brought her here to this June Saturday morning, hiking with Audra and Tyler.

She recalled the accident began with a simple tire coming loose from a road.

This had pulled a ton and a half of steel, aluminum, various synthetic fluids, vinyl, cloth and carbon-based organic material across a painted stripe comprising mostly reflective substance and Yellow Dye

73

No. 5.   Then there was impact like the fucking of two asteroids, only smaller.   Chrome merged with chrome, steel with steel, aluminum with aluminum.   One automobile wrapped itself around the other like an iron fist, the cars performing something like a Fandango.   Their human cargo became components in a twisted steel salad, whose lives proved as fragile and non-substantive as croutons, perhaps, splitting open with matter and viscera leaking forth onto a bed of asphalt lettuce.

The employee had threatened her a few weeks later.   And although the threat turned out – as these things often do – to be more an articulation of the employee's passionate disappointment than of his intention to actually hurt Donnie, still, it was unnerving in a way that had, at moments, utterly subjugated her.

All of this was an unpleasant dwelling place, anomalous in the calming greens, browns and reds of the forest, amid cedars, Western hemlock, salal, fir, madrona, gigantic ferns and ceramic fungi.   Her marching steps had begun the day with vigor.   But now she plodded, scraped fallen needles and pebbles into the pathway, skirted the lips of the broken road and suckhole embankments, startled squirrels and nuthatches.   Donnie was disappointed she couldn't shake her disquietude, not even for the sake of fellowship with Audra and Tyler.

Although the three were in superb hiking shape, the briskness of their walk into the park earlier had exacted a price from each of them, on the walk out.   Donnie, through her bleak outlook, had begun to sense a grinding wrench with every step – it started where her femurs connected to the pelvis, deep in there, and took turns shooting down her legs.   There, at each point of contact with the trail, her moist feet shifted a fraction inside tight socks.   She began to raise kernels of blister.

Then, almost as if the three of them possessed a single volition, they had veered from the mottled road, entered the woods to the north and trekked across a game trail.   The river noise broadened.   The ballast and great height of coniferous trees gave way to the lissome copses of vine maple and aggressive, hairspun nests of wild blackberry and salmonberry.
 They emerged from the tree line, mostly red alder at the river's terrace, and the Carbon River valley opened up like a promise.   The transition from wane sunlight filtered through cedars and hemlocks to this – this

brilliance – staggered them. For a moment, it had been as similar for all three as a spell of vertigo, and manifested so. They had had to pause for a moment and let their pupils grow pointed, adjust to the urgent rush of light.

The tableau: an alpine river fed upstream, now almost six miles, by the thickest glacier flanking the tallest mountain in the state. The water here was silty, the color of dusty milk, and flowed at fifty-six cubic feet per second across rapids and in channels and rivulets. Although the river bed here was, perhaps, a quarter of a mile wide, flow was down in early summer. The onset of the dry season had reduced the main conduit to a boiling runnel a foot and a half deep and eight feet across. At this juncture, the main channel was closer to the south bank than the north, but the three could look upriver, east, and downriver, and see that it meandered, as did its parallel, tributary feeders.

Here and there were pools, and stumps moved through seasons down the valley sides, almost glacial themselves, to akimbo deposit amidst the river boulders. Donnie paused to watch a waterskipper skate across a pool. The bug moored at a minuscule periwinkle shell clamped, like a tiny vise, to a riverstone. Donnie, Audra and Tyler climbed over limbs thrown down during winter storms, even fully networked branches, segments of driftwood – all lay on a nest of gray, red, brown, black, white rocks. Filaments of web spun from waterspiders stitched the driftwood together or glinted in breeze-blown arcs.

"Let's cool our feet," Audra had suggested.

Tyler and Donnie left their knapsacks at the bank, set their staves against a tree trunk, scrambled from the terrace out onto the riverbed. Before long, Tyler was leaping and cavorting over smaller channels, finding purchase on some boulders, slipping a little on others, not being very careful. Audra and Donnie followed, though, and giggled when Tyler made an ill-advised selection for foundation. The rock turned under his boot; he fell ass over tea-kettle.

"The great outdoorsman bites the dust," laughed Audra. "Are you OK, Tyler?"

"I'm fine, it didn't hurt a bit," he said. "Really." Tyler's grin belied a confession – it hurt quite a bit, but whether it was his pride or his backside, he wasn't saying. The women leveraged him up and they walked together, slower now, over to the main channel. It was hotter here in the sun, and Audra chose a large rock for a chair and started to unlace her boots. Tyler and Donnie followed suit, and soon six pink feet were drying in the light.

Donnie placed her bare feet on boulders in front of her. Warmth captured in them resonated and colonized her soles, the instep, toes, the ball, up her pretty ankles. For just a moment, the exigencies of life outside the Carbon River valley faded and the warmth traveled up her in a waveform of thermal abundance from star to stone to shin.

This pleasantness was abruptly truncated. Donnie remembered again the digital pager at her belt, that it might go off at any moment. She recalled a squadron of meaningless deadlines Monday and Tuesday, so many that she would never be able to meet all of them. Now that her company had merged with another, it was "right-sizing." This, she understood now, was euphemistic for firing absolutely everyone. She was in the locus of a bloodbath, had laid off forty percent of her shop. The criminally absurd part of it was that no one was being allowed to reduce the amount of work she or he was expected to accomplish. No one was enjoying a "concomitant reduction in work statement," as a paper snowflake, falling from the desk of some senior-management stooge, had dared to print, there, in black and white.

Donnie had somehow agreed to move up in her career by accepting a supervisory position, not really knowing what it would mean during a difficult time such as this. The union of two companies is a weird puzzle, especially when the other company has "won." It's as if the Catholics and Lutherans had re-unified, forswearing old wounds, she thought. Now Lutheran deacons are running around the College of Cardinals trying to manage things, and this is simply too much like the ripping of a cicatrix. Somebody had better tell them to let that scab heal before they do any more pulling!

Donnie realized she was having bizarre thoughts again; she'd been lulled into an imaginative state by the gurgling of the river. These days her imaginative states inevitably turned black, needled onto her skin – deeper, in fact – a tattoo of resentment. She looked up and saw Tyler and Audra skipping stones down the river, side-arming flat rocks that would plane the turbulent flow three of four times before disappearing without sound into the milky rush.

She stood up, letting her weight settle onto the boulders, feeling the heat from them in her insteps again, letting that kinetic wave work up her calves, knees, thighs. Donnie reached to her right hip, clasped the pager between her thumb and forefinger, articulated its fastening hasp, pulled it from her side. She performed this act as a surgeon, extracting the blemish from herself, observed it in her open palm as if it were a lump of malignancy. She skipped the tumor downstream; it slapped off the river's surface only twice, then disappeared into the milk. Goodbye, Company Property.

Tyler and Audra stared, first at Donnie, then where the pager had disappeared, then at Donnie again. To explain, she simply she shrugged, then added, "Screw them."

That's when she let her senses overtake her. That's when she noticed the pure blueness of the sky, the isolation of the river valley, the fluidity all around her, the pairing of hawks. That's when she felt the sunlight laying like justice on her skin from above, a hot, almost erotic counterstroke to the warmth rising from her bare feet that joined and sparked somewhere deep in her chest. That's when she looked at the sun, put her hand up as a visor, saw the matter of light captured in the soft hairs of her wrist.

She heard a splash over the river sounds. She looked down again, back at Tyler and Audra, who were plonking huge boulders into the main channel. Tyler would look around, find the heaviest stone he could lift, and heave it in. The pair took delight in the plashing, in the raising of geysers of spray and droplets, in the fractalizing and rainbowing of June sun.

To Donnie, this looked like fun. It looked like something purposeful, something where when they were done, they could step back, point, and say, "There: Look what we have accomplished." Whatever came of it, it would be the physical articulation of their thoughts, their will, on the landscape around them. It would be their special achievement, the reforming of land – the damming of the Carbon River.

Donnie bent to heft the largest rock she could manage without serious strain; it was, perhaps, ten inches in diameter – roughly the size of a basketball – probably weighed between thirty and forty pounds. She had no idea what kind of rock it might be, supposed it igneous, formed in heat and pressure and fire, lifted it up to the extent she could, and putted it through a weak arc into the stream. Its splash must have raised ten gallons into the air for a few seconds, sent water clear across the channel, splattered the dry rocks on the other side with droplets. Donnie, feeling twelve years old again, let slip a loud whoop and clapped her hands with delight.

Tyler and Audra continued throwing rocks into the channel. Now that Donnie had joined them, they established a sort of hefting rhythm. They would lurch to the bank with these heavy mineral bombs. Then, using their arms as pendulums, they would swing – first away from the stream then at it – releasing the boulders at the extremity of the arc, and watch the splashes rise and rise and fall.

At first it seemed as if the trio was making progress, that they might raise a barrier here at this point. They started to work from the edge outwards, so that soon they had established a rocky foray a couple of feet into the channel, like a jetty. They even imagined that the water rushed more urgently through the constricted channel that remained. This may have only been an illusion of early, fresh ambition though, because beyond the point where they made this observation, the river never seemed to get any fuller of stones. After a while, they wondered whether it might be deeper here than had appeared.

Forty-five minutes passed; Tyler's and Audra's zeal flagged. It was almost three in the afternoon and time to start thinking about completing the mile-and-a-half hike back to the cars. Donnie was still hurling boulders into the channel.

"Donnie," Audra called. "Hey, Donnie!"

Donnie stopped mid-swing, held the boulder, then let it drop at the bank's edge. She nearly crushed her bare foot as she looked up at the pair.

"It's time to head back," Tyler said. "It's almost three."

Donnie had driven to the gate and parked her car there, joined

78

Tyler and Audra, who had driven together. It was understood from the morning that they must get back to the cars by four o'clock – Audra and Tyler planned to be back in Renton by six-thirty for their niece's birthday party.

Donnie didn't want to leave yet.

"You know what?" she said, forsaking boulder throwing for a moment and trailing the toes of one foot out into the icy, swift current. "I think I'm going to stay a while."

"Donnie," Tyler started a protest.

"No, really," she said. "Just a while. It'll be O.K. – I mean, it's hot, summer, hours of light – I know the way back, Tyler." She looked over at him, sized him up.

"I know, but, uh... that's not the question," he said.

"He's worried about leaving you alone in the woods, Don," Audra said, an effort at invoking the logic of personal security. "That's all."

"Oh," Donnie said. Just "Oh." Then she paused, looked around at the valley face, the sky, the thousands of boulders, the Carbon River. "Don't be, I'll be fine. I really want to stay for a bit."

Tyler and Audra exchanged looks, surrendered. Donnie could be obstinate. Sometimes there was no cracking her. Tyler held up his hands, a penitent to the deities of long-suffering – "Whatever," he pronounced. Donnie smiled.

As Audra and Tyler balanced their way back across the boulders of the riverbed, back to the terrace of the bank, she sat again, set both feet in the water. There, she luxuriated in the contrast of skin and body made warm by the sun and exertion and the swirl of starkly cold water around her toes, across the tops, through the instep, over the ankles. She leaned her body backward resting on the palms of her hands stretched out behind her, arched her neck, her head back and hair flowing out behind her, stared straight at the sun and closed her eyes. She would just rest a minute here. Just a minute, maybe two, before resuming with the boulders.

USFS Ranger Mark Gottardi woke earlier than usual to the absence of something, a needling discomfort like a folding, chopped-off finish of a dream. He lay nested in sheets with the beginning of light seeping in through curtain fabric. He wound himself in the sheets, pulled blankets up around his shoulders, and realized he must urinate, mightily, very soon. So he rose from the mattress and crossed the half-light to the bathroom.

Afterward, Mark made coffee in the kitchen. He forgot the unease of waking up, puttered, poured milk over cereal and sliced a grapefruit in half. After breakfast, he opened the front door to retrieve the newspaper, forgetting it was barely dawn, maybe 6:20 or so now – the paper wouldn't be here yet, clear out here in tiny Carbonado.

The air outside his cabin was silent. Not void of sound – he could hear sporadic birdcalls and the rustlings of forest rodents up in the branches, but an ambient sound was missing.

"What the hell?" he thought, stepped off the porch around the side of the cabin. He drew up short as he rounded the back, where the property abutted the Carbon River. He stood there with his mouth agape.

The river and its background music were gone. Only a greasy, silty runlet with holes of standing water remained. He took a step closer to the bank, looked up the channel at a confusion of bent rootwood, long-submerged boles. He looked across the chasm at the watermark – its crisp declination was as straight and sure as striations in a rock face. He looked downstream at more waterlogged detritus. Everywhere were round, wet boulders that hadn't known air for, perhaps, centuries, but would now slowly dry in the crisp morning, with languidness at first then in a sudden evaporation as the sun rose and dappled the canyon with lambent, soft light. The arc of a bird's flight caught his eye. It settled in silt, drove its beak in for a morsel. Mark stood and watched the bird feed, until an itch distracted him.

He scratched his cheek, felt the stubble there.

Movie Stars' Kids

Down at the Hicks group home the kids would play a game in which they were the children of movie stars. Ricky, for instance, was the son of Kirk Douglas, and would imagine his father as Spartacus. The resemblance was unmistakable – chin dimple and all. Candace went for Doris Day, and would skip through the Hicks's halls mewling, "Que sara, sara, whatever will be, will be." The Hicks grownups would play along, since the kids didn't have real parents – their folks dead in car wrecks, castaway drunks or simply, in sallow Evan's case, vanished, leaving him bawling on apartment linoleum.

The kids didn't know the details.

They just played the game, and it lasted so long and became so important it was transformed into something nearly real. That they might be the offspring of these Hollywood people took on the characteristics of the almost-factual, a maturation of fantasy, wish, hope.

Raymond was the son of Fred MacMurray, the Absent-Minded Professor, intent on discovering the real-life formula for flubber. Jill, daughter of young Natalie Wood, Maggie Dubois in The Great Race. Randy, the sallow one, Bela Lugosi's boy, young Dracula. The five of them would flop on the carpet in front of the Hicks's black-and-white RCA set and wait for a glimpse of their mothers or fathers, and Mrs. Hicks would pop corn and bring in soda. She would join Mr. Hicks on the sofa behind the Hollywood kids.

"When will we see them?" one of the group children would ask, as the tube faded to a single white dot – a unitary, alone sun in a blank universe of greenish-black glass – and the quintet made ready for bed. "When will they come for us?"

"You're just staying here for a while, while your parents make pictures," the Hicks would explain, and gradually the grownups stopped winking when they said it, so the kids started to believe that it might, perhaps, be so. Never mind the inadequacy of this explanation, its latent cruelty. Let the kids believe what they will believe. Better than to disclose the real nature of those who gave them life, then walked away, especially for beautiful children of such innocence.

"Perhaps you'll see them soon," was the best encouragement that could be offered from the Hicks's, and the children were hurried off to shared rooms, bunks, sheets of flannel, their restless dreams.

Ricky turned eleven that spring, the first that all five children were together. The Hicks arranged an outing, a picnic lunch at Leverich Park with a tablecloth, baskets, yard darts and a plan for badminton. But the afternoon soon featured mustering clouds from the west – they marched and rose against the clear, blue sky of the morning and mid-day. By the time Mrs. Hicks had unfurled the tablecloth on a sheltered picnic table, the first drops were falling. The kids continued throwing the darts, clapping at their arcs and proximities to targets, Raymond postulating possibilities were the darts composed of flubber rather than their pointed, steel tips and plastic fins.   Then Mr. Hicks gathered them from underneath a downpour, and they bustled under the shelter soaking.

Ricky's present was an Instamatic camera and two rolls of film. Mr. Hicks showed him how to load the mechanism, advance the brown tape into the camera's gears, click shut the cover. He cautioned Randy not to open the back panel while the film was wound, lest he expose it to light and ruin his snapshots. The other kids gathered around, offering further, spurious cautions, rain leeching their sweatshirts. Water from them dripped onto the lumber of the table's benches, forming puddles.

Ricky remembers how at one instant the clouds opened and the sun cast an urgent, material swath of light into the park. He recalls its play across cedar trunks, casting them in barky columns of zealous orange, so that they appeared to ignite and burn from within. The sward of grass seemed to leap there, in front of the movie stars' kids, until it vibrated green. Sunlight penetrated a curtain of rainfall that had moved east, over the valley cut by Burntbridge Creek, and inscribed a perfect multihued arc hovering over the encroaching neighborhood.

"Look!" Jill had shouted, "A rainbow!"

Ricky wanted to make a snapshot, to record his birthday rainbow. It seemed a lucky thing, to have a rainbow on one's birthday. A special present, from God himself. Ricky raised the Instamatic, scanning for the arc in its viewfinder, locating it splendidly, feeling the cool button of the shutter under his fingertip. But Mr. Hicks snuffed Ricky's ambition matter-of-factly, but with a precise gentleness.

"Ricky, it won't turn out," he said. The boy dropped the camera from his cheek, looked questioningly at his foster father. "The rainbow," Hicks explained. "It won't show up on the film. You'll be wasting a picture."

Ricky remembers Hicks went on with some formal explanation, invoking science and light particles and the manner by which lenses trap light, and emulsions and shutter speeds and – well, a lot more Ricky can't recall. The effect, that afternoon, had been an unwanted but immediate truncation of his enthusiasm regarding the present. And the onset of an evolving distrust of the illusory. Ricky remembers that during the course of the afternoon, after the arc faded and the clouds closed again, after rain set in for good, after gobs of potato salad and fried chicken and soda, after the wind kicked in and they began to shiver, he was changed. He remembers that damned camera now, how his chest filled with joy as his fingers tore wrapping paper from around its box. And how the original joy warped and fragmented, cascading in shards through itself into resentment, denied his first photographic subject. No amount of pictures taken afterward – group shots, individual portraits of his Hollywood brothers and sisters, his foster parents – none of these mitigated his ache for a picture of the rainbow, whose real image was later strangely lost to memory, imprinted for a while only as a shade of discontent.

The son of Spartacus was, for many years, a child of disappointment.

Rick can hear the pounding of woofers as he climbs out of his car. Lamplight casts forth from Ray's place, windows beckoning party-goers inside, and Rick steps up the walk adjusting his leather jacket and running his hand up through his hair. He steps to the door and feels the bass thump through its wood. Realizes a knock will go unheard, so twists the knob and steps into warmth and sound.

Friends and acquaintances fill the front room. They're dancing to Frampton Comes Alive. Rick scans the room for Ray, sees some old mates from high school – they wave plastic beer cups, sloshing the contents around a circle of garrulous smiles. Some heavy-footed dancer Rick doesn't know causes the turntable to bounce, and the needle skips. An inebriated chorus of boos meets this gaffe, and then the mistake is quickly forgotten.

Ray emerges from the kitchen door, tottering, fingers lacing the neck of a VO bottle. He sees Rick inside the doorway, breaks out in an idiot's grin.

"Son of Spartacus!" he announces to the party, his boom stentorian, eclipsing even the Frampton launched from massive speakers. "He comes!"

Rick crosses the party, carefully nudging aside too-close dancers and staggerers, mouthing *how are you* to those he knows and *howdy* to those whose names he cannot remember, but whose faces seem familiar. Ray falls into his embrace, and Rick can smell the bourbon reek of his breath, but it doesn't matter. The two movie stars' kids squeeze each other like large mammals, Ray smacking a drunk kiss on Rick's stubbly cheek. The smell of crushed leather rises, joins the bourbon. Ray makes a present of the VO. Rick pulls hard on the bottle, grimaces as the whiskey rolls and catches down his throat, and lights his guts.

"I gotta surprise for you," Ray says, guiding Rick away from the front room through the kitchen door. "Come in and get a beer first." Ray points Rick in the direction of a keg next to the refrigerator, inspects Rick's drawing of a first draught. The amber fluid drops into Rick's plastic cup, half head, and he says, "You better pump them taps, bro. This is all head." He tips the cup to drain foam into the sink, returns to the spout to draw more airy beer. Fills the cup and drains half of it.

Now properly refreshed, Rick asks about the surprise.

"Candy," Ray says.

"She's here?"

84

"Yeah, she's down from Seattle."

"Doris Day's kid?"

"The very same," Ray says. "Looking good, too."

Rick is intrigued and excited. He hasn't seen Candy for more than five years, he thinks. Last time was at his high-school graduation, which the Hicks and all the Hollywood kids attended. They'd stayed in touch with the Hicks – Rick had left when he graduated. The other kids had moved on to other group homes – wherever the state of Washington told them to go – jobs, high-schools, before his departure. Jill had even gone to college in the Midwest, and no one had heard from her since. But from time to he'd run across Ray and Randy, Ray more often since he still lived in town.

Rick refreshes his beer, has another pull off the VO. Ray guides him through the front room, down the hall. In one of the bedrooms, merry-makers have convened a mini-party, one for those more seriously intent on modifying consciousness. A sweet odor wafts from inside, hazy therein, and he sees Candy sitting cross-legged on a futon through strata of dope-smoke. She is applying the tip of lighter-flame to a waterpipe's bowl. She sucks the smoke in, releases her thumb from the carburetor as the dope in the bowl kindles to ash. She holds the hit for a long time, unaware as Rick stands evaluating her. Then she exhales an enormous gout, sips her beer, and looks up.

Rick has prepared himself for her to leap, cross the haze, and fly into his embrace. It's been so long, and of all the movie stars' kids, they had been each other's favorites. She has grown stunning, changed her blond hair for highlighted brown – even from her seat Rick can see how she has matured, curves in the right places, face made up not too much, but some. Her eyes, lightly shadowed with lashes thickened, appear to be the eyes of royalty in retreat. They are at once gorgeous and troubled. Aware of themselves, their beauty, but hunted, or haunted.

Her lips move as if she searches for a word. She squints through the drugs and alcohol as if searching through a book, reading to discover a reminder of his name. A smile spreads across her full lips, but instead of rocketing from the futon, as he had expected, she says, simply, "Ricky."

"Candy," he says, deciding to cross the room himself, not unaware of the three other pot-smokers attending his childhood princess, but ignoring them nonetheless. Suddenly he stands over her. She gazes from the height of his waist, the soft skin of her cream neck visible, blouse collar plunging to lace, pretty chin pointing. "Stand up and give me a hug," he says.

"Come down here and give *me* one." She hands the bong to a pair of hands that have materialized from the corner-frame of Rick's focus.

He accedes, dropping to the futon next to her, gathering her in his leather arms. She kisses him on the lips – he flashes on a pre-adolescent afternoon when he was a prince. A strong, narcotic scent rises from their embrace – she turns so that her chest pushes hard into his, but this is the extent of her response, as if the movement has required all she has stored within. She is quickly limp in Rick's clutch and he is aware, instantly, that she is utterly stoned. They come apart, and she mumbles something about a cigarette. She fumbles inside her own jacket, hand trembling as if with a palsy.

"Let me help you," Rick says, drawing a package of smokes from her inside pocket, aware the skin on the back of his hand brushes her blouse, her warm breast beneath fabric. He experiences a minor arousal as he excises a cigarette from the pack, lights it for her, places it between her lips. His visceral interest falters though, when he remembers she is, in some ways, practically his sister. It flees at the unbidden thought that despite her beauty, she may be a husk. Still, they were children once, movie star's kids, royalty. She bestowed his first kiss, ever, and the years that spanned that kiss and this one tonight apparently had been gentler with Rick than Candace.

She draws on the cigarette, staggers against the smoke, eyes shut tight. She neglects to thank him.

Rick glances back to the doorway to see whether Ray can offer any explanation or, at least, a silent, shared communication. But Ray is gone – he has returned to the dancing guests or to refill his cup. The pot-smokers continue to smoke, passing the bong and hacking. They offer Rick a hit, which he accepts. Candy reclines against the wall behind her, eyes still most often closed, although her lids flutter and she utters mixed-up phrases and clauses from time to time. "Don't worry about her," one of the strangers says. "She's messed up tonight. Completely zoned."

"On what?" Rick feels the hit kick in.

"Oh..." and laughter breaks in, "...you name it. Speed. Coke. Must have smoked about a quarter-ounce of this bud herself."

Rick floats on this information for a while, long enough to hear someone change the record in the front room. Music resumes, it's a Ted Nugent album. He refuses the next offered hit. Rick doesn't drink too often, smokes pot on even rarer occasions. Its okay for him periodically, but he never has suffered it habitually. He listens to the first cut, muted through the walls, sound waves canted strangely through the orifice of the door. He is awkwardly aware of Candy next to him, the warmth of her thigh against his, and he realizes she is nodding onto him, leaning, her head has dropped onto his shoulder. A shampoo and conditioner smell rises faintly from her hair.

A Guess Who record is playing outside, but Rick is in Leverich Park playing yard darts with the other movie stars' kids. And they are with the Hicks in front of the television set, fortified with blankets and pillows and popcorn. Their parents sing and dance and say beautiful things on the TV. Then he is with Candace sitting on the lower mattress of the bunk-bed he shared with Randy. She is giving him his first kiss on a dare, just her soft lips are all, and he likes it. Something makes him want to open his mouth, to open her mouth with his. To feel what it feels like for one tongue to touch another. Her mouth remains closed, her eyes open. He is not embarrassed to gaze directly into them, forever.

Rick is alone with her, the potheads have departed. Candy seems to be sleeping, her breathing even and shallow. He nudges her off his shoulder, lays her carefully on the futon. Her jacket rises and falls, a slow oscillation that simultaneously fascinates and concerns him. He leaves her there, searching for Ray, finds him in the kitchen with the party's late-stayers.

"Have a beer," Ray slurs. "Filler up."

87

Rick waves him off. "Candy. She's out of it, man."

"She's just fucked up," Ray says. "She can crash here."

Rick shakes his head in refusal. "Naw, she can crash at my house. I don't want her to wake up to this mess."

He expects Ray to be offended, but if anything's clear, it's that Ray is only capable, maybe, of summoning enough mental exercise to draw another beer from the nearly exhausted keg. The VO bottle is clear and empty on the counter.

"You wanna help me get her to the car?" Rick asks.

Candy wakes on strange sheets, rises with a thrumming head to search for a toilet. She finds one in time – there she flings the contents of her stomach, turns, jerks down her jeans and folds in on herself to pee. She hasn't closed the door, and Rick stands in the doorway, wakened by her noise.

"Ricky," she utters from a savaged throat.

"Candy, it's okay."

"You can't just stand there. I'm peeing."

He closes the door gently, so as not to bring a great noise into her fragile morning. The hasps and latch click like a whisper.

Candy wipes, rises and flushes, stoops to drink water directly from the bathroom faucet. Examines herself in the mirror, borrows his comb to draw tangles from her hair. Her empty stomach clenches, and she is hungry and it occurs suddenly to her that she may have slept with Ricky last night. She wanders around this notion for a moment, decides it didn't happen: She awoke fully clothed, and there was no telling drainage from between her legs, no feeling other than the need to urinate.

She steps from the bathroom – Rick is there with a cup of coffee.

"You want sugar and milk?"

"Black." She follows him down a short hall to a kitchenette. Sits after he sits at a small table, hovering over a steaming mug of his own.

"Thanks," she says. Rick thinks she means the coffee. She means for bringing her here.

"It was brewing."

"No... for bringing me... is this... where you live?"

Rick nods yes, surveys her in full light. She looks older than twenty-three. He decides for sure what he suspected last night: She has been living harder than he, possibly harder than anyone he knows.

"You didn't..." she says. "You didn't sleep with me last night." It is a statement or a question, Rick isn't sure which, so he gestures through the kitchenette's open spanway to a sofa with a knot of blankets. Her eyes follow his hands. She utters only, "Oh."

"I wanted to, kind of," he says, thinking this disclosure – which is only half sincere – will kindle warmth in her. Maybe will offer her a boost.

"I would have let you. But I'm glad we didn't."

Okay, Rick thinks, that settles that. Good. He attempts another track.

"What are you up to?"

"Just hangin' out," she says. "Do you know where my jacket is?" She wants a smoke, and he gets it for her.

"You were loaded last night."

"I'm loaded every night."

"Like that?"

"Mostly." She states this as if it is a feature of her, the defining characteristic of what it means to be Candace – Candy – motherless, fatherless, hopeless. Artificial love and stimulation have been her companions for years. She sees no reason why they will not be faithful, adequate, for years to come. They may be absolutely relied upon, and she hates them wholly, if tepidly.

"You could get some help," Rick offers, instantly regretting it. This is none of his business, really. But he pushes, "There's people, places who could help you." She's silent. He blurts out suddenly, "I could help you."

Candy snickers while her head hammers. "I don't need any help."

"Yes. You do."

"There's really no use."

"You're use enough."

89

Rick's insistence doesn't produce resentment in her, only a desire to change subjects. "What do you do these days?" she asks.

"I'm a shooter, a photographer."

"Oh, God, I remember. Do you? The time in the park – it was your birthday. We all, well, the Hicks I guess, gave you a camera."

Ricks nods, memory welling. "Come here," he says. "Lemme show you something." He rises, indicates she should follow, guides her by the forearm through the spanway into the living room. They stop at a bookcase where he retrieves a scrapbook. He shows her clippings, color photographs cut from newspapers and outdoor magazines. "I shot these," he says.

He turns the page to a fold-out section of a travel magazine. The panorama shows lush green peaks, rocky outcrops overhung with a tapestry of clouds. The sun's light has penetrated the photo and there, arcing from peak to peak, is a perfect, glorious rainbow.

"He said it couldn't be done," Rick says.

"What?"

"Taking a picture of a rainbow, Hicks said it wouldn't turn out."

Candy holds the scrapbook in her hands. She scrutinizes the print through her own fogginess, even as the caffeine begins to kick in and clear it away. The quality of the photograph is so precise, so well-delineated, that the arc's colors leap from the page and bathe her in scattered, visible light. The spectrum reproduced here is perfectly diverse – the inner rim of the rainbow an angry red to match her pain, then orange some kind of enkindled anger, bitterness yellow, green that suggests transition, blue for the coolness of her prince. And a violet, salving hope at the outer boundary. A hope that still, despite all of this – that Doris Day never came to collect her, nor her own mother and father, that she had been relegated to the heap of loss – has not died, and never will as long as she wakes in the morning.

"It's beautiful," she says. Candy remembers, too, Ricky's birthday party. She remembers it was not long afterward that she kissed him. And she sees now that Ricky has shared this photograph as a gift, a promise. She hands him the scrapbook. Anything is possible.

"Ricky," she says, stops to abridge her thoughts. "Rick," she

90

pronounces, finally. "Will you take my picture?"

"Yeah, I'd like that." She stands with her arms at her side, observes him move to a closet, remove a bag full of gear. He withdraws a tripod, erects it as she watches. He tops it with an expensive-looking black box. Starts to set up a halogen lamp on a second pair of sticks, to screw into fixtures a small silver umbrella that will refract the light precisely, pauses as he notes she has stepped from her jeans and is slowly undoing her clothing.

"No, Candace," he says, holding out his hands, palms toward her. Her fingertips pause at the last button. Both sides of her blouse have fallen away, revealing the front hasp and lace hemispheres of her bra, the valley of her cleavage. Her underpants are partially occluded by the blouse's fabric, by her hands, which are frozen there over the final button. "With your clothes on," he explains.

There may be – will be – time for the other, later.

The Names of Moss

With a light touch Andrzej Pliszka parses through furrish tendrils of *Kindbergia oregana.* Most days he is never so happy as when his fingertips commune with the bryophytes of moist forests. Nevertheless, Andrzej's spirit is incongruously heavy. Or is he only annoyed? Andrzej always has been confused on this point.

There may be several reasons why Ranger Kelly Neville remains aloof – even to the point of discourtesy – after four days. They weave around and through his head in the same way his hands invade and separate the Oregon beaked moss he is preparing for exhibit: *Because I am not like her American men. Because my English is marginal, more so when spoken. Because my nails are chewed to the quick.* The reasons could run to lists. Maybe she thinks he only wants *dupczyc.* It's true; any man would find her desirable. She is pretty, with the cheekbones of a princess and clear, soft-looking skin. Her blond hair is gathered in the back with a pin. He imagines that if she unclasps it, the hair will fall gently about her shoulders, but no further. But if she thinks such a liaison is the first thing on Andrzej's mind, she is mistaken.

Ranger Neville stands at the counter tightening a knot of tourists into a hiking party. She will guide them on a one-hour walk through the Hoh Rain Forest. Just now she is speaking casually with a swarthy, bestubbled man whose neck dangles an enormous camera. The capped lens points precisely at her right breast.

"I know, I've driven that route many times," she says. The camera-man has just offered a comment about the great distance he has come, with his family, from Seattle. Andrzej recalls the drive as well. It had lasted a long time, Kelly – Ranger Neville, as she had introduced herself – collecting him at the University of Washington's Forestry Center, then driving the U.S.F.S. Ford Explorer down to Olympia, and on to Hoquiam, then north again on the coast. Andrzej first glimpsed the Pacific through gaps in trees as they sped by. He had thought Ranger

Neville might stop the Explorer, let them get out and stretch. It seemed improbably close inside, particularly since she offered few words of any sort – no encouragement or enthusiasm for his presence, nor any interest in his project. Four silent hours from Seattle, they turned into a valley and followed the Hoh River nineteen miles. The road climbed as they went. To their right, the pale, silty water cascaded toward the ocean, rushing among gravel bars and moraine boulders. Sopping leaves clotted the road's shoulders. Fog – hovering just at the tops of coniferous trees – threatened to drop onto them as she drove. Her lips were set in a line.

Had she said as many words to him during the entire transit as she had just said to the man with the camera?

"Dozens and dozens of different moss types thrive in the Olympic Rain Forest's wet environment," she tells the party. "We'll see them on trees, nurse logs, covering the forest floor – they can be just about anywhere where they'll be drenched in water and nutrients." Members of the party nod like eager students. And their instructor's lesson flows also to Andrzej's ears. It is plain that she is at ease with strangers, yet not with him. "The types on trees are called epiphytes," she says. "They live their whole lives above the ground and are not parasitic, meaning they do no harm to the trees. You'll see them hanging everywhere, especially in a glade of broad-leaf maple we'll visit."

The park's visitor center is tucked back into trees whose tops often disappear into the fog. They are western hemlock or giant Sitka spruce, sylvan behemoths whose age seems more geologic than graspable by humans. It seems so to Andrzej, anyway, twenty-four and a research fellow from the University of Agriculture in Krakow. The department of Forest Botany sent him to America to study mosses – well, bryophytes, to be exact, which includes true mosses, peat mosses and liverworts. But not lichens, hornworts and selaginellae, as he has explained to Ranger Neville two or three times, hoping to interest her in his work. In each case she has nodded and returned to her tasks.

Andrzej returns to the mortarboard, on which he separates moss from moss with gentle tugs. He is looking for a perfect strand in order to best illustrate Oregon beaked moss. His exhibit, a project for the Forest Service on behalf of the University of Washington, is an interactive catalogue of the types of mosses to be found hereabouts. Interactive in the sense that visitors to the center will be able to touch the strands of different moss types, to caress the soft, green tendrils as they would the hair of a loved one or the fur of a pet. The specimens will – when the project is complete – number nearly a hundred. Each will be affixed to its own board and set in a large tray atop four table-legs, so that the effect is similar to that of a card-file, and it will be possible for visitors to file through to look at all the mosses.

Why won't she talk to him?

He had tried to reach her in her own language of instruction. Each morning she picked him up at the oceanside inn, where he would spend these two weeks. He climbed into the Explorer's passenger-side seat, said "Good morning," and received her curt nod. For forty-five minutes they drove the twenty-five miles from the inn to the park's visitor center.

"Moss lacks the true root," he had said the second morning. "The things that makes it supporting and conducting to the nutrients are being carried out by filamentous structures that are known by the scientists as rhizoids."

Ranger Neville had nodded as the wipers cleared mist from the windshield. When she offered no comment in return, Andrzej tried to engage her with questions.

"These trees are being very tall and old, isn't it true?"

"Five hundred years, some of them," she said.

"And what are some of them being called?"

"You got your western red cedar, Douglas fir, the spruce of course, the giants – those are the evergreens. Big leaf maples and alders mostly, for the deciduous."

Many words, admittedly, but offered as if reading black type on a page. Bankrupt of emotion or friendliness. Clear of the desire for communication.

"Is it raining here all the time?" he asked.

"Fourteen feet a year," she said. "That's four or five meters, I forget which."

Andrzej sadly recalls this exchange. He sifts sporophyte stalks

94

and spore capsules from *Claopodium crispifolium* – rough moss – with his aching fingertips. He bites the nails more often when he is unnerved, and he has scarcely been more so in years as he has been the past few days, here with Ranger Neville. As he affixes a sprig of step moss to its board, it occurs to him that perhaps she is simply a bitter young woman. Like so many Americans, she thinks the world revolves around her and her wants. What she doesn't have or cannot get she resents. Everyone should line up and do whatever she wishes. They should all enact her plan. He writes in block letters on an index card glued to the board: *HYLOCOMIUM SPLENDENS*: STEP MOSS, ALSO KNOWN AS MOUNTAIN FERN MOSS. Then adds, with the pen, THE AGE OF STEP MOSS CAN BE DETERMINED BY COUNTING LEAF-CLUSTER INCREMENTS. Satisfied with this fact – and with the knowledge that thousands of visitors will soon know this – he moves on to the next board: *Pseudotaxiphyllum elegans*. Elegant silk moss.

After visiting hours, Ranger Neville and another ranger whose first name is Jack but whose last name Andrzej has forgotten or never learned make entries in folios at the counter. They take inventory of the books, postcards, and posters for sale in the store and cash out the till. They briskly examine the center's interpretive exhibits for any damage that may have occurred during the day, which, if found, they will note on a government report and fax immediately to their superiors in the Forest Service. Andrzej rushes to finish the board he is working on – the club moss that is so ubiquitous here and drapes the giant maples on the walk through the park known as The Hall of Mosses.

He had come along the first day on one of the walks – with Ranger Neville and a group – and had been impressed with the club moss. It hung everywhere like coarse, verdant hair. The weight of it pulled the maple branches toward the moist earth. Ranger Neville explained that sometimes the club moss became so laden with rainwater that its weight would break its host branch. The branch and moss thus became part of the ecosystem's cycle, joining the humus of the forest floor and making this soil some of the world's most nutrient rich. For this reason, she explained, the Olympic rain forests are registered as a World Heritage site. Members of the group squinted upward in appreciation. The Hall of

Mosses trail was three-quarters of a mile long, with slick leaves, rocks and protruding roots underfoot, steep climbs, narrow paths and fallen, rotting logs to traverse. Andrzej had been pleased with every moment of the outing. Out of nearly every bit of space grew a living plant. Nurse logs presented nurseries for ferns, mosses and saplings, and colonnades – orderly rows of mature trees in their positions as originally nourished by long-decomposed nurse logs – rose away from the trail in all directions. Someone asked Ranger Neville whether the rain really ever stopped.

She shook her head. "There aren't many times where it's too dry here. That's why it's called a rain forest." Some in the group laughed. "When it is dry, for a few days maybe in the summer, mosses cease photosynthesis and become dormant. They reawaken only when rain comes again."

The group had completed the walk, chattering in the forest, stunned and amazed by the enormousness and age and ancient beauty of the place. Someone remarked it was a place older than time. A boy said, "It's like Jurassic Park," and when no one seemed to have heard him, said it again.

"Are you ready?" he hears her ask. "We're finished."

Andrzej looks up from the worktable.

"I should cleaning up this," he says.

"You can leave it for morning, if you want," Ranger Jack says.

"Is this being O.K.?" He turns to Ranger Neville. She shrugs her shoulders without answering, so Andrzej lays the glue-stick and pen gently on the table next to the club moss, dusts his hands on his pant-legs, and follows the rangers to the exit. He wonders again why she is such a *suka*, such a bitch. He hadn't expected such unpleasantness in America. Ranger Jack drives away but Ranger Neville wants to use the women's toilet, and as dusk drops and rain quickens once more, Andrzej finds his gaze drawn magnetically to the tops of trees again. Ancient, he thinks. When these trees were saplings, my country was a mighty power. Krakow was an important center for commerce. Was Columbus sailing the oceans then? Trees so enormous and primordial – Andrzej suddenly thinks of them as sentient. And witness to so much.

She comes out while he is still looking, mist dropping coolly on his upturned face. It's almost dark as they climb into the Explorer.

The Roosevelt elk is among North America's largest animals. An adult male – a bull – may weigh as much as 1,200 pounds. A collision between this giant ungulate herbivore and a Ford Explorer could be cataclysmic. None of this is on Ranger Neville's mind as her headlights sweep a moving, tawny monolith and she swerves. Wishing there were more shoulder, she steers into the slide. The tires bounce on uneven turf. A wall of bark looms. There is a colossal jerk and crunch. Something explodes in Andrzej's face, the dashboard mounted airbag. The Explorer rolls. Andrzej's head feels like the end of a horsewhip. His temple bangs against something. While he fades the Explorer comes to rest, driver's side down.

After a moment he feels her hands on his neck. Still belted, he is upside down with his cheek dragging Ranger Neville's thigh. The dashlight is weak – in fact, most of the light is coming refracted from the Explorer's beams off the surrounding trees. Of course, the engine has quit. She's whispering something so softly he cannot make it out. She may be telling him that she is bleeding hard or that her legs are broken, boots ensnared in the pedals. She may be saying that her skull has fractured on the left, upper plate and that swelling is already gathering insanely underneath. She might be mentioning that one of her ribs has shorn and ripped a jagged laceration across her left lung, or that her stomach has been punctured, or that her duodenum and spleen are severed and leaking. She may be whispering that the radio is smashed and inoperable. All of these things are true. She may be finally talking to him, but so inaudibly that it barely keeps him from wafting in and out of conscious-ness. She has gathered the strength to lift her blood-slathered hands onto the skin of his neck. Through her touch she asks him to go for help. There is no other way.

Andrzej climbs out of the Explorer. His boots search for purchase, and as Ranger Neville grunts he realizes with horror that he has trodden on her. He lifts himself with brilliant pain through a door that seems as far away as the bent tips of hemlocks. Atop the crumpled metal he sits for a moment, guessing at bearings. He thinks he can spot the road. The only sound is the river, to his left. If the front of the Explorer hasn't flipped during the roll, then the park exit is to the left and ahead. But did they go off the road on her side or his? This he does not know. It had happened far too quickly. It's all Andrzej can do to make his brain wrap itself around these calculations. If he moves toward the river sound and encounters the road before the river, then he should simply keep the river on his left on the hike out. How far is it? How far had they come? Fifteen minutes maybe, so, say, eight or ten miles. So maybe ten to go, or were there houses or little stores after the turnoff on the way to the center? Yes, he thinks so. So not quite so far. Six or seven miles.

He realizes it will be pitch black. Surely there must be a torch – what he has heard Americans refer to as a flashlight – in the vehicle. He peers into the interior through the open passenger door. Ranger Neville lies in a silent mass against the far wall.

"I have to find a torch," he says. She doesn't say anything. "A light!" he shouts. "Are you hearing me? I want to find the light!"

It comes out of her heavily and glottal, as if spit through blood: "The glove box."

Andrzej reaches into the maw of the fractured Explorer, lifts the deflated airbag out of the way and opens the box. There is a torch secured by a pronged, metal clip. He retrieves it, then speaks down into the hole. "I am going for the help. I will go to find quickly help." He thinks he sees her eyes flutter.

Then Andrzej stumbles toward where he believes the road lies. Slipping and falling, his ankles are snared by exposed wet roots. Even after he toggles on the flashlight, he finds himself constantly on his knees, or pulling himself to his feet again, hands grasping the fronds of soaking-wet ferns. The light from the Explorer's headlights is behind him, to his right, and casts a strange light like a city on a horizon. Its aura climbs up into the boughs but is interrupted by the huge Sitka trunks. He glances back one last time before he gets to the road. Already the light is barely discernible.

Then there is a water-filled ditch. He slides down its bank, cold mud coating his trousers and jacket and hands. He drops the flashlight in the water but quickly snatches it back. The road is in front of him, and the Hoh River just beyond the asphalt. He fears he has come only a small distance, that there are hours and hours of hiking and pain ahead of him before there's a chance at a telephone or radio. The air smells dense and he can smell his own sweat. His clothes already cling to his skin. He wishes he could burst into tears, but knows that men do not do this, even when they are alone and the odds are insurmountable.

Could he run ten miles? Or twelve, or however far it is? He thinks about this a moment, standing there dripping at the roadside, and realizes he is wasting precious time. It might take him four hours to walk out, or two to run and jog. He could rest if he got tired. Andrzej wonders how much time Ranger Neville has, and starts running downhill. The flashlight plays across the trees in front of him, light shifting and shadows undulating with the bounce of his feet.

To pass time, he thinks the names of moss: *Racomitrium aciculare... Leucolepis acanthoneura... Sphagnum geniculata... Fissidens crispus... Antitrichia gigantean...* The names are a comfort as his feet work like never-stopping pistons. *Scouleria aquatica... Metaneckera menziesii...* Somewhere he sheds his jacket: it is far too heavy and wet, and he is as warm as a fever. This goes on for some time.

Andrzej spots a light ahead. As he draws nearer, he can see that it is high in the air, on a pole perhaps, or a hill. At half past ten, he stumbles against the bare wood stoop of the Hoh River Store. His fists hammer on the front door, hands breaking glass. An alarm goes off. As he slumps against the siding, then falls completely to the stoop, the proprietor rounds the corner of the building with a shotgun.

"What the hell?" he shouts. "What the hell?"

Andrzej Pliszka cannot at first say, but at least the man has lowered his weapon. It's clear there lays no aggressor here. This man is a pitiful mess, soaked, not adequately clothed, hatless, pale, chest heaving and – when light is trained fully on him – considerably bloody.

Soon the Hoh River Store's proprietor understands everything. The sheriff is summoned and Andrzej is offered steaming coffee of the weak sort Americans drink. He accepts it gratefully, and the fluid scalds so that for days his tongue and mouth will be a reminder of this night, and then after that, there will only be his memories.

Or maybe it happens this way:

Kelly says she is cold. He can barely hear it. Her voice is as meek as a strand of tufted feather moss. What she says is offered so softly that Andrzej wonders whether she really spoke at all, or whether her declaration was not spoken but otherwise communicated. She asks him what happened.

"We are wrecked," Andrzej says.

"Are you O.K?"

"I am O.K. But are you going O.K.?"

Kelly doesn't answer right away. She seems to be taking stock and deriving a self-assessment from what she finds. "I don't think so," she whispers. After a long silence, she says, "It hurts."

Andrzej unclasps his safety belt and, using all the strength he can muster in his limbs, climbs around his own body and the seats and the center console so that he is just behind her. He kneels on the ground or, more to the point, on the window on the ground. In the dashlight and the glow from the headlights off the trees, he sees that she is irreparably broken. He doesn't know anything about medical trauma but it is plain Kelly will not live.

"The radio," he says. "Where is it?"

She lifts a hand to point, but her fingers will only hang from her palm. The radio has been torn from its brackets by the impact of her knee. In the tiny light he can see her ranger slacks are torn where it happened, just on the kneecap.

"It is wrecked, too," Andrzej says. Their breath commingles, though hers is coming labored. "I will having to run for help," he says.

Her hand bunches at his wrist, clasping with strength he would not have suspected she still possessed. "No," she says. It is louder, this negation, almost as loud as her normal voice. "Please don't." After a while she says she is afraid.

"Let me going for help," Andrzej pleads. He is crying, although Kelly isn't aware of this. But she will not let him, but instead asks to be held. Andrzej reaches around the seat and grasps her. She is warm and wet – it's blood, he realizes – and soft. His face is next to her ear. His forearm lies across her breast, but it means nothing.

"I'm sorry," she says.

He assures her that he is O.K.

"No. I've been so rude." Andrzej can think of nothing to say, then finally says, "All right."

"There was a man," she says, "who hurt me. Do you know what I mean?"

"I am not him," Andrzej Pliszka says. "I am not that man."

She is quiet again for a long time. Then she whispers, "I didn't tell anyone."

Andrzej thinks about this a little while, then asks her whether she would like to hear the names of moss. She nods.

"*Kindbergia praelonga*," he says, "which is being commonly called slender beaked moss. I am mounting that on the board tomorrow. Then there is *Rhytidiadelphus triquetrus*, also called electrified cat's tail. Is not that a funny name?" Kelly Neville makes a wet sound that may be a laugh through fluid. "Tufted feather moss," Andrzej says, "*Scleropodium cespitans*."

Sometime during this Kelly passes away. But still Andrzej holds her. And whispers sweetly into her ear the delicate names of moss. Until dawn comes, and discovery.

Yes.

This is the way it happened.

This is the way he will always remember when he thinks about it.

Displacing Water

A barely understandable shape rises out of the lakebed toward Danielle. Past lidless schools of rainbow trout and freshwater bass – scaled beings suggested only as brief glints of silver-black near the surface – the form ascends. Bubbles rise from the catatonic fish as sediment endlessly falls through strata of murk and lakeweed. The man who was her grandfather drifts upward. She stares into the dark water over the dinghy's gunwale. There. *There.*

She is seeing him now for the first time in nearly thirty years – what she *can* see from the light of stars, plus some distant floodlights on shore. It's not much, but enough for now.

Wavelets kiss against the hull. He is displacing water on his approach.

Danielle had made an odd decision. Stealing from her home in the strangely ideation-populated hours after midnight, she drove across forty miles of summer-night freeway under a new moon and rote constellations. Her objective was imprecise at first – it had been a simple calling the same as the plush sounds of mated loons. But as she drove, alone but for an occasionally passing trucker, the goal resolved. First, as water, as a pre-form of itself – the wetness, coolness and fluidity of it. Then as water contained, shorelines and volume – not a sea, which is the absence of containment, but as a lake or pond encircled. She saw a beach of variegated pebbles, cedar and madrona roots clawing at soil on the water's edge. She imagined she heard the shouts of children leaping from docks... small, squealing cannonball people. She saw the physics of oarlocks, heard the squeak of them dry and rhythmic. She felt lake reeds braid through the spaces between her toes, wrap her ankles and calves as she swam. She tasted and breathed lake water, gasping, only to burst into sunshine, laughing and tasting and spluttering at the same time.

Finally, after Danielle turned left off the freeway at Gorst, traveled Highway 3 for ten miles through an empty, post-midnight Belfair, and hooked up with State Route 300 – as all of this came together in a dreamlike concatenation – she appreciated her destination. The goal materialized as a lake of her own childhood.

It was at first called Prickett, after a homesteader. But the man abandoned his summer cabin there sometime in the 1940s, and others erected vacation structures on its shores, renaming it Trail's End. Barely three-quarters of a mile long and half a mile across – a spot where the water table had risen above the land. It was, as lakes go, barely a depression in the ground. A large, soaked field. Its greatest depth at the height of the rainy season – which goes long in the Pacific Northwest – may have been twenty-five feet. In the mid-60s, Danielle's paternal grandparents had purchased a small lot on the lake. There, they constructed a tiny A-frame cottage for summer visits, respites from a life of middle-class complications in Seattle.

Danielle's mother and father, as well as her brother, spent weekends sleeping in the lofts, in the cabin's closely held heat, listening to the shake shingles overhead pop with expansion and contraction. Too, they would hear squirrels scrabble over the cedar roof, the beat of their tiny claws a signal of the onset of morning. Danielle learned to float in Trail's End Lake by inhaling as much air as her lungs could contain, holding it there for a full minute, laying back in the water with her arms spread wide, legs splayed, hair fanning out. The waterline of her body hit right at the ears, so sound would alternate between muffled and clear until her ears gave out, stopped up with lakewater. She remembered a saturated happiness emerging from the lake after a day of swimming, waterlogged, fingerprints occluded by pruny ridges and valleys. She would run dripping to the cabin, a towel draping her, as hungry as ten horses. A breeze off the lake might raise gooseflesh on the bare parts of her browning skin.

Danielle remembered these impressions as she turned from SR300 onto Trail's End Road. The asphalt wound upward, a steep grade that frequently suffered washouts – great relaxations of earth that carried sections of the road into a draw at her right during spring or fall rainstorms. The water table of this country was high, and nothing was ever far from saturation, even in the high summer of August and early September. The soil held and released water on a schedule of its own.

She entered where the road began to circle the lake, remembering the way in the same manner birds migrate. It had been eight years since she had been here, and the directions to her were a series of vague impressions – a rise here, a stand of madrona trees there. She recalled a community boat launch at the west end of the lake, a leftover from when power boats were permitted. Now, of course, only craft propelled by oars or paddles were allowed. As she recalled the place, it materialized. Her course, barely recalled, was thus validated – it was like a pilot whispering through clenched teeth that he knows the flight is over because he is on the ground. And she realized she was like that – tense – teeth clenched until she caught her jaw aching. She drove past slowly, so the sound of her engine wouldn't disturb anyone.

Familiar shapes resolved in the light, or shapes that were at least archetypes – forms she knew somehow but had forgotten. They had been here all along. They comprised the articles of a playground mounted on a shore: a picnic cover, a plywood supply shed, a swing set, a large slide, a sandpit. A wooden dock jutted out across the water, exactly as she remembered. She could imagine which planks were loose, the green algae that had affixed itself to the styrofoam floats underneath. Someone had tied a dinghy to cleats at the end of the dock.

She pulled the car into the playground's tiny lot, killed the motor. She cut the headlamps. The absence of light was so nearly perfect as to astonish. Its fullness was mitigated only by the digital clock on her dashboard. It read 2:24 in bright blue rectangular numerals. The colon flashed with passing seconds and she was reminded that time, tonight, was a resource, although as a means to what end she was still, at that moment, unaware.

The engine clicked as the block cooled. In full light, her knuckles would have been colorless, gripping the steering wheel.

What am I doing here? she wondered. What magnet could have drawn her from the nest of her bed, from the closeness and security of her husband? What had drawn her across the freeways and highways, forty miles? What compelled her to visit this playground, a lake of her youth, the death place of her grandfather?

They'd found him in swimming trunks, almost thirty years

before, floating face down. A rubber inner tube around his waist kept him from sinking, but not from drowning. Actually, the doctors weren't at all clear whether the cause of death had been the infarction of an abnormal heart – a condition unknown to him and all around him – or whether his lungs had filled with water first and caused the attack. It was all rather academic anyway. Her grandfather was just as dead either way. Except as a warning to future generations – if his heart's condition was, for instance, congenital. Otherwise, it was simply another story of a man dying before his time.

He was in his mid-fifties, and Danielle remembered most about him that he had a Clark Gable-style pencil mustache, and that his hair – in which she remembered a sort of salt-and-pepperish gray – had swept up and back. When she saw photographs of him, he seemed to have a reddish button on his chin. It was not quite a birthmark, but a tone and skin quality that suggested a fellow who often rubbed and pinched his jaw. She imagined this meant he was a thoughtful person, and that the world had been robbed of his thoughtfulness too early. Her grandmother, who was still alive, would only say that he was a *good* and *special* man, that God had blessed her with him. For His own reasons, her grandmother claimed, her husband had been *called Home* earlier than most.

Danielle sat in the car and speculated about his last moments. The day would have been hot, midway through July. He was industrious around the cabin, never resting, always performing tasks, probably sweaty and overheated to the core of him. He would have finished a project – moving a pile of bricks or digging a runoff trench – enjoyed a cola drink and traded soiled work clothing for trunks. Then he would have stowed an inner tube in his rowboat, pushed the craft lightly off the waterfront. He would have rowed out to the family's float, tied up the boat and climbed out onto the wooden decking with the tube and a towel.

He would have squinted into the midday sunshine, breathed in the odor of the lake and admired its forested shores in every direction. A heated breeze would have caressed his salty skin. He would have been the locus of his universe, all pale Caucasian flesh and tropical Hawaiian trunks, golden sun glinting from his wedding band and the caps of beckoning wavelets all around him. All the cosmos would have radiated from him, surrounded him, and focused upon him. In all of this, he would have seen the signature of his Creator. He would, at that moment, have been at the center of God's lens. Then her grandfather would have stepped into the inner tube, reached down to draw it up around his waist. He would have, under a blemishless blue sky, leapt into the opaque greenness of the lake.

As he crossed into the totality of water, it squeezed his chest like a vise. Danielle imagined his last cognition was the smell of tire rubber, his nose next to the inner tube as he struggled for air, for light, for benediction. She imagined his legs kicking out, *the shock of the cold water,* he thought at first, then he knew the bull muscle of his heart was tearing and shorn. He wanted his wife, his sons, his daughters, his own mother – one last embrace – and then he knew, *he knew,* and then surrendered and walked into the waiting arms of Jesus.

All of these *things* she manufactured about her grandfather's last moments, as if it was her task to tote up some maudlin summation of all the last *things* that happen in storybooks and whispered anecdotes. If she properly toted them, if the equation she derived and solved was managed correctly – she would cease to fear the unexpected but sure tragedy that crouched to spring into some other compartment of her life. She would be equipped with certain immutable properties in her defenses against such dislocations. Then, finally, she could live free from fear of the unknown, unspoken, unpredictable.

Was it an unconscious but conscious hope of *this* that drew her?

She exhaled in the place of cynical laughter. She knew she was – at the center of herself – a tentative, uneasy person. That she lacked fundamentally what might be described as *courage.* But it seemed absurd that an irrational outing to a place that had ceased in its relevance at least two decades ago would change any of that. But if that wasn't it, what was?

She opened the glovebox to retrieve a flashlight. The miniature bulb inside cast weak, yellow light onto the passenger's-side seat, made her bare right arm glow palely. She pushed the door open and the dome light flooded the car. It poured out resolution onto the gravel aside her, and Danielle stepped out. She closed the door slowly, just felt the latches catch before she pressed against the cool panel with her hips, slowly, solidly. She felt the fabric of her dress slide against the metal. She heard the latches engage inside with a single, solid *chunk*, quiet in the night, controlled and muffled without the slamming kinetics normally associated with a car door closing.

She knew where the oars for the dinghy were stored. That they had always been kept in a plywood shed next to the fence was an unmistakable part of her personal history, although one she frankly didn't remember. She knew that if she opened the door – which was not locked, had no reason to be – she would find inside old-fashioned, bright orange life jackets with tie-together canvas straps, canoe paddles, beach balls, nylon rope, spider webs. And carefully placed, in one corner, the oars.

It was exactly so when she opened the door and trained the beam of the flashlight inside. And when she felt the stout hardwood of the oars against the soft skin of her palms, when she lifted them silently from their storage place in the shed, she felt she had acquired the means to an unavoidable locomotion. Toward what, she had no idea – surely it was the same destination that had brought her across three counties in the deep night to this place of her childhood and these thoughts of her grandfather. The hinges made small squeals of untended protest as she let the door settle back on its jamb. Then, an oar in each hand, she walked across the playground toward the dock. The flashlight made minute leaps in front of her, laying open the truth of the playground – its struggling grass and sand, agates and bottlecaps. As she approached the shoreline, sand and an aggregate of tiny stones began to proliferate, and finally the front of the dock emerged from shadow. Its planks were black in the flashlight's beam, timbers running into darkness beyond the light's circle.

She played the light out onto the dock, believed she barely caught sight of the dinghy moored there at the end, but couldn't be sure. She heard the call of one night bird to another and smiled. Then she stepped up onto the platform, felt the weight of herself move the sections of dock in an undulation, so that it briefly adopted a serpentine life and adapted to the act of her mounting it. She heard water splashing beneath in reaction, then a series of deep, hollow thumps: the dinghy's sides bouncing against the end of the dock, no doubt. It occurred to her to extinguish the lamp, that if her eyes adjusted to the dark after a few moments she'd be able to walk the length of the dock safely and have a better chance at doing so undetected. The beam clicked off and darkness enveloped her again.

She stood without moving, listened to the meter of her own respiration, and that of her heart pumping. As her eyes grew accustomed to the darkness and gathered the small light afforded by her environment, she began to appreciate the features of the lake and boundaries of objects. There was the shoreline, where the reflections of stars off of water ceased. The opposite bank could be understood as that point equidistant from the floodlamp of a cabin across the water and its mirror image on the lake's surface. She could see the dock now, a black runway stretching out to the vanishing point, and her eyes swept the distance and gathered more light. She took a slow, exploratory step, balanced with the moving foundation, and followed it with another.

She found herself over the dinghy with no appreciation whether much time had passed since she stepped onto the dock, or whether she had arrived there in only seconds. She could see the boat perfectly, its oarlocks folded down, the twin bench seats, the blunt bow and squared stern. It bounced gently against the dock itself, and she knew waves were moving out from the dock from her footfalls, messengers of greeting to all that the lake held. She fed the oars into the boat then crouched, bringing her center of gravity low. Then she crabbed over the edge of the dock into the boat, steadying herself with one hand on the dock, her foot hooked under the dinghy's seat, another hand on the gunwale. Balanced so, the rowboat barely dipped as she climbed aboard, then shifted slightly as she sat erect and slipped the oars into their locks. The lake rose to accommodate her.

Danielle slipped the rope from around the cleat, pushed off with a small wake rushing in to fill the trough left in the water. The splash caused her to look up and around. She expected sentry lights to snap on, searchlights to flow out over the water, alarms, bells – but the water settled out and she drifted away from the dock. Keening mosquitoes, no-

108

see-ums, and other night bugs flew around and into her ears, drawn by the nectar of her sweat. She took the oars in each palm, clasped the handles, and pulled with a determined gentleness. The dinghy leaped at the center of Trail's End Lake.

As she rowed, she tilted her head back and stared at the sky. It was Empyrean, with stars on stars. Making her way in the city, she had forgotten how dense, how layered, they could appear without competing light. The Milky Way bifurcated the bowl of night like a milk river, and she recognized familiar constellations: Cassiopeia, Cepheus, Cygnus the Swan, Lyra. There was Ursa Major and the Big Dipper, with its second, binary star in the handle. She loved the legend – perhaps apocryphal, perhaps true – that Indians used that remote dual star to test for keenness of vision in their small children. She could see it yet, with small children of her own. Her eyes traced the imaginary line produced by the first stars of the Dipper's ladle, arrived at Polaris. And as she mused that these heavens were unchanging – she certainly *had* reclined in a boat or on a dock at this lake and seen *exactly* this before, precisely as tonight, the only difference being the time that had passed behind the beholder's eyes – a meteor shot across the firmament. It left a streak as long as half of the universe, then vanished.

She turned her head down from the sky and contemplated, again, the shore from which she had debarked. Then she swiveled, rested with the oars a moment to ascertain her progress. She thought of a progression paradox: her goal was the center of Trail's End Lake. How would she ever make it if in order to reach the center, she must first row half way to the center? And if in order to reach half way to the center, she must – indeed – first row halfway to that halfway point? Then, of course, she must first row halfway again, and so that the closest she would come to her goal would be to arrive just short. How could she circumvent the first half of the next, proscribed half-distance? If one is constantly covering only half-distances, how can one ever arrive?

She shrugged and resumed the rowing, reveling in its mechanics, the strain against the biceps and triceps, how the low muscles of her back and abdomen contributed. It wasn't a cold night by any means; the temperature had dropped from the high seventies during the day to perhaps the low- to mid-sixties. She had broken a sweat, but there was no wind, and she found herself in calm, flat water. The physics of rowing are a displacement as well, she thought – one creates a pressure wave from the digging of the oar's blade. It's like an airplane propeller or a wingform. An oar creates lift toward the absence or reduction of pressure.

She played at these sorts of mental reductions as she rowed into the lake's center. She heard an owl or owls hoot, the splash of droplets from the oars when she rested. She realized she had left the flashlight on the dock. She heard, at one pause, a dog bark in the distance, from far beyond the opposite shore. She wondered whether animals on the beach could see her – deer perhaps, which had forded streams and crossed valleys to come bathe in the lake – or whether, in fact, she was beheld at that moment by more magical beings.

She entered a whorl of mist on the water, and the lake collected and sighed beneath her. She sensed this, and it made her consider again the physics and metaphysics of displacement. A woman places her hand in a bucket of water; its level rises. She removes the hand and it falls. In a moment the water in the bucket is still. Was her hand ever there? She leaned over the side of the dinghy and trailed her own soft hand in the lake water. It was tepid and silky, like a secret fold of moist, impassioned skin.

Her grandfather sits in the stern of the dinghy. His whisper, so light it might be an aspiration of breeze, colonizes her. "It's O.K., Danielle," he says. "You don't have to be afraid. You can go all the way. You can."

She remembers, or he places the memory in her, that when she was a little girl he used to collect her in his large arms. He would hold her so closely and breathe the smell of peppermints onto her skin, her small neck, the tiny form of her. He would offer her a lozenge from a roll he had stowed in his trousers-pocket, and wink as she sucked in air to cool her mouth from its minty fire.

"It's so hot!" she would say.

"No sweetheart, it's *cool*."

She would suck longer on the lozenge and then understand. "I've been watching you," he says, from the stern of the rowboat.

She remains silent, studying him – he who was and is more than a silhouette in the night, but only barely. His features seem to effervesce from an internal place, features she remembers as if they had recorded themselves in her small-girl memories only moments ago, but that she knows are ages old, perhaps ancient. The Gable mustache. The swept-up-and-back hair. His grandmother's token of union, the wedding band on his knotted left ringfinger.

"Did you know that?" he asks. "That I have been watching?"

"Yes," she says. "Will you still?"

"Yes."

"Forever?"

"Yes." He holds out his hand with the band between his forefinger and thumb. With his other hand he grasps her palm, holds it upward, open, leaves the ring at its center. "Forever."

He stands in the boat and ascends. She rises to follow but he holds out a hand upward, the gesture that speaks without voice both *no* and *stay*. She sits again, watches him disappear toward Cygnus.

The noise of gulls on the hood of Danielle's car.

At first the scratching of their talons on metal seem an interference with an elaborate dream. Their steps draw her from a well of pleasantness suddenly and dropped her in this place of heat and glaring light. Her skin feels sticky. She tastes old food, unbrushed teeth.

She stares at the playground. Her nightdress and hair are sopping wet. She looks down, sees that water has pooled on the upholstery. A moment of near-sleep again, where she believes she went up with him. That she departed and is no longer here, now, in this place. She can look down and see her car, and the dinghy pulled up on the shoreline, and its wake from the center of the lake even though it dissipated hours ago. From this great height Danielle can see that she has been in the lake, that she has, in fact, experienced a displacement, and has

111

exercised a displacement on all that was around her.

But she opens her eyes again. The sun shines through the passenger-side window. She sees the open glovebox.

Danielle looks at her soaked nightdress. A waterplant, some kind of sleek reed, emerges from the neckline. She pulls it forward, sees it wraps almost around her breast. She feels another reed through the fabric, at the small of her back. It winds down her thigh, emerged from the hemline.

Believing she will hold and contemplate his old wedding band, she unfurls her other hand, (It will be dirty with sediment and algae. She will rub its surface, burnish free a clear, exquisite undercoat of gold.) There is nothing.

She pumps the accelerator twice, reaches forward to turn the ignition. The engine roars to life.

Hughie and Moira Stand in Freezing Air

Hughie and Moira stand in freezing air outside the driver's door of Hughie's Eldorado. Their breath makes twin plumes in the night, and ice crystals are already forming on the windshield. Its frozen skin crawls imperceptibly up the window from the dash to the roofline, forming a skein so slowly that watching the sweep of a clock's hour hand would seem, in comparison, like tracking the movement of light. But this – the propagation of ice crystals on smooth safety glass – they do not watch: instead they watch Hughie's keys hanging from the ignition through the driver's window. Lisa comes up from behind and asks what's the matter.

"Dammit, Hughie," she says, after his palms-up explanation. "It's fucking *cold* out here."

They've just eaten a post-midnight supper inside the Denny's, Hughie a chicken-fried steak and the girls both pot pies. They sat in an upholstered booth, Hughie between the two young women like a tended sultan. Although they are not consorts, simply devotees. They had talked for an hour and a half after finishing their entrees, cream spiraling into bottomless coffee mugs. Talked about being clean and sober, in the program, the Big Book, twelve steps. The Fellowship. The Promises found on Page 84. Hughie is older than the two of them put together, a sagacious mentor who can, somehow, get a pair of young women to run around with him on a Friday night with ardent alacrity. He gave them a ride to the clean-and-sober dance. They worship him, now, because what they worshipped for so long – albeit a short time in comparison to some others – was no longer working. Moira and Lisa know this: When Hughie speaks in meetings, he speaks wisdom by agency of fable and parable. It's the wisdom they crave now, more than the drink. He's got it – they want it. And not the *other* – intimacy or sex – probably not, anyway.

"I know darlin'," he says, sighing, resigned to the frigid fact of his inattentive gaffe. "I know."

The three make an assessment, bare hands stuffed in pockets for warmth. The night is as clear as glass, with stars visible straight overhead, although not at the horizons where their light is overcome in neon and klieg. Even though it's past 1 a.m., cars continue up and down Auburn Avenue, headlamps sweeping the puzzling trio as drivers traverse the intersection in front of the restaurant. It's twenty-five, maybe twenty-six degrees.

"I'll go see if they got a coat hanger inside," Moira says. Hughie thinks a coat hanger won't work – the Eldorado has electric locks.

"We gotta find somebody with a slim-jim," he says. "Who knows where, at this time of night."

He thinks a slim-jim would work, despite the electrics – they can work the lock mechanism from the slot between the window and its rubber stripping. Poke and lever around down in there with the cold metal strap and maybe – just maybe, if they're lucky and the Higher Power grins down on them – pop the mechanism.

"Jesus, it's cold," Lisa whines again. "Kind of thing makes you want a good shot of bourbon."

Hughie eyes her with a level stare, a look that communicates he is about to impart a zealous *saying*. The kind of thing members have on their bumper stickers. "There's no problem, ever, that alcohol can solve," he states. Then adds, to make clear he understands she was only half-serious, "except, perhaps, virginity."

The girls giggle, their laughter rising like bubbles toward a bright, fresh star overhead. Hughie has a notion maybe they could jimmy the trunk – one of the girls might be able to wriggle through the support struts that give form to the back seat and separate it from the trunk space, if there's access and room to squeeze through there. He can't remember ever noticing. But the trunk's lock isn't electric. Maybe one of the girls has a key that will fit.

"Let me see your keys," he says. Lisa points through the back window to a dark mass on the seat.

"Mine are in my purse."

But Moira has a set. From fingertips already going numb, she extends them to Hughie. Their jingle overfills the Denny's lot like a tardy echo of the young women's laughter. It occludes the sounds –

114

momentarily – of passing autos as it whorls and eddies into a bottleglass-spun heaven. He examines each key for one that might fit the trunk's lock, finds a likely candidate, shoves it in the hole. But it won't turn.

"Maybe they got a paperclip inside, or a stiff wire," Moira suggests, accepting Hughie's return of the keys, stowing them in her jacket's pocket. "You could pick it."

Hughie grins – it's been years and years since... but he could do it, *has* done it in the past. Picked a lock, that is. He nods, his affirmation indicating one of the women should go in and inquire. Lisa says she'll go, shuffles across the frosty asphalt, leaving Hughie and Moira to assess, further, the gamut of possible solutions.

"Maybe we should go in and warm up for a second," Moira says.

"Naw, she'll be back in a minute. We'll have this open in no time."

A police cruiser rolls by on the Avenue. Hughie and Moira watch the officer watch them – Moira suffers a mote of paranoia that is habitual. For her, so green, so recently on the deficient side of right and wrong, the feeling that she is iniquitous – *guilty* – is inherent in even the most innocent encounter with any sort of authority. She has only, just in the past few months, migrated toward that fulcrum where most of humanity breathes in the filigreed oxygen of ethics. She has only understood, recently, the mishap of her past six years as the manifestation of disease, an allergy with anguishing consequences. Hughie, though, has defeated this concept – that alcoholics possess some unique measure of original sin. He has grappled with it as Jacob wrestled the angel and overcame it, receiving unto himself a New Name: Israel. Even so, Hughie knows that guilt snarls at the heels of the freshly picked even into the initial stages of recovery. Possibly years into it, if the guilt has set down deep hooks. He spent decades hard-plowing the fields of booze, piled up his own tottering list of transgressions. But that's all over now. And this is *his* car; the title's in there to prove it, clamped to the sun visor. His registration, proof of insurance and drivers' license are in order. He is a productive citizen needing protection and service. He wants the cop to stop, on a number of interesting and provocative levels.

But the cruiser continues down the Avenue in spite of Hughie's

115

raised, beckoning arm.

"Shit," he tells the night. "He didn't even slow down."

Moira is glad the policeman continued his patrol rather than stopping to help. She offers Hughie no rebuttal, and Lisa is halfway across the lot anyway, grasping a bobby pin one of the waitresses had dug from her purse. Lisa tenders the ersatz key to Hughie, who smiles at its latent utility. Hughie takes the pin.

"The light," he says, and gestures so Moira can see how her shadow falls across the lock. He nudges her to one side with firmness but gentleness, and streetlight flashes from the chrome hasp. Hughie kneels, knees on the cold blacktop, holds his mouth in a moue of concentration and will, inserts the pin. By minute probings and explorations, he charts the lock's topography. Its architecture is revealed to him through subtle pressures on his fingerpads. Numbness has not yet colonized them, but it will soon, so he must survey the lockscape briskly. It reveals its guts to him and his bobby pin. He records the positions and ridges of tumblers and pins. Now that he has mapped his mission, he turns the pin twice, depressing one, then two, then three tumblers. Moves the pin horizontally and down at fifteen- or twenty-degrees approach. The lock clicks, gives, the trunklid raises on its springs.

"Ain't lost my touch," he says, trunk yawning as a wishing well. He stands over a balding spare tire, the jack and lug wrench, a couple of boxes of literature, remnants of carpet that used to go quarter-panel to quarter-panel. The odor of mildew emanates. He explains there may be access through the backseat, in doing so indicates his round body is no candidate for the squeeze that may be required. Which one of them – Moira or Lisa – will climb into his trunk and see whether there's a way in? Lisa says no way in hell is she getting in that trunk, climbing through all that crap, feeling around in the dark. All that musty carpet and rusty bare steel...

Before Lisa can conclude her list of excuses Moira is over the trunk's lip, hands down in the clutter, ass in the air. "Don't you dare shut it on me," she orders as she disappears into the cavern. Her head and upper torso vanish, the onset of a spelunking that may produce discovery or disappointment. Hughie, who thinks of himself as past, or nearly past, the age where he is much influenced by matters carnal, is surprised in a pleasant way that he cannot remove his eyes from the curve of her bottom, its tight jeans, the way they hug and caress the valley between those well-proportioned half-globes. The way she moves back and forth as she probes, up there where he can't see, as if she is midway through the act of female-dominant sex with an invisible partner trapped in pleasure underneath.

There used to be a neighbor Hughie, as a young man in his twenties, would watch in her window. He'd step onto the veranda of his apartment with a tumbler of whiskey and a cigarette, sit in a folding chair, ever hopeful. Sometimes she would shower with her bathroom window open wide, step from the hot steam into view. She would apply her towel and deodorant, raising her arms to reveal the soft curve of breasts. Hughie would gulp his bourbon, draw at the smoke like a hog attacking a rasher of bacon. She'd step through her wall into the bedroom – curtains never drawn – take a station at a settee to leisurely apply makeup, still nude. He would stare and grow hard, disappear into his house to masturbate.

One morning Hughie stepped onto his veranda, disappointed to discover her curtains drawn. But as he waited, she swept them aside and stood in the window full on, breasts high and round, pressed almost into the glass. The view ended just below her navel – he was left to imagine the sill-eclipsed sweetness where her legs joined. The woman's gaze was as vacant as the alley between them, forty feet between Hughie and her nakedness. There was no acknowledgement, no seduction, no exhibitionistic motive, no approbation nor reproach apparent in her stare. Slowly, she redrew the curtains and, as far as Hughie knew, never opened them again.

"What am I looking for?" he hears, muffled, from deep in the metallic cave of his Eldorado.

"See if you can feel for any of the seat fabric," Hughie answers, bends down into the trunk as if closing the distance will make his instructions all the clearer. "I'm trying to figure out whether there's a solid wall of metal between the trunk and the seat, or if the seat just kind of rests there and makes the wall itself – do you get it?" Where Hughie has placed his head, he can just discern where Moira's leather jacket hangs open and her blouse has come untucked from her waistband. When she moves at a certain angle, one cup of her brassiere, slinging her breast, is discernible – even if almost entirely imagined in the small, stingy light. Even so, Hughie finds the imagining delicious and prodigal.

"Yeah, I get it," Moira is saying. Her fingers wander across hard nubbins of metal that are bolts cranked around nuts, sealed, and painted over. Little flanges where steel has been spot-welded together, the nipples of rivets. There are no cavities where she can thrust her wrist and feel for the inside springs or fabric of a seat. It's all solid. A barrier that cannot be breached. "There's nothing here," she declares.

"All right," Hughie says, and Lisa utters an impatient oath in the chill behind them. Moira hoists herself backward from the cave, Hughie arrested and still with the shape and arcs of her, the movements of her pistoning legs and lunging hips as she extracts herself from the fruitless attempt.

"Watch your head," he adds, as he monitors her thighs. But he recovers himself, reaching in to protect her neck and skull from the sharp flange where the trunk's hinges wait like jackal teeth. He'd hate for her to bark that creamy skin on one of those nasty hinges. The open trunk births her back into bitter pre-dawn, a birth of flummoxed justice in which even the best, most honest and willing attempts to render problems powerless, instead, leaves their solutions unrealized. Hughie tenders the bobby pin, which he has been grasping, to his trousers pocket. He notes in the vicinity an adjacent semi-tumescence.

There is a moment of bewilderment as the trio contemplate a next course of action. This is not at all what The Promises on Page 84 say: *We will intuitively understand situations that used to baffle us*, or some such guarantee. The solution is fleeing them rather than coming home. They circle the car like tugboats, crystals having sheeted, now, both the windshield and rear window. Their vapor wafts like smoke from three burn-barrels. But now Moira has an idea:

"What about a locksmith?"

"At this time of night?" Hughie asks. "I bet that'll run a hundred, hundred and fifty bucks."

"Oh," Moira says, disappointed. She would like to be the one who solves Hughie's – *their* – problem. And stop Lisa's looks of accusal and impatience. She's starting to see, again, Lisa's bitchy side, with which she is well-acquainted. Moira and Lisa have grown up together, but Moira has evolved toward the demure, assuming everyone else is always right, while Lisa makes a point of how stupid and ridiculous everyone else is, how her will and her plans must take precedence. She is having a rough go at acceptance, and always will. Her recovery, therefore, will be anguishing, if it holds. Moira looks at Lisa now, who is shivering, glaring at Hughie with impatience.

"Well maybe you better do *something*!" Lisa nags.

"You got a hundred and fifty bones?" Hughie asks, still calm, but pointing at the fuming Lisa. "Either of you? 'Cause I don't."

A silent fuming descends on them.

"Why don't you just go inside?" Moira suggests to Lisa. But Lisa only offers a pout. After a moment, Hughie suggests they do, all three, go inside and warm up for a few minutes. The two women are about to agree when the three of them hear a strange, whirring sound and the popping of rubber tires on sidewalk. A man in a motorized wheelchair trundles toward them, humming and singing snatches of a song. His progress is slow and zig-zaggy, not a straight line as a wheelchair might more efficiently draw on pavement. He has, they suppose, emerged from The Dot, the tavern four businesses up the Avenue. The man looks up and sees them gathered around Hughie's Eldorado, takes their measure – friends or foes? – motors his chair through a gap in the curb and pulls up. He surveys them, wonders through grain alcohol about their situation. Maybe they'd give him some money, if he asks.

"What up?" the wheelchair man stammers.

It looks as if his legs have suffered some withering catastrophe. They are too small for his body, even dangling, as they are, from a down parka that hides most of his frame. Hughie can tell just because of the size of his head. He scrutinizes the chair-bound man, wonders whether this miserable drunk can possibly represent a contribution. In Hughie's experience, the Higher Power has sent his agents in more baffling

119

disguises, that's for sure. But a bird-legged booze-hound mumbling *What up* in the icy night – it seems unlikely.

"Locked my keys in," Hughie says.

"We tried everything," Lisa adds, "for about an hour."

The wheelchair man accepts this information as if it is a passing comment about the frigidness of the air. "Hmm," he observes. He engages the chair motor with a flick of his gloved hand, the chair lurches to a slow orbit around the Eldorado. "Tried a hanger?"

"Electric locks," Hughie answers.

"Slim jim?"

"Nobody has one," Moira explains.

The drunk man pulls up aside the driver's window. Tries peering in but can't see over the lip. Frost has begun to assemble there as well, so even if he could get the angle he'd be unable to verify Hughie's keys suspended there.

"You checked your pockets?"

"Oh, they're there," Johnny says. "We seen 'em."

The man seems to gather thoughts like yarn into a ball, from tangled, wooly strings saturated in dipsomania. His assembly of options, parsing through them like a slow, stumbling megahertz hierarchy, resolves in one simple action.

"Howard DeSchutes at your service," he announces, reaches behind him to a tube affixed to the back of the chair, withdraws an umbrella and wields it like a ball-bat. Before anyone can react, he has wound up, and powers – with biceps and forearms toned from years of self-propulsion before he got the electric-motored conveyance – the umbrella through a resolving arc. Its curled handle strikes the driver's-side window, its contact like a gunshot. A system of cracks webs the safety glass. Before Hughie can protest, the man swings again, reaming a small, baseball-sized hole at the web's nexus, shards like a failed pearl strand or falling teeth showering inward.

"Jesus God!" Hughie shouts, and Moira and Lisa step away. But its too late – the wheelchair man winds up once more and cavitates the window with a third sweep. Little pieces of safety glass lie everywhere, inside and outside the Eldorado, some even gathered in the wheelchair man's parka'd lap. He offers Hughie the umbrella.

"Do you mind?" he asks. "It's easier to get out than it is to put back."

Hughie accepts the annihilator of his Eldorado's driver's-side window – the agent of its destruction, but the solution to their immediate problem as well. He wonders for a moment whether he should knight the man with it. Hughie has a foreign urge to bring it down on this besotted idiot's skull, to crown him king of vandals. Smash his fucking pumpkin-head to a pulp. He is convinced such a blow would uncover wet-brain, mush like a booze pudding. Instead, shaking his head, he returns the umbrella to its plastic sleeve.

"Jesus, man," he starts, and wonders what in the hell he can possibly say. "Uh, oh shit." He looks from the man back to his window, or rather, its absence. "I didn't exactly want *that*. I mean, well, *I* could have done that."

"But you didn't," their deliverer states, gesturing at the shivering women, offering an assessment of accusal. *They're freezing*, his look seems to indict, *close to hypothermia. Have the courage to change the things you can.*

Truly, in that moment, Hughie forgets the destruction of his window and what it will cost to replace. He stands corrected and humbled in a night that seems arctic outside, but has grown tropical in his guts. There is a certain wisdom in this rolling drunk. It is a certainty, the Higher Power can utilize anything or anyone It wishes. And has done so, here, now. It is an odd acceptance, borne of years of practice, one that Moira and Lisa would not understand. While they are amazed Hughie doesn't retaliate, they – Lisa particularly – are grateful they will soon be home under warm blankets. In fact Lisa, absurdly, now offers the man a ride home. No thanks, he says, vodka-hot and stumbling over an explanation that he lives only three blocks away on Third. He'll just roll on home now.

And so he does, engages the lever again, lurches forward mumbling as if mildly perturbed by the new power of a good deed executed with great risk, but yet missing a proper compensation. "You're welcome," he calls back over the chair, and the whirring of its motor

121

fades in the more urgent passing of auto exhaust from passersby.

Hughie reaches through the wreckage of his former window and retrieves the keys. Holds them up for the women to see, displays them to Lisa's lame clapping and exclamation: "Yay!" He unlocks the door, it opens wide in his grasp, glass spilling onto his loafers. Bits cover the benchseat in front, have sprayed into the backseat as well, on the floormats, on the dash like a hoard of diamonds. He removes his jacket to sweep them off the seats, hands Moira an ice-scraper he keeps under the front seat. She starts scraping the windshield as he polices the shards from inside the car. Lisa stands hugging herself, immobile, useless and watching. When Moira has cleared the front window, she hands the scraper pointedly to Lisa.

"You can do the back," she orders, and her demand is as frost-coated as the window itself.

Cleanup finished, Hughie clicks the lock lever, the buttons leap up like sailors at attention on a scrubbed deck. Moira slides into the front passenger seat, careful to ensure there is no more glass she might sit on. Lisa joins her purse and keys in the back. Hughie sits behind the wheel, hauls his door closed and fires the ignition. They all engage their safety belts. Hughie toggles the thermostat on full, engages drive and pulls from the lot, wind picking up in the space that used to comprise the window. Lisa squeaks in the back seat, the airstream's edge growing increasingly arctic with each mile per hour Hughie accelerates. She slides across the back seat, buckles in behind Moira. They are all silent and freezing as Hughie crosses town to Lisa's apartment. They drop her there, waiting at the curb to ensure she arrives safety at her doorstoop and is inside. She barely uttered a goodnight as she left the car.

She will drink yet tonight, for the first time in more than seven months. Lisa, as she hunkers up the walk, knows a bottle of whiskey waits for her inside, a decanter she refused to purge from her apartment in those early weeks. Knowing, somehow, it would come in handy for post-trauma such as this morning's. Fool!

Hughie and Moira drive toward Moira's place, an apartment nine blocks from Lisa's. They are quiet – although there could be much to discuss, and they have consumed enough coffee for a small battalion.

The thermostat strains, blowing heat across them and out past Hughie and the empty frame. It cannot keep pace with the icy air blowing in. Finally, Moira asks, "You got a seat belt in the middle?"

"Yep."

"Mind if I move over?"

"No – but watch it, there might be glass I missed."

Moira unbuckles her belt, slides over next to Hughie. Clicks the harness across her midriff. Despite the cold, despite the fact Hughie is at the confluence of two independent, pressurized streams of air, one hot from the blower, one freezing from the windowframe, her scent is discernible, and pleasant. He is at the locus of a weather front, where hot meets cold, and could form a thundercloud.

"I'm sorry about the window," she says. "And about Lisa."

"You need to keep clear on what you are responsible for," he says. Ah, in his confusion he reverts to proffering advice. "You aren't responsible for any of that."

"I'm still sorry."

He thinks of another window, another time. The nude neighbor and his habitual voyeurism. That is something he is not proud of, but which he has – he believes – dealt with and made, in his own way, amends for. Now, next to him, is a pleasing surprise. She is like a visitor whom he hasn't received for two, no three, decades. He's fifty-four, she may be twenty-three, twenty-four – something like that – and clean but a few months. He is sober nineteen years. This is absurd. Still...

The are outside Moira's apartment. She asks whether he will come in and get warm.

Can this be? A sudden, surprising offer for her to make, even as the words escape her teeth. Does the inquiry in her soft, gray eyes belie confusion or state clarity?

Her question may envelop an entire cosmos. Considering this, Hughie and Moira stand in freezing air.

Never

He waits, peeking out the upstairs window, listening for the sound of his father's truck turning up the drive. Is that it, a thrum of motor? No. Someone else's vehicle passes the driveway, proceeds up the street.

After commuting from my job, I pull up to the house in a white Chevy Suburban. There's my nine-year-old boy emerging from the front door. As I step down from the high utility vehicle, he's moving down the sidewalk toward me, short-sleeved in a Star Wars T-shirt despite the February rain.

"Hey Buddy," I say, with my briefcase in one hand, coffee cup in the other. I shift the travel mug to the briefcase hand, juggle the items for a second, so I can tousle his hair.

"Hi Dad," he says, but doesn't look up at me. He's looking around instead, beyond me at the truck, around the front yard, up at the bare crowns of defoliated maple.

"How's it goin', Champ?" I use all those names with him: *Buddy, Champ, Tiger.*

"S'alright," he says, still looking around. We walk together up the sidewalk. The front door squeaks through its arc as we enter together, and then there's the dog and two cats and his mother and sister – my wife and daughter. We're a tidy little family unit on a weeknight like a thousand other weeknights.

Now I'm inside and evening hugs have been dispensed. My daughter returns to *Entertainment Tonight*; my wife steps into the laundry room to change loads. I've patted the bozo dog's head, and start performing the daily sift through envelopes and bulk mail. Drop some of it straight into the recycling bin. I notice my boy is underfoot a little, seems to be walking around the kitchen in exactly the places I want to walk, at exactly the same moments.

"Buddy, back off a little, will ya?" I say. It's been a long day, but he doesn't sense my need for slow, measured engagement, has no way of understanding it. He moves away, but continues to hover four or five feet off. I filter through the letters and bills, the circulars. Then I get wrapped up in some documentation for an insurance claim, and it's impossible to tell whether our outlay is going to be covered or not. This small frustration festers some, and I turn the piece of paper over in my hands and look up: he's now at the table across the kitchen from me. He's sitting in a chair with his arms folded and resting on the table surface, chin on overcrossed wrist. He's just watching me, but looks away quickly when our gazes meet.

"What?" I demand.

"Nothing," he says, resuming brief eye contact, then glancing away again.

"Honey," my wife comes in the kitchen from the laundry room. "Can I talk to you for a minute?" I'm looking back at the reverse of the insurance claim again, hearing her through a sieve of renewed concentration.

"Hmm?"

"Upstairs, maybe?"

"What?"

"I need to talk to you upstairs."

"Oh," I finally respond, attention severed at last from the form I'm turning over again and again in my hands. "Sure."

I follow her into our bedroom where she tells me this: The father of one of my son's classmates has committed suicide. Hanged himself last night. For a moment, standing there in my bedroom, I can imagine the news spreading through the elementary school that morning like spilled black ink. Across the playground, whispered in words that cannot comprehend: *Devon's dad kilt his self.*

Now I understand my boy's attentiveness, his position under foot. His uncharacteristically shy greeting, the hovering. How he peered at me as if around corners, but quickly glanced away when discovered.

"Our son is terrified." My wife's eyes are overfilled with

disquiet.

"I can imagine." I am calmer than I should be under the circumstances. I have only just been informed, and this response reflects my detachedness while I struggle to appreciate what my wife has said. As far as I know, my son is unacquainted with the concept of death self-inflicted. Funny, at age nine, I've delivered to him the sex talk, the drugs talk, the never-hit-girls talk. But I never thought to cover this.

"He needs you to talk to him," she says.

Agreeing, I descend the stairs to find him. He's sitting in the La-Z-Boy manipulating the buttons of his Game Boy like crazy.

"Hey Buddy, why don't you put that down for a minute and come talk to me?"

He doesn't look up. His fingers are working the toy over good.

"Buddy, come on," I say.

"Just a second, Dad." He moves the device closer to his face, studies the screen, grimaces lightly, and flicks the pause button. Looks up.

"Come on," I say, indicating with a jog of my neck that he should follow me. He climbs out of the big chair, follows me down the hall and up the stairs. For some reason, we end up standing in our walk-in closet. I start weakly: "How ya doin'?"

"O.K.," he says.

"Mom said something happened at school today."

"Uhh..." He looks at everything but me – shoes, hanging suits, cowboy boots, the gun safe, ballcaps, the ceiling – grasps the fingertips of one hand with the other behind his back, arches his back. Moves his body in the manner nine-year-old boys will when uncomfortable.

"I'm talking about Devon's daddy," I prompt, watching his face.

"Oh," he says, a lot, really, with a single word. He's still looking elsewhere, but I'm silent for a moment, and experiment with looking away myself. When I glance back down at him this time, he's looking at my face, then immediately feigns distraction.

"Do you have any questions about what happened?"

"Uh-uh."

"About anything you heard?"

"Uh-uh."   He's shaking his head as if he comprehends everything, as if I have asked him whether he needs help with his times tables.

"Are you worried about it?"

"No."

"Really? You're not worried at all?"

"Uh-uh." But he is worried; he's *terrified*, my wife had said.

"I would never do that," I say. "I would never leave you that way."

A tremor across his chest and a glance up, directly at me, come simultaneously. The irises of his eyes are light green; his gaze is clear. He senses an oath, the boundary of enormous relief.

"O.K.," he says.

"I love you," I tell him.

"Love you, too."

"You'll have to be very nice to Devon, especially now." I think he needs to know that the best way to be rid of one's pain and confusion is to concern oneself with relieving another's. He seems to understand this.

Then his tears fall as he reaches for my embrace.

I skip the board meeting I had planned to attend. He lies in my arms on the sofa, an afghan thrown over us in the dark. We watch *Jurassic Park: The Lost World* together on the VCR.

Two-Man Crash

When Glenn and Andrew piled Glenn's small airplane into the Gifford Pinchot National Forest and walked away from the wreckage with only a few scratches, they took just a moment to thank the powers that be, then staggered over to a moss-cloaked nurse log and abandoned themselves to broad laughter that began, before much time had passed, to resemble dementia.

There had been engine trouble. A pop like a backfire, the jangling sound of metal on metal from under the cowl, then smoke. The propeller feathered. They dropped like a coal-sack from seven- or eight-thousand feet – just above the nimbostratus deck. The pair of ex-roommates plunged through the gray on this unplanned trajectory, Glenn churning the yoke, plunging at pedals, trying to figure out which way was up. Needles spun in the instrument dials. Andrew, for his part, simply could not understand it. It was as if – as the old saw goes – he were having an out-of-body experience. Or watching someone else's incident in slow motion. He felt weightless. He didn't wrest the understanding from what went on that this was happening to him. When the craft broke through the underside of the clouds, they saw the forest rolling below.

At the last possible instant the deities of aerodynamics must have blessed them. From a chaos of airflow impossibly twisted upon itself emerged a brief miracle of lift. Glenn sensed the plane carve an arc into the air about them, scribing just enough stability to yank the craft from its uncontrolled spin and level the wings. Although the nose was still pitched hard earthward, Glenn sensed the most minuscule resumption of control. Was it enough? Suddenly he could feel the flow across the ailerons and elevators with the same exactitude with which he demonstrated calculus for his students at the high school. The pressure passing over and around his airplane felt precise, confident and perfect, yet smooth and soft – the same way it would feel if he caressed Cynthia's cheek, or the small of her back. At least now they would impact in near level flight.

Three seconds, perhaps, from the time they had fallen through the clouds. Three seconds, and there were evergreen treetops.

Andrew closed his eyes as the first limbs banged the plane's underbelly. Glenn bellowed an oath that sounded like, "Hooooo!" They hit something hard at starboard. A trunk sheared off the outboard third of the right wing. The craft yawed in that direction and rolled up. The empennage crashed into another tree just aft of Andrew on the port side. The canopy cracked next to Andrew. It resounded like a detonation in his head. They dropped toward the forest floor, raking limbs and treebark all the way to the understory. The whole works came to rest against a Western hemlock. There was incomprehensible silence. Then Glenn thought he smelled fuel.

"Get out, get away now."

Their harnesses came unbound like magic. Glenn pushed the fractured canopy up and aside. They leapt from the cockpit onto the port wing, which was astonishingly whole, and slid down its slippery surface onto cones, ferns and salal. The airplane lay on unremarkable groundcover.

And that is when they thanked the great Giver of Mercy, staggered to the wet, fallen log, collapsed onto its mossy, rotten bark crown, and began to bray into the woods. After a while their guts hurt from laughing and their cheeks hurt from grinning. But it was a good hurt.

"We must be a hundred miles from anywhere." Glenn burst out giggling anew.

"I can't believe we ain't dead, bro."

"My airplane – she's dead." They hooted like drunken owls for another two or three minutes.

"Jesus, Glenn, what are we going to do now?"

Glenn stood, placed his hands at the curve of his back and stretched backward. He looked up through the branches. The sky seemed close. Rain fell, but changed to mist as it bounced from branch to branch through the canopy.

"See if the radio still works, I suppose. Shoot off a few flares. I don't know, build a fire, hunker down for the night." Glenn stopped grinning and turned toward the broken craft. "It would be better to stay with the airplane. In another hour and a half they'll wonder where we are. The plan I filed said we'd be to Chehalis by 1700 hours."

"They'll wonder where we are? You sure?"

Glenn nodded. "Yes, you'd think. It's my dad. It's his airport, I mean."

"It doesn't sound like you're convinced, bro." There was an edge of disquiet in Andrew's voice.

"Drew, that's what a flight plan is for. I file it for one, and only one, reason." He swept his arms in a circle. "This."

Andrew checked his watch. "I can't believe this. I mean, can you believe this?"

Glenn lifted his hands, palms upward. He saw a deep cut in the webbing between his right thumb and forefinger. And he saw something else too: that his hands shook.

"Look, I don't know. I don't know what happened. I'm standing here now telling you I'm glad to be alive. And I'm glad you're alive with me. You and I could be jelly in the bottom of a smoking crater." He took a giant breath and let it out in a cloud. "Of course I can't believe it."

Andrew seemed to study some space in front of him, although Glenn could not discern whether it was a space close or faraway. Andrew trembled also.

Both men remained silent for some time. There was a gradual resumption in the sorts of noises forests make – small animals pipping in dim light, mountain birds fluttering from limbs. The throaty calls of ravens.

"Dude, how cold do you think it is?"

Glenn considered this for longer than it seemed to warrant. "Oh, forty, maybe. Or a little less." He glanced from Andrew up, at the sky, again. "Dusk will be falling pretty soon. We'd better see about that radio. Then we'll figure out what to do about a fire. I smelled fuel over by the wing, so we'd better make the fire a good ways over there." He indicated a general direction away from the wreck. "I have some flares behind your seat. There's three or four handhelds, and the flare gun with a clip of three shells. We ought to be able to get a fire up and hot with one of those." Glenn turned in a circle with his eyes on blow-downs and

130

sodden moss. "Even if everything is completely soaked."

"If the temp drops any more we're gonna have snow, huh?"

"I guess that's possible."

"What if it starts to snow hard?"

"Then it snows hard."

Andrew thought about this for a moment. If the weather turned, who'd come out to search in the mountains?

"They won't come?"

"Maybe. Maybe not."

The radio was inoperable. The sky darkened. A few fat flakes fell. The two retrieved their jackets from the stowage space under each seat. Both sniffed for the odor of spilt fuel, but neither could any longer detect it. The fuel cells in the fractured wing must have been low, drained, and already dispersed in the wet soil. Glenn took two flashlights from clamps to the left of his seat. He gave one to Andrew.

As his friend took the light, Glenn studied Andrew's face. Again, that sense that he was thinner than Glenn remembered. The cheeks hollow and paler than the average man's. And some pretty grim circles under the eyes. Before the museum, it had been sixteen years since he had seen his college roommate. Four months ago they had met, purely by coincidence, at the Oregon Museum of Science and Industry in Portland. They'd been waiting in line – one in front of the other – for the IMAX. Cynthia had been with Glenn. Andrew had been alone.

After the pleasant surprise of unexpected reunion, they shared coffee in the museum's cafeteria. Andrew explained that he had returned to school at Willamette University in Salem to study history and music. After fiddling with college on and off for the better part of twenty years he hoped to graduate, finally, in the spring. Glenn had spent fifteen years in the finance departments of three mid-sized companies in the Seattle area, and then bailed out of the psycho race for a job teaching entry-level economics at Clark College in Vancouver and calculus across the street at the high school. When he had lived in Seattle, he'd spent weekends in Chehalis learning to fly his dad's airplane. He got his license four years ago.

Cynthia sipped her coffee and smiled. She and Glenn held hands. Andrew pointed out, again, that he was about to get his degree, in the spring. Glenn invited Andrew to go flying. "Over the mountains is best." Andrew had never been in a light airplane. They had agreed Glenn would phone and they'd select a date.

The odd coincidence of their meeting played through Glenn's mind as he showed Andrew where to pile smallish sticks and limbs – maybe twenty-five yards from the plane – and lit the flare. Its bloom was stunning, a jet of energy like that leaping off a welder's torch. The snow fell faster and started to stick. They placed the brilliant flare amongst the branches and soon had glowing vapor billowing from the pile. At first it was more condensing steam, as moisture cooked away from the saturated wood. But then it kindled and the area around them soon was filled with the incense of woodsmoke. When the flames caught, Andrew straightened from over them and thrust his hands in his jacket pockets. Glenn glanced up at him. A puzzled expression lodged for a moment on Andrew's gaunt face. He pursed his lips. Then he appeared to check the front and back pockets of his pants, and his jacket again. He brought the flashlight out of his back pocket with his left hand.

"What?"

Holding the light, Andrew reached inside to his vest pocket with the opposite hand, but withdrew it empty.

"I think I dropped something. I'll just go look for a second." Although it was not yet necessary – the afternoon had dimmed but was not yet dusky, nor even really a half-light – he clicked on the flashlight. He combed the ground in a line back to the airplane. Glenn returned his gaze to the fire for a while, then gathered a few stouter sticks and dropped them onto the pyre. They hissed, sputtered and threw steam.

Soon the fire was roaring. Glenn checked his wristwatch. Five minutes after five – they were now officially overdue. His father wouldn't yet be concerned, of course. He would assume that his son was simply flying in later than planned. He might start to wonder if, in the next fifteen or twenty minutes, he didn't receive any radio communication. Glenn thought of his father waiting there, in the faded

132

green shack next to the giant oak that, in summertime, dropped aphids onto the hair and shoulders of people who loitered underneath. His dad would be hunkered over a cup of hot black coffee, gazing out at Chehalis. Lights across I-5 would blink on as gloom gathered and dusk fell. His father, in the falling light, would study the composition of the clouds – their tessellations, their rounded masses, the direction of their wind-blown precipitation trails. His dad would read how they settled and soughed around the hillocks across the freeway, the shapes mist took as it wrapped those green, water-laden foothills of central Washington state.

The wettest spot in the USA, his dad liked to say.

Glenn left the fire and returned to the airplane. He found Andrew shining the flashlight into the tight spaces behind the rear seat, then playing the beam across the ground where they had climbed out. Glenn watched as Andrew searched the area near the nurse log, all around where they had – almost two hours ago – been nearly consumed by hysterical relief.

"What are you looking for? Have you lost something?"

"Nothing, man. It's not important." Andrew, as darkness encroached, looked anything but convincing.

"Are you sure? We have time to look. The fire's going great guns." Glenn gestured over his shoulder. "We ought to look quick though, before there's much more snowfall. It's sticking pretty good."

This offer seemed only to agitate Andrew. "Look, I said it don't matter. It's not important, bro." Glenn saw twin glints of flame reflected on Andrew's pupils.

"O.K. with me. Hey, I was just offering."

Andrew gathered himself and breathed in deeply. He closed his eyes and held the breath. He slowly exhaled and reopened his eyes.

"I know. Thanks. But let's worry about what we're going to do for the night. I mean, what do we do? Sleep in the seats here? With the top back on?"

"You got it."

"Shit."

"You got that right, too. But just remember, it's better than jelly. And I hope in twenty years you've learned not to snore. I'm still

133

catching up on all the sleep I missed when we were roomies."

"Oh, that's rich. You are so damned funny." Andrew seemed himself again.

Glenn opened the emergency kit and withdrew two objects that looked like silver bags. He zipped down the end of one of them, then unfolded it.

"Emergency blanket."

Andrew rolled his eyes. "That doesn't look the least bit like a blanket, bro."

"Hey, I'll use both of them if you want." He held out the second silver packet. Just as Andrew's fingertips were about to close on it, Glenn snatched it away. Then he offered it again, then pulled it away. Andrew, laughing, put his hands in his pockets.

"Look, man, just give the thing. I promise I'll stop complaining."

"You'd better. Because I'd rather you snored. And we probably won't sleep much anyway."

Andrew nodded. His teeth chattered. "We could take turns. Or maybe we could just stay up. Sit by the fire with those blanket things. See if somebody comes."

"We could shoot off a flare once every hour, at the top of the hour."

Andrew seemed to further brighten at this.

They walked together back to the fire, snow falling around them. Both pulled the emergency blankets up over their heads and around their shoulders, and squatted near the flames. They let the heat colonize their fronts, then turned with their backs to the warmth. No food. No heavy coats. No radio. No idea where exactly they were. Just the warmth.

Glenn shot the first flare at seven o'clock. The snowfall had abated. Glenn believed by now his father would have notified the FAA that he was overdue. Airplanes in the area, with pilots alerted to a missing craft, might be making overflights. A search plan could be forming, even now, in Portland or Longview.

The flare roared from the launcher's muzzle with a percussive whumph.   Its trajectory was like that of a Fourth of July firework, bathing everything in the vicinity with 15,000 candlepower.   After two seconds it reached the top of its parabola and stalled.   Then it seemed to float.   Silently it fell back and winked out.   Six seconds in all.   Andrew watched from under his emergency blanket, shaking.

Glenn returned to the fire circle.   "So much for that."   He placed the empty launcher – basically a wide-muzzled bright orange pistol with a clip holding two more of the shells – on the ground between the two of them.   It settled into the snow.

"You really think anybody's up there?   That anyone will see it?"   Andrew's eyes were large in the firelight.   The tops of his cheeks twitched.   He squinted and blinked.   Glenn saw that he was trembling from his shoes to his head.

"We have to try.   We have to assume so."   Andrew's shaking bewildered Glenn – it didn't feel terribly cold to him next to the fire.   Andrew had been crouched before the flames for more than an hour.   How could he be shivering?   It occurred to Glenn that Andrew might have been hurt internally in the crash.   Maybe something was wrong inside and Andrew had simply not said anything.   But to say nothing seemed unlike his friend.   Too, when Andrew's hands weren't jammed in his pockets, he held them in front of him and moved the thumbs and forefingers vigorously as if he were rolling bearings between them.   He kept this up for a long time.   Glenn grew more perplexed and concerned with each moment.

"Hey, are you O.K.?"

"Yeah.   Fine."

"Because you're shaking – is it just the cold, or are you hurt?"

As if to halt Glenn's line of inquiry, Andrew held up his palm.   It trembled uncontrollably.   "I said that I'm fine."

"Drew, you are going to have to tell me if you're hurt.   I'm not shitting you.   We've been as lucky as lucky gets today, but we are in a damned serious situation."

Andrew closed his eyes and wrapped his arms around his own torso.   "I gotta jones, man."

"You're what?"

135

"I'm jonesing or tweaking or something. Coming down. I lost my rig and my shit. That's what I was looking for earlier. My dope."

Glenn couldn't believe what he was hearing. They were nearing forty years old, for God's sake. Sure, they had smoked a little grass in college. Even used cocaine a time or two. Was Andrew talking about something like that? Or something else? Something worse?

"What are you talking about, Drew? You're high?"

"It's not like it used to be, bro. Lots of normal people are chipping."

"Chipping?"

"Using once in a while."

"Using what?"

"Smack. Horse. Junk. Heroin, man. It's not like it used to be."

Glenn heard the words, but his mind was racing. Apparently much unexpected could, and did, change in sixteen years. What happens when someone goes through heroin withdrawal in the wilderness? No hospitals, no doctors, no 9-1-1. No... Glenn searched for the names of drugs he had heard about on TV, on cop shows – the kinds they use to stabilize people in withdrawal. People with a jones, as Andrew had said.

Anger welled in him. Andrew had brought dope on his dad's airplane. What had he planned to do, shoot up in the john at his father's airport? Come out wasted for the return flight?

"What were you thinking, man? Coming on board my airplane with drugs. Crossing interstate. You know, they confiscate people's airplanes who use them to do that." Andrew remained silent, hugging himself. "You were stoned the whole time?"

"Bro, I'm sorry. I was so high. I wanted to see the mountains."

Glenn sat and shook his head. God, tell me this isn't happening, he thought. He stared at the flames. What bizarre setup of random effects had brought him to the center of nowhere with a busted airplane and an addict he thought he knew, or once had known? And now that he knew, what?

"So what happens now?"

"I don't find my shit, I'm gonna burn and shake all night. I'm already starting to sweat."

"You've been shaking for a long time."

"Feel like I'm gonna puke pretty soon, too. You gotta help me look again, bro. If I can fix, I'll be fine the rest of the night."

Every passing moment struck Glenn as more outrageous than the previous. Three hours ago they had been staring through cockpit glass at the splendor of Mt. St. Helens's empty basket-shaped cone. Mt. Adams and Eastern Washington flowed like a grain-colored blanket to their right, as far as they could behold. As they crossed the divide they saw clouds stacked against the western slopes of the Cascades range. Snow clouds. It had all been so spectacular. A plea that bordered on a whine broached Glenn's thoughts.

"You gonna?"

"Am I going to what?"

"Help me. Help me find my shit. It's gotta be around here somewhere. We didn't walk that far."

Glenn looked around at the flame-lit limbs. At the tree trunks all about them and the canopy above. Pitch in the fire popped. He stirred to rise. Although he was in good physical shape, his muscles protested from the cold and stasis. He took in a huge breath.

"Drew, there is no way in hell I am going to help you shoot heroin in the middle of the freezing fucking woods. Who knows where the hell we are, or when somebody's going to find us. I take you on my airplane, my dad's airplane. I ask you to go flying after sixteen years because it's nice to see you. I mean, here we are – I've crashed my dad's airplane, as soon as he finds out I'm alive, he's going to kill me. You don't seem to get it. You're too busy worrying about your heroin, which I can't even believe. 'Lots of people are doing it,' you say. Now I've heard fucking everything."

Glenn realized that he was shouting. He stopped. Andrew was quiet, with the emergency blanket drawn over his head. It almost covered his face. In the aftermath of Glenn's frustration, a hush.

Even the flames seemed to consume their fuel silently.

Then Andrew staggered to his feet. The emergency blanket fell from him. Half of it evaporated in a flash-melt over the flames. He

137

pointed at Glenn.

"I'm warning you. You better help me find my dope."

"You're what? You're warning me?" Glenn braced himself.

"You and your business. Well aren't you successful? Too good for other folks just trying to get by. Got it all together, with daddy's airplane. Mister gave it all up to be a perfect teacher. More like Mr. Can't Fly a Plane for Shit. And your airhead wife, that's unbelievably totally amazing. She's just damned beautiful, isn't she…"

"Cynthia?"

"Yeah, your blond, stupid honey-pot I met at OMSI."

"Don't you even say her name. I don't want to hear her name coming out of your mouth."

"Cynthia. Cynthia. She give you head every night? Take it in the ass for you?"

Glenn cocked back a fist and let Andrew have it in the mouth. Andrew dropped next to the fire. Then he moaned. "Whuh'd you do? Whuh'd you do?" He pushed himself up onto his forearms in the snow. Both men saw the flare gun and its extra shells at the same time.

"You are gonna help me find that shit!" Andrew reached for the pistol, fingers closing on the grip. With his other hand he tore away one of the flare shells from its clip. He fumbled with the gun, not appreciating its mechanisms or understanding its operation. Glenn snatched it, and the shell, from Andrew's clumsy grasp.

"What the fuck, Drew? What were you going to do?"

Andrew rolled onto his back and stared straight up. There were stars.

"What were you going to do just now?" Tears welled, then spilled from Glenn's eyes. "Were you going to shoot this at me, Drew? Were you?"

Andrew vomited.

"You couldn't get it loaded, huh? Well let me show you." Glenn snapped a shell into the magazine. He closed it. He pointed the launcher at Andrew's head. "Simple as that." Andrew turned his face away. Then Glenn pointed the launcher at the sky. It went whumph and the forest glowed. "I'll show you again." He shot the third and last shell.

138

Then he noticed, too, stars through the branches.

Andrew retched desperately in the snow.

Some time later, Andrew mumbled that he heard sounds in the woods. A while after that, he suddenly described in vivid detail an approach of angels.

"That's all right, Drew. You're O.K." Glenn soothed his old roommate, remaining wrapped around Andrew in an embrace. He took his jacket off and put it on his friend so that Andrew wore two. He saw that at some point he had knelt in Andrew's vomit. He stretched the remaining emergency blanket around both of them. Andrew's shaking climbed onto Glenn and set its hooks into him, so that he began to tremble as well. When Andrew pissed himself, Glenn simply held him closer.

In this way, they passed the night. And shortly after the sun rose – gleaming off of the crumpled fuselage and casting rays sidelong through the last wisps of smoke from the night's fire – Glenn heard the unmistakable signature of helicopter rotors.

Andrew looked up into the light, no longer shaking.

The Last Living Elk in North America

The newspapers are reporting that I poached the last living elk in North America. It happened, the articles write, in an apple orchard in the shadow of Cascades foothills near Leavenworth.

I remember being in the orchard. I was hunting feral pigs. There was a warm breeze soughing through leaves and hardwood branches. The flat light of early autumn and the odor of fallen, corrupt fruit laid about everything. There was a shortage of itinerant pickers. (This also has been in the news.) But you were there.

You have to help me remember. Because when I connect the moments before we were in the orchard with the moments after I find a broad hole. I remember with exact clarity the beginning and end state, just not the middle. The middle – this hole whose lip I want to stumble on and topple in. To fall and fall until I get an answer.

Beneath every tree were hundreds of apples. The skins no longer were bright red, but a wilted, blood color. There were craters and pits where larva had burrowed. You perturbed a cloying mass of them with a stick and fruit flies thrummed in a small, buzzy cloud. We may have ingested some of them by merely inhaling as we stumbled backward. (Isn't there a Buddhist law or koan or something that warns of this?) My rifle on its sling slapped against the side of my jacket. When I stepped backward, blown-down sticks snapped under my feet, and more rotten apples squished beneath my boots. It was possible to track our retreat by the imprints of our soles on warped apple skins.

I know I looked desperately at you then. What was left of daylight caught in your hair. It laid upon you lambent as the sun dapples a near-calm lake. A fall chill had risen with the first onset of dusk – your exquisite skin seemed the single source of warmth. I remember an overwhelming sense of intoxication. I unslung my rifle to shift it from one shoulder to the other. Its burnished wood stock, its blued gunmetal muzzle: light leapt from these surfaces in sparks and flares. Glow girl! Need burned in me like a coal forge. For the same reason sky-gazers will not point a telescope directly at the sun, I had to look away from you. There may, indeed, have been a solar eruption, the magic of sunspots, an alchemy of coronal flux that changed longing into act and conjured up a ghost, or ghosts.

Sunstroke? Radio transmissions were garbled; strange, alien blotches tainted developing x-ray film. The entire spectrum of light bent impossibly over the fulcrum of desire. The magnetic weight of want on both ends – the onset and conclusion. And null space in between.

I'll confess only this: I saw the elk. To say it was magnificent discounts what really stood there before us, between apple trees. A simple stating of the facts, a reduction to something so simple as narrative, produces a short-enough, utilitarian-enough depiction: The last living elk in North America walked into the orchard. You gasped.

Its antlers had six tines each, plus the eyeguards. Their beams stretched almost a meter and a half behind its withers over its back. The stout hair of its undermane shone with oil, and its pelt faded to a tawny buff front to back. It was as large as a mid-sized horse, with obsidian eyes that bore down on us the way a king's would – with assuredness and superiority. The ears fanned wide to receive more data about us, to catalogue and categorize our intent. Its nostrils flared and blasted. It stamped the floor of the orchard twice, threw its giant head back and bugled. Its cry rent through the half-light and on it was unmistakable, incomprehensible sorrow.

What was it you then said? What should we do?

Stay still, I whispered. Stay put. Let's just watch him.

When I was a boy I would accompany my great-grandfather on elk hunts. This was back in the day when hunting was legal, an accepted rite of Western life, a thing a boy did – a man did – all his life. Game was rich in the range. Deer, sheep, mountain goats, black bear. Elk.

141

That was thirty-five years ago, before the viruses. Before the game laws changed. Before the threatened species acts. Before the only things that could be hunted were pigs, nuisance beasts that pulled down fences, rooted through crop rows and stole infants.

My great-grandfather would hum softly as we worked about camp or hiked in the woods. I would follow him from task to task – whether chopping wood or coaxing fire from tinder – in order to be near him. For the contact. My own father had died. My grandfather was ill by then. And as I say, my great-grandfather would hum, and his humming assumed the patterns of scales. His humming erected mathematical constructs as arpeggios. Being near him was to be immersed, always, in perfect tone.

I recall a morning in the field, he and I, overlooking a forest clearing. We were warm in our coats and wool trousers, sitting on fallen logs in the sun. Great-grandpa had his .30-06; I held a Model 270 whose kick would have left my shoulder raw and bruised had I fired it that year. He was humming.

Grandpa? I whispered.

His humming stopped. He looked at me. There was gentleness and magic in the points of his eyes.

Grandpa, why does music come out of you all the time?

He asked me whether I knew my history, whether I knew of the Second World War.

I nodded.

He asked if I knew about the Germans, the Nazis.

Yes.

Well, he said, when I was a boy, there was a camp of Germans who were prisoners. And that camp was near my home, with my dad and mom.

I watched his mouth moving at the center of whiskers.

My dad and mom lived in a town called Battle Creek. You know of Michigan?

I nodded again.

That's where I was a boy, he said. The Germans in this camp were prisoners of war. When they first came we would ride our bicycles down the road to the fences and watch them exercise in the fields there.

My great-grandfather had a look in his eyes as if he were standing at the edge of an impossibly wide ocean, yet watching the shore on the other side. He went on: The prison was an old hospital with a tall fence around it. On each corner was a tower. At the top of each tower stood a soldier with a rifle. The soldiers in the tower would shout down to us to go away, but we liked watching. The Germans would stare at us, then look away. Once one smiled in our direction.

After a couple of years one of the prisoners started to give piano lessons. Looking back, I don't understand how this was possible. Why it was permitted, I mean. But it was, and he did. I took piano from him for about eighteen months. He spoke English with a heavy accent, using the sound for a V when we would use the sound of W, and always a Z for an S. Practize your zcalez, he would say. Ven you are ready, ve will have a rezital. It vill be zoon, ja?

I laughed at my great-grandfather, much too loudly for a pair out hunting elk, a pastime requiring, more or less, silence. But we didn't care, my great-grandpa and I. There was no one else in the world that morning but the two of us. The two of us and his memory of a kind German prisoner in Battle Creek, Michigan.

Vhat vas hiz name? I said.

My great-grandfather giggled as if he were my age. Then he stopped laughing and stared at the treeline for a moment. Then he looked at his hands. Then he looked at me.

I can't remember.

Do you recall how the elk stamped his hooves in those apples? Or is this just a detail I made up, a conjuration from a dim, invented pocket of my memory? Did this particular element of recollection indeed take place? Or did I muster it up, laboring with steam and sulfurous incantations, summoning it like a daemon? Please, be my memory. Guide me through this night. Help me find water. Navigate for me this map that is the gnarly concatenation of dream and fixed fact. Ameliorate my effort to ford the confluence of these independent rivers – the one in

143

which floats the uprooted timber of liability and the other in which never-a-backward-glance skims across the surface. Pull me from this current, this undertow.

Are you going to stand there with no expression on your lips? Are you going to help me out?

You stand now, but you laid down for me then.

Never mind the apples, you said. Never mind the elk.

In the orchard you laid down.

The season before he died my great-grandfather took me to the top of a small mountain. To get there, we hiked up game trails for hours. I was thirteen or fourteen – he must have been nearly ninety. He never broke a sweat, never stumbled on exposed roots, never slipped in mud or groundcover. His rifle rode his shoulder. I put my boots in his prints before me. Made a game of it, stepping exactly where he stepped.

We emerged from the forest on the mountain's crest. Around us the world fell away. Hills folded into the distance, their misty crevasses holding secrets. The forest was a green algorithm, the divisors and products and sums all solving in green. And stacked over the forest was a blemishless blue sky. Blue was its numerator. Blue was its denominator. So the blue product was unified, was one. And that unified, single one was a near star in that calm, bottomless ocean of blue: the sun. Our sun, my great-grandfather's and mine and yours. Our sun was in the west, and sinking.

Now watch this, my great-grandfather said. He set his rifle against a boulder, took off his coat and held up his arms like a wizard. A mountain breeze gathered and began to swirl around us. First it stirred the hair on my great-grandfather's arms, then his head. It gained momentum and purpose, penetrating my warm clothing, my quilted coat and wool trousers. It blew through my flesh and tendons, into my bones, into the marrow, into porous pits of phosphorous and calcium girding the osteocytes therein.

I remember then that the sun stood still over the earth. And that after some time it began to slip slowly backward, reversing its course.

144

Shadows that had been long performed a slow retrograde and became axial. The sun shone down from overhead like pure justice.

Tell me, my great-grandfather said, what you think has happened now. Off this mountain, I mean. In the world, outside.

But I couldn't speak. I had no memory of words.

Of course, you say, I shot the elk. The newspapers are reporting the truth; I should expect the sheriff any time. There is no disputing it, you say. I dropped to one knee, took the rifle's grip in my upturned left palm and placed the butt in the crook of my right shoulder. I flicked off the safety lever with my right thumb. My right fingers laced the trigger-guard and I slipped my forefinger through its gate. The trigger was cool to the touch. My nose was next to the magazine and the scent of gun oil produced a pleasant enervation. My pulse quickened and I took long, calming breaths.

You were there beside me.

I found the elk in the lenses of the riflescope. The optics' reticules made a cross; at its nexus was the elk's heart. I inhaled and exhaled. My finger drew taut. You whispered, take him. I inhaled again, let half of the air out. The rifle barked and kicked. The last living elk in North America shrieked and buckled at the knees. A fierce tinnitus rang instantly in my left ear – oddly, the one on the opposite side of my head from the rifle – and there was the beautiful smell of spent gunpowder. I pulled open the bolt and the spent shell flew end for end from the magazine. Fading light glinted off the spinning brass. I engaged a second shell, throwing the bolt home and jacking it shut. But this second bullet – even the loading of it – was superfluous. The elk was writhing, spewing blood from an entry wound so authoritatively placed that its lethality was a foregone conclusion. Its rear legs gave out. It collapsed. It tried to get up, but was drawn inexorably toward the earth, toward the apples.

Lover, you said.

Its eyes were still bright when we stood over it. Its antlers were incredible – far larger and more extensive than we had thought from even a few yards distant. They possessed, as near as we could tell with its

145

head canted to one side and motionless, perfect symmetry.

You said, look at that hole.

One shot, I said.

You put your finger in it, took it away bloody.

By then the life in his eyes had faded.

My great-grandfather made the sun reverse its course in the last year of his life. Just months before his death, he rewound an autumn afternoon so that the stream of time halted and flowed backward. Perhaps, sensing his own end, he sought a cipher to recover more than a mere afternoon. Or maybe his casting of this spell was a gift for me, so that I might one day recollect it and evolve a faith that time has no limitations, is no barrier, holds no prohibitions or impossibilities to hinder me, you, us. I could go back in time and clean up my messes, alter the now-consequences of my then-choices.

My great-grandfather set out on the long, drawn-out desert route to death, but not before attempting to make his wrongs right. I saw him try. He wanted me to see.

When he was in his twenties and early thirties, he spent twelve years in the state penitentiary at Walla Walla for raping a young orchard worker outside of Selah.

I find it impossible to stop speculating:

She was picking fruit. (I have never heard what kind – apples, safe to say.) He was a foreman or field boss or had some such position of authority. He saw her picking alone, a distance from others, and moved in close. He came up behind her. His one wiry arm wrapped her torso and pinned her arms. He raised his free arm and tried to clamp his fist across her mouth. He forced her to the ground by pushing his knees into the backs of hers. She cried out so he smashed his fist into her open mouth. Still from behind, he pulled at the fabric of her dress. He tore away her underclothes and shoved his dry, hard cock into her. His clamped palm held her screams, and she bit down on his hand, but the pain only made him burn hotter. He stroked five, six, maybe seven times and came. Then he went away.

146

The wounds in the meat of his hand were an angry, infected reddish-orange when the sheriff came.

Sorry Emmitt, the sheriff said, I bet them cuts on your hand fit the teeth a that Mexico whore perfect.

Better you come around than her brothers, my great-grandfather said.

You were there, yes?

We watched him die together, the bull elk with the perfect antlers, the single shot, one entry wound, his lifeblood flowing out onto the decaying apples. You said, look at that hole. One shot, I said. You put your finger in, took it away bloody. By then the life in his eyes had faded. Your eyes filled up with red. They glowed like embers in the dusk. You opened your mouth in the shape of a moist O. A sound like a dove came out. You were the devil.

You put your finger in the bullet hole. You opened your legs for me there and it was as sweet as ripe, ripe fruit. Laying across the back of the last elk in North America, you gave me the prize, the trophy hunt, the one-shot deal. Blood on our hands, our faces, arms, stomachs, sexual organs, tongues. In your eyes.

Is this how you have filled that broad open emptiness I suffered? My lack of memory? My inability or disinclination to recollect? Is this the story you are telling? Is this the terrifying music that comes from you? And must I listen?

When I was a young boy my great-grandfather took me to a hill where time went backward. The sun froze, then headed east. He sought it like a magi. He longed to bring it gifts, to confess, to propitiate. To cross the incomprehensible expanse between him and God.

He appreciated a wise course of action. He knew a smart move when he saw one. His magic just wasn't strong enough. Mine's an altogether different thing.

You were there with me. You're coming along now.

147

The Newark Marriott

The Newark Marriott is as good a place as any to toss under bedcovers. Eleven floors of rack 'em and stack 'em, built right into New Jersey's busiest airport. Has one of those lobbies where road warriors tug black rolling cases across faux marble. The wrinkled-khaki men have chins with eighteen hours of stubble, or hopelessly creased business suits, or both. They have surrendered just that last tie-torque, loosened the knot, popped the button that hemmed – for hours – a swollen larynx. They surrender no real eye contact. The women are brittle skinned. Hours in the pressurized hulls of airplanes have wrung the moisture from them. They are no longer even able to shed tears.

After offering his company card for an imprint at reception, Neil had settled, for a moment, into a stuffed chair. It was one of those oversized thrones ubiquitous in lobbies worldwide. For a hundred-thousand dollars, he could not have described its upholstery just moments after standing again and moving off. Next to him was a minuscule glass-topped table. Behind it, a vase the size of an oil barrel. From the vase sprung a 90's sort-of arrangement – stiff, twirling tendrils of variegated color, synthetic broadleaves, what appeared to be an unbound sheaf of wheat dyed in hues not encountered in nature, fake moss. Dust nowhere in the lobby but on those fake fronds.

At the revolving door two staff members carried on a conversation. They spoke as he imagined Jersey Shore people would. The one, a Hispanic man in a vest and cummerbund, was shaped like a fellow who loved his tripe menudo. He seemed to be proffering advice to the other, a slim acne-pocked youth, an apprentice bellman perhaps, a mere boy with hair clipped closely on the sides but long and gelled back in a flourish on top – a sort of hair tail, if one thinks of that dust and ionized gas that trails a comet.

"All kinda spears gettin' trown in here today." The older bellman waved his forefinger to emphasize a point. "You gotta learn to be careful, but at the same time, let it roll off."

"What you talkin' 'bout, spears?"

"Like darts, man.

"Darts?"

"Dey trowin' at yo back."

The apprentice nodded in a pretense of under-standing. Yet the teacher knew that, still, his meaning went unappreciated.

"Look," he said. "It's sharp roun' here. You get cut." Then the wise bellman turned to pull open the door for another bag-tugger. "You gotta watch yo back, and yo friend's."

Suddenly the captain of the bellman hovered above Neil, then spoke. "Sir, may I assist with that bag?" An authentically first-generation timbre and diction – what was that? East African? Ethiopian? Eritrean?

"I'm fine, thank you." Neil routinely declined this service. His expense reports allowed no provision for gratuities. Their rows and columns were straightforward: meals, lodging, room tax, transportation. You couldn't recoup a courtesy. In fact, Neil had developed resentment, over the years, for hotel staff who offered. Bellhops with their eyeballs on his bags. Departing room-service porters pausing expectantly at the door before shrugging and slipping across the threshold. Maids who came to turn down the bedcovers. (This last curiosity so perplexing in its valuelessness.) He thought of them, in time, as inconsiderate half-people whose role in cosmology was to stack one inconsequential embarrassment of his own hyperfrugality upon another until they became consequential just in their dimensions and bloated complexity, until there was a heap of alienating stinginesses that made him question – fundamentally – his own decency. After all, on the other hand, these are just folks trying to get by. And isn't it true to say that we are all just trying to get by? Aren't all of us simply squirrels trying to store a few nuts away for stormy times? For winter?

Now, three time zones to the east of home (wherever that is), Neil's body rotates like a planet above a strange mattress. He had made the mistake of checking his e-mail before bed – just a quick dial-up and audit of the in-box to see if there was anything truly pressing. But each line presented its own distraction, some projects going awry, one or two with admonishments that the sender had not known Neil would be out of the office, implying that this had set back the day's goals, and demanding what now to do or some other satisfaction. Too, there were several of the variety Neil called "blistering snot-grams," electronic lectures or reprimands or inelegant missives of displeasure over something he had, or had not, done before he left town. Usually from the same whiney passive-aggressive shits who refused to pick up the phone or walk over to his cubicle – people utterly horrified at even the smallest prospect of confrontation. Even if such a thing might prove ultimately fruitful.

All these e-mails said, "Tell us what to do." They said, "Respond to our needs. Give us what we desire. Do better next time."

Every night a different pillow. All of them too hard, smelling like chemicals or someone else's head. And these sheets that aren't fitted, that come quickly undone at the corners. Comforters that refuse to shed their raised crop of rayon pills. The smoke alarm blinks. Asynchronously, the diode-sized light on the black brick of his computer surge-protector blinks as well. The absence of timing between the two lights sets up a dissonance that distracts and fascinates Neil for a brief time. Then there is the incessant march of the digital alarm clock to note. Early in his career he was never quite sure whether he'd successfully set these clocks. Now Neil always leaves a wake-up call.

The e-mails, the telephone messages, his boss's most recent poorly managed meeting that went on for an hour and a half beyond its scheduled end, the last gathering in which Neil had made a presentation that was soundly ridiculed by all present in a macabre game of pile-on – all of these indignities – Neil tosses in the sheets because of these. His seething hatred for all of this coils upon itself in a conspiracy to drive sleep further away. As the moments gather and sag under their own weight, Neil begins to think he might well rise, log in again, and dispatch some of his own correspondences. Send a finger-wagger back to some other unfortunate, or let fall some toxic snowflake from his own electronic pen. Somewhere, someone, tomorrow morning – this morning – would open his or her in-box and read the imprimatur of Neil's metastasizing loathing for this job, this vocation he had chosen, this pursuit that was never an occupation, but a position – as in *assume the position* – BOHICA: bend over, here it comes again.

Neil hears the scratching of mice feet on the carpet at his room's door. Through the ribbon of hallway light that bleeds under the doorcrack comes his statement in a hotel envelope. This is something Neil likes – that he can check out by pressing a sequence of keys on the television remote. He can avoid the hotel people at the checkout counter full of their vacuous how-was-your-visit questions and automaton-like efficiency. The person who thought up this modern convenience should have got one of those big prizes like the Nobel or Pulitzer, or an Addy.

Neil launches himself from the alien mattress. The covers go to the floor. His bare feet hit the carpet. He has decided that sleep will not come tonight – perhaps he'll be able to recover some of it on the airplane. If there's not much turbulence, and if he isn't seated one row in front of the lavatory, if there isn't a two-year-old screeching brat nearby whose ears hurt, if the flight attendants don't pester him every four seconds whether he wants a drink or headset or magazine or pillow, and if the plane doesn't explode in mid-air or auger into the side of a mountain range (although if that happens, it technically wouldn't keep him from sleep).

In the dark, Neil reaches for the trousers he flung over the room's desk chair. He tugs them on, one leg at a time. Clicks on the lamp and locates his socks. Laces up his shoes. Instead of the Oxford button-down, though, he wiggles into a sweatshirt. To protect the world from the sight of his bed-mussed hair, he pulls on a Colorado Buffaloes ball-cap from his luggage that is just for this purpose: you never know when the fire alarm might go off. You don't want to be showing the other hotel guests your particularly virulent strain of bed-head.

Neil checks to confirm that the plastic card-key is still in the pants pocket and opens the door. The hallway is long and maize-colored. The carpet stretches to his left and right. To his right the hall turns a corner a few rooms down – the tableau puts him in mind of those scenes in *The Shining* where the little boy keeps circling the hallways on his Big Wheel, encountering terrifying things. Neil turns left – which is, anyway, the direction of the elevator shafts. He arrives there in the little elevator lobby with its silly credenza, two stuffed chairs and ashtray with the

151

hotel's logo pressed in the sand (what marketing propagandist thought that one up?) with one half-buried non-filtered Camel snuffed therein like a burrowing emphysema-projectile. Neil pokes at the L button. A ring of light around it glows. There is an electronic chime from halfway across the cosmos and the doors slip sideways. Neil steps into the box and waits for it to drop.

The lobby is the same cavern it was earlier in the day except that it contains no life-forms milling about. Every step he takes sends an oscillating reverberation across the dead space, so that his footsteps return to him in fading echoes. A single clerk concerns himself with paper behind the reception counter. If he glanced up at Neil's footfalls, it must have been before Neil noticed him – for he does not glance up now. For a moment Neil contemplates exiting the lobby through its monstrous revolving glass doors into the New Jersey night. Fresh air, he thinks briefly, then wonders if New Jersey has any. These are swamplands, right? Gas-lands? Garbage-heap and toxic-chemical dump-lands? Meadowlands? He had passed, in the taxi from the city, Giants Stadium. They say Jimmy Hoffa's body is buried there under one of the goalposts. Funny how the night lends itself to free association, particularly a night such as this where sleep – that unattainable commodity – may as well be as far away as some exotic precious metal unknown to earth and available only in the ores of the eighth undetected planet from Proxima Centauri. (Closest star to Earth for you factoid buffs, yet still 4.3 light years or 10 trillion kilometers from us – roughly 1.2 parsecs distant. In other words, un-fucking-attainable.)

Neil is like a zeppelin that has lost its rudder. He wonders how far from here the Hindenburg blew up (the answer, fact-freaks, is about 50 miles). He wonders why Americans obstinately refuse in the manner of the most obstreperous donkeys to convert to the metric system. He wonders whether, even now at this ungodly hour, e-mails continue to flow like tainted fluid into the electronic reservoir of his in-box. Whether e-mails, like water, refined petroleum, sloe gin, magma, piss, mercury above -36 degrees Fahrenheit, blood, bull semen, Kool-Aid and corporate policy, are governed by the laws of hydrodynamics. Do the same principles of ideal and viscous liquids apply? The same tenets of turbulence? Are boundary layers, diffusion, shock waves, intersections of surface discontinuities, and flow over fixed bodies part of the equation? Could Polynesians derive fabulous stick-maps by reading the shapes of these disconsolate waves? All this hard, mid-night thought of fluids.

Neil hears the small sound someone makes who is shedding tears. The sound of quiet weeping.

A woman is seated on a long sofa behind the giant vase. Her luggage is arrayed at her feet. She is work-attired, her long and admittedly attractive legs in nylons, hair in place. A mid-forties businesswoman, but clearly aggrieved, clearly distressed. The tissue in her well-manicured hands dabs at her face, and Neil sees that her tears have left her eye makeup in disarray. All of his experience and conditioning tell him to avoid this woman, to cross the lobby and exit into the gas-lands night, to abandon her to whatever private troubles she has. To let her wallow in the consequences of her choices, or sins. Yet he stands immobile, the soles of his shoes immensely heavy and unified with the lobby floor. He cannot move, he cannot flee. What alchemy transforms him from the most cynical, disgruntled man alive to something, someone, less so, if only for the briefest instant?

And so, against all probability, he asks, "Do you need something?"

She looks up, her tissue frozen in space. "No, thank you," she says. "I'm fine." This amazing lie we all tell.

"No, really," Neil says. "Obviously something has upset you. I'd be happy to help."

Her shoulders slump and she folds into herself. The temblor of a sob shakes her.

"Sit with me," she says.

Her husband lies intubated, hooked to all manner of monitors and other medical interventions, in Dallas. He has suffered a cardiac infarction the size of a small Jovian planet. He lives at the boundary of life. And while there are several flights from Newark to DFW – even from JFK and LaGuardia – none are leaving now, and those leaving first thing after dawn are overbooked.

Even so, she awaits a cab. She believes she'll have a better

153

chance of getting home today if she's physically present at the terminal.

All of this information flows from her like a dam-burst, Neil at her side. Her perfume commingles with the scent of her grief. Normally, Neil would be unable to separate himself from her scent, her woman-ness, the essential fact that he sits in intimate proximity to an attractive female who is not his wife, yet whose smell washes him. He should become aroused. The full length of his thigh and the full length of her thigh are pressed firmly together. But now, instead, in this nameless, faceless cavern, he merely laces her fingers with his, and holds her hand until the cab arrives. They do not exchange names or business cards.

Whether her husband lives or dies.

Whether she gets a flight.

What her company or business is, whether she has kids, whether she likes living in Texas, whether she likes living – life – at all.

He will never hear another thing about her –

Incarnation on First Avenue

The street sweeper pokes his broom into a recessed doorway, recoils at the bloodpool. At the center of the puddle, a crushed pillbox. Blue plastic rustles next to the hat as a finger of breeze, lifting from Elliott Bay and refracted through streets and edifices, whirls through his legs around the broomshaft. The wind lifts the sack's corners. Plastic lace of the hatbrim has absorbed blood in a maroon stain. He leans the broom against the doorjamb, stoops carefully to lift the hat and the sack. Blood clings to them, the separation a moist, stringy thing as he lifts, gingerly, examines the bag and its contents. *Books inside*, he thinks, *I wonder whose*. He drops the bag and hat in the wheeled refuse container behind him, retrieves the broom, makes a couple of cursory sweeps around the pool. Moves on.

Darren ran across Jesus on a wet storefront sidewalk in Pioneer Square. At least he thought it was possible it might be Jesus, so it was best to take no unnecessary risk and comply with her teary request. She was wrapped in a cherry red, full-length coat missing buttons. It draped her, revealing a stained blouse and short pants that ended just below the knees. A small lace-trimmed pillbox nested in her curls – her scabbed calves dropped from the coat's frayed hemline, ending in exposed feet, open-toed sandals. Water dripped down her from standing in the rain, soaking her feet raw.

"Sir, I don't have no place to go," she mumbled. "I'm cold." Her eyes, he thought, would have appeared watery regardless of whether she shed tears, which she was doing, now. Brown eyes, with specks of almond, set in jaundice. The tracks of veins networked them as she pled.

"I think I got a couple of bucks here." Darren dug in his hind-pocket for his wallet.

"I'm trying to find a blanket." Her lips formed awkwardly

around the explanation. "Do you think you might have five dollars?"

Darren tilted his wallet away from her so he could inventory the denominations folded inside without her seeing. He honestly didn't know what he had. But he hoped there were some small bills. It seemed absurd – disrespectful even – to ask her for change for a twenty. Two ones, two twenties, some ATM slips. He withdrew the ones, dug in his coat pocket for castoff change. He presented her with the bills and coins.

"This is all I can manage," he said.

"God bless you." Her palm reached to receive the donation. It shook, her brown, saturated hand with a palm the color of his. She stuffed the money in her coat pocket, sniffed and shuffled away, up First Avenue towards downtown. Darren watched her walk away, pinned beneath conflict. You never know when the Lord is going to show up, or one of his angels. It could be on your street any time, could be a black or white person, even a Chinese. *Do this for the least of these, and you do it for me.*

If he were wrong, she would spend it on booze or crack. If he were right, he'd have a favorable tick-mark in Heaven's righteousness ledger. Either way, it was in the Lord's hands. And that was a good enough place for him to leave it.

Darren turned, stepped down the sidewalk in the opposite direction she had departed. As he walked, grimy water flicked up from his heels, dampening the back of his pants-legs. The walking felt good after being pent-up in his hotel so long.

Another two blocks toward the core of Pioneer Square, and he stood at the entrance to Elliott Bay Book Company. Darren loved the independent bookseller, the old brick interior and wooden-slat floors that squeaked and gave way when you walked on them. There were so many books inside a person could spend a hundred grand in there and still – so many titles, so many writers.

He wandered to the "Staff Selections" rack, caressed the spines of a few titles. He withdrew "The Restraint of Beasts" by Magnus Mills, read the synopsis on the back jacket. He wandered a little more, twenty minutes in all, settling on the Mills book and a collection of short stories by Geling Yan. Paid cash at the checkout, offering both twenties, receiving change.

Grasping the bagged books, something was unsettling yet: a thought he had not completed his business with Jesus/the homeless blanket-seeking woman.

A simple blanket was all she was asking for. Darren knew he and his wife probably had a dozen of them in their closet – Afghans, woolens, you name it. They would be plenty warm on any given winter night, having perhaps, even, to crack a window. If the woman in the red coat couldn't find four walls, she'd spend the night outdoors downtown under a bridge or behind a hedge – the temperature would drop to the mid-thirties discounting wind chill. And if she couldn't score enough change to buy a blanket – with her sopping clothes she might freeze to death.

Darren examined the change in his hand – three fives, a one and coins. He'd have to find her.

He had set out from his room in the Four Seasons – sprung at last after nearly forty hours. Darren had come downtown from a Seattle suburb to spend the week as a minor functionary in the support regime for his company's interest in a trade conference. The World Trade Organization had descended on Seattle's business core, convening commerce mucky-mucks from the world. But also gathering were a maelstrom of anti-free-trade, environmental, animal-rights, labor, and other special interest group who took issue with the trade group's agenda. They vowed to shut down the convention.

His company's security personnel had warned of the dissidents, discussed solemnly precautions each company representative ought to take, even passed a rumor of a possible anthrax release by a fringe group. And now protesters were rallying, shutting down intersections with peaceful but disruptive confusion. The mayor, whose police force had been unprepared in spite of lessons learned by other big cities hosting similar extravaganzas, petitioned the governor for National Guard support.

And so everyone connected with the trade convention had been, at turns, cautioned to remain inside their hotels – chained in for their own safety, in some instances of vast overreaction. The mayor imposed a curfew, Seattle's first since World War II, after the first volleys of tear gas and rubber bullets had been ineffectual.   So, suffering a bout of cabin fever and back pain in one of downtown Seattle's five-star hotels, Darren fled the venue at his first opportunity. Just to stretch his legs. Besides, he was walking in the opposite direction of all the unrest, and so, had found himself headed south on First Avenue, away from the mayhem, with the bookstore in mind.

As he walked, wind quickened. Rainfall, for which Seattle is famous, cycled between sporadic drops and full-bore sheets. During the latter, he would duck under canvas awnings over storefronts. Once, waiting at an intersection for the pedestrian light to change, a delivery van cornered too tight. Puddled water splashed his trousers, and he worried they might stain. Still, he had continued toward the bookstore, toward his possibly holy encounter with the black homeless woman who might be an incarnation of the Christ.

He had barely seen her approach. Why had it taken so long for her to register? Her coat was brilliant red – most residents or visitors to the rainy city dressed in subdued blues and browns, Northwest colors, Eddie Bauer, L.L. Bean and Old Navy wear. A red as bright as a new automobile should have been discernible from a couple of blocks away. It puzzled him – from whence she came, how she suddenly appeared – it was if she had simply materialized from behind a lamp post, a parked UPS truck, or, possibly, from simply nothing.

And there had been something about her face – the way her lips bunched and shook with her plea. Or maybe it was her eyes, or rather, the depth behind them. These were not the surface eyes of a con artist. They had not shifted left to right with fear, they didn't appear to be the eyes of hapless frailty, the eyes of a person expecting to be struck or moved along. She had looked straight into his gaze, into him. There was complex content there, down deep. The kind of eyes with which Christ might have rebuked Sanhedrin as he scandalized them, consorting as he did with whores and tax collectors and generally unsavory Judaean scofflaws.

If she were anywhere, she'd be up First Avenue still, he thought. Darren tried to recreate their parting moment – which way had she walked off? North, he remembered, and set out from the bookstore, face into the wind this time. Twilight had fallen, and Christmas decorations in storefronts and on city light poles cast surreally their holiday cheer. An odd juxtaposition, all this chaos downtown with the symbols of Yuletide cheer as backdrop. He wondered for a moment about the perceptions of the delegates: they had come from everywhere packing bags of heritage. There were prickly French, Third Worlds with attitude, arrogance and momentum from China, the economic humilitarians of a battered Japan. Tonga, Iceland, Zimbabwe, Slovenia – they had all sent representatives. He'd seen them, wide-eyed on the TV in their business suits, confronted by lines of bearded, ball-capped, dreadlocked activists who were, in turn, besieged by gas-masked, baton-thumping policemen.   Seattle's media reporters were in the thick of it, always at the locus of high tension, gagging live on the gas. It was an absolute mess.

Darren passed an adult video store, a pawn shop, an importer of lavish Middle Eastern carpets. Across the street was an Irish pub, a used-book store. He crossed Cherry Street, weaving around and through knots of other evening walkers. He scanned through the rain and falling light for a red full-length coat.

Of course, there were numerous side streets she could have taken. But if she was still in need of a handout for the blanket, it seemed likely she'd work First. It was simply, to Darren's mind, a matter of prudent odds-making – there were more people shopping, walking, or just hanging out on First Avenue, and most folks didn't care to wander up side streets in this part of town.

The rain quickened, soaking Darren's hair. Cold drops furrowed down his neck under his collar.   He waited for the light to cross Columbia, surveilling all the while. She couldn't have gone far – unless she had already collected enough to get the blanket.

And then he speculated, for a moment – if she was Jesus in the guise of a homeless person, could not she then simply conjure a blanket?

No, he decided – that would have been out of character, a surrender to temptation. Exactly like Christ's forty days in the desert, harangued there by the devil. Better, safer, Darren decided, to conceive of this afternoon's events in this way: to engage fellow mankind in an exercise of grace, a test of compassion, Jesus had dawned the scarlet cloak of a soaked, freezing indigent.

Darren noted other down-and-out folks, curled like bristling infants in doorways, at the entrances to alleys. Could they be a Heavenly Host? He walked, with the light and other pedestrians, across Marion Street, then Madison. A stiff wind rustled the plastic of his book bag – the books, though trade paperbacks, felt heavy and wet in his bare palm.

He glanced up Madison as he crossed. Then *there!* – in his periphery – back up First on the opposite sidewalk. At the next intersection a flash of red in the sodium streetlights.

He looked straight at it, but the red was gone. Perhaps down Spring Street toward the waterfront. His pace quickened to a jog, moving around slower-moving walkers, sidestepping paper-boxes and sidewalk trees. He crossed to the south side of First Avenue, headed downhill to Western, sure the red coat was just out of his sight but, nevertheless, ahead. He reached the corner and spun in a circle. There was no sign of her. It was as if she had executed an ascension.

He looked north on Western to where Pike Place Market jutted out over the waterfront. He hadn't paused to note how far north and out of his way he had come. Then, just as a dream begins and is over, he spotted red on his side of the street, midway through the next block. He broke into a run past a streetcorner preacher holding a Bible splayed and calling down Armageddon

"Tell it, Brother," he shouted as he passed. The man smoldered and burned in acknowledgement, returned to his prophesying.

Darren looked back up the street – again she was gone. He drew up short, two problems evolving from the back of his mind to the front. One, her movement. How could she move so fast, appear and disappear in such a weird manner? She had been clearly unhealthy and – well, sort of kinked up. Yet she appeared to be, without rancor or premeditated avoidance, moving away from him quickly and with no pre-determination. Two, his location. Once off First Avenue, he wasn't entirely reconciled with his surroundings. Nothing looked familiar except the Market, up ahead. He presumed if he kept in this direction, he'd locate some known landmark soon, or he could double up the hill, get back on First.

He heard the staccato *whulp whulp whulp* of helicopter blades, canted his gaze upward to see police choppers circling. Their searchlights, given columnar form by the streetlamps reflecting off rain and mist, dropped down and scanned somewhere to the east of the Market. He started walking north again, crossed University and headed back to First Avenue, climbing the steep hill. Immediately on breaching the rise, he saw police everywhere, black-booted, with batons at the ready. He turned left to head up First.

"Excuse me, sir," he heard. He turned to encounter one of the cops.

"Yes?"

"Sir, I wouldn't go up that way," the cop said. "You're likely to run into trouble."

"Oh," Darren said. "Where could I go?"

The policeman pointed east, up University, with his baton. "Better move in that direction," he instructed. Now Darren knew where he was. The Four Seasons was three blocks further uphill. He could simply head back to the hotel, his leg-stretching and book-buying complete. He'd contributed to the woman's blanket fund. Surely she would find other Samaritans, maybe even someone who'd take a moment to show her where to buy one.

But from the corner of his eye, up First again, he saw her.

"Thanks," Darren said. "But I've got business up here."

"Suit yourself," the cop said. "But be careful – there's a mess further on up near the Market. I wouldn't get too close."

Darren took off at a brisk walk, but she had vanished again. And as he crossed Union Street, from the mist and fog and light in front of him emerged a tableau of street theater. The commotion must have included a thousand people crammed into the next intersection – police standing in a line, protesters milling about, armored vehicles, a half-dozen cruisers with lights swirling, cops on horseback – *Horsemen!* It was like a bizarre, apocalyptic carnival.

As he approached he saw a mayhem of unorganized dissidents running toward the police line, teasing the cops like unwanted insects. Behind them, people wielded picket signs denouncing the trade talks:

161

WTO KISS MY ASS! Darren read, and *THE RIGHT TO ASSEMBLE!* People had dressed as harlequins, devils, in black leather, ski masks. They hooted and catcalled to the police. Media lights bore down on the crowd from all four corners of the intersection, and Darren wondered how he could possible locate the woman in this morass. He heard a siren, saw lights from approaching fire engine further up the street.

A cry went up from the crowd: "They're going to hose us! They're going to hose us!"

But as the engine approached, it became clear the driver simply wanted to traverse the intersection, en route to an emergency somewhere away from the area. The crowd split, and police horses stamped nervously as the engine crawled through the mob. Some of the crowd beat on its sides with pickets or bare fists.

Suddenly, Darren was through the police line and surrounded by the carnival. Everywhere he looked people were smiling and shouting, egging each other on, daring the police to take action. He overheard bullhorns warning that the intersection must be cleared immediately, that the crowd would soon be in direct violation of the curfew and would be dispersed. From everywhere around him came, as one voice, a tumultuous jeer in response. He looked west over the crowd, toward the waterfront. The PUBLIC MARKET sign was baking neon, and Christmas lights bloomed their merry message from every lamppost, every shopfront. The helicopters above sounded like the locusts of Revelation, so close and loud Darren thought for an instant, illogically, *they must be preparing to land here.*

The crowd jostled him to the east side of the street, past a Starbucks shop with cracked windows, across the façade of an Italian eatery. Pressed to the building by the crowd, he looked up into a full-length street window, his nose six inches away from two women simulating copulation for those gathered. The pair had dressed themselves in almost nothing and, amused by his closeness to their act, giggled inside. He looked up and out from under the awning: LIVE GIRLS pulsed a sign. He looked back to the pair, who were simultaneously bumping and grinding, and motioning with coy index fingers that he should enter the establishment and taste temptation. They pushed their breasts against the pane – Darren feared the glass would melt or break. *Come out of the cold.*

The women turned to rub their slim asses on the inside of the glass, peering like coquettes back at Darren over their bare shoulders. "Come on in," one of the woman mouthed, turned, kissed her compatriot, plunged her tongue deep between the other woman's lips.

Darren turned from them, simultaneously embarrassed, disgusted and... he had to admit, momentarily lured. "Lord reach out to them," he prayed, quickly, and stepped off the sidewalk into the crowd again.

The horde parted like the Red Sea before fleeing Israelites. And at the focus of its part, the vanishing point of an expanding cone, she materialized. Jesus in the form of a lost, broken lamb, enveloped in a red coat. She stood cradling her pillbox hat, and as Darren crossed the street and approached, it appeared to have been crushed. As he drew closer, she seemed increasingly disoriented, as if her location, and the means by which she may have arrived there, were for her a source of profound confusion.

It wasn't clear whether she recognized him. He stood before her. She leaned against a recessed doorway for a pearl shop, whose display windows were empty. The owner, apparently, had feared more vandalism and excised the merchandise from his window. And this made her, to Darren, appear all the more desperate – emptiness before emptiness. An empty vessel, exactly as a testing Savior might choose to appear.

"Excuse me, ma'am," he out-shouted the commotion around them. She beheld him with diffusion at first, but then directly. "Do you remember me?" he asked.

She appeared to conduct an internal search, an audit of interactions for the past hour. She paused, gathered, shook her head yes.

"I gave you some money for the blanket," Darren prompted.

"I remember."

"I, uh... I have some more," he said. "I wondered if you still need it."

The woman nodded affirmatively, damp curls dropping down over her cocoa forehead. Darren drew nearer to her, into the doorway, as the crowd milled behind him like a rapid tidal cycle. He thought there

163

might be a Salvation Army store nearby, he explained. Could he take her there, buy her the blanket?

She considered this, silently, for a moment that was strained, stretched and snapped with the explosion of the first tear-gas canister. Reflected in the empty window, Darren saw a plume of smoke like rocket exhaust. It was the contrail of a lobbed canister streaming acrid smoke. He turned in the doorway to watch its arc, to hear its steely *plonk* on the asphalt, to have sight go white with its concussive explosion. And then the air was filling with noxious matter. It rose and pulsed, and Darren saw the silhouettes of people, low to the ground, fleeing from the police line, lamenting *Gas, Gas!*

More canisters came, the intersection shrouded in oily stench, and the gas entered their eyes and lungs. Darren found his vision tearing, esophagus catching itself like a snapping animal trap at the back of his mouth. The gas had not completely filled the recessed doorway – more precisely than overwhelming them, it had an effect as if they were on the periphery of the cloud. But the crowd was beginning to panic, to press urgently in. Darren realized they sought cover as he heard the sharp reports of gunfire. Rubber and cork bullets were finding their marks in the street. Through the smoke he saw a half dozen protesters double over and fall, retching the gas, writhing, holding themselves where the pellets had impacted. He could still hear helicopter rotors overhead, bullhorns admonishing the people to disperse.

Yet he felt strangely unafraid. *Fear not, sayeth the Lord,* he heard, whispered. *For I am with thee.* He turned to the woman, who, eyes closed and hands clasped, was praying. He covered her body with his. *Yea, though I walk...*

Giselle shrieked as the black, hooded form rained blows on the man who'd stopped, again, to help her. "Oh my sweet Jesus!" she cried, repeating the supplication in rhythm, as the baton raised and lowered against the man's skull and shoulders.

As he crumbled in the doorway, she tried to move around the

164

tangle of his legs and place herself between him and the striking policeman. She heard the cop's command, muffled from behind a gasmask that made him appear horrific, buglike:

"Back off, lady, right now!"

"Right now," he repeated, when it became clear she intended to place herself between them.

The cop appeared to hesitate for a second, reluctant to strike her.

She spat at him, "Thou art Jezebel, the Whore of Babylon!" and rushed him. He brought the baton down, but her reflexes appeared hypertoned, blessed, sanctioned with the resolve and precision of Samson, a holy strength-beast. She caught the club in mid-strike, grasped it in a fist of denial. "You shall not strike me, but that the Son of God shall crush your head beneath His heel!"

"Lady," he said, backing away, "I am placing you under arrest." Another cop joined him, then there were two and three, a Legion, and they pummeled her to the ground. She felt them, through ebbing senses, yank her arms behind her back. The bite of zip-ties drawn taut around her wrists.

Giselle woke in a roomful of bodies, some sleeping, some awake. She stirred. Pain swam through her joints and bruises, through her head.

She lay wounded in dampness under a wool blanket and waited to be processed.

Hey Now, All You Sinners

T.J. arrives home to find the pumphouse door smashed in. Not only the door but the jamb, too, a deconstruct of splinters. In a wasp nest of sharp pokers, the hardware gleam of brass and oil. The failed, fucked lock jutting out. There's a streak of bootblack next to the keyhole.

T.J. thinks *Whuh?* and stands before the crushed woodwork. He peers into the gloom inside, thumbs hooked in his carpenter's belt, and sees a torn network of webs crossing the suggestion of wooden handles and unmade forms: pump-house guts, a scythe, hoes, rakes, axes, a dozen kinds of shovels. Shit under tarps. The concrete bunker of the wellhead – its cement discus cap. Spiders and their sacs. He looks through the door as if he surveys a desert prairie at twilight, waits for a crescent moon to rise above a massif horizon.

Now he is in a 1974 Plymouth Roadrunner raising a creosote cloud trail across hardpan. Then there is cloth sliding up damp skin, the urge of fire, the shape of her, penetration and movement above seat fabric that has held the day's violent heat. His vision sweeps through the dust of windows – saguaro, stinkweed, bur sage, Joshua tree – and he stands now again in front of the pumphouse like he's never left, never been anywhere but here, now, at this moment. He is pierced with ache, run through with one of the pumphouse implements.

This is Michael's work. His bipolar son, who repeatedly breaks into the house and steals, has now expanded his megalomanic range. The drugs are not working, or Michael's not taking them. One of the two. But the pumphouse, for Christ's sake. Why the pumphouse?

T.J. peers around the fractured door, seeking afterimage. He senses vacuum, but not, at first, its shape. Light is diffused herein, its migration across old panes occluded by untended grime. Motes of it barely bleed in – it suppurates, one might say, like a picked wound. Its wan presence reveals nothing, and T.J. has to invoke another sense. After a minute he resolves a protoform: rubber, chrome rims and spokes, handlebars. It is a bicycle, gone missing. His daughter's bicycle is the thing that's not here.

Of course. T.J. has recently forbidden Michael use of the family car. But the boy has places to go, people to see. Manic episodes to spew. Roaring empty raw desolations of depression to ford. He's going to get his fucking wheels one way or another. Thus the smashed-to-bits door and missing bike. Kendra, T.J.'s daughter, is going to be pissed.

True, she comes home from school, discovers the trashed shed and her missing locomotion. "Dad! Mike's ripped off my bike!"

"I know sweetie, I know. He'll be back with it." T.J. hopes. And in the same breath, hopes not. The little bastard. The shrinks said – no, they *promised* – the meds, the counseling, would work. Instead he's running around like a goddamned ape. The rural town has become Michael's jungle of waves. He crests, he troughs. The town watches and suffers. Seventeen, dosed and potentate-of-the-world/pile-of-shit. Sheila, his wife, keeps saying, "Give it time, Teej, give *him* time." She would.

A (partial) list of Michael's thefts:

Money from his father's wallet, on numerous occasions. Money from his mother's purse, as often. His father's portable CD player he kept in the garage, because Michael is self-medicating and needs cash. His father's coin collection, also for the fence.

Other transgressions:

Truant from school, Michael was locked out of the house – he arrived home before T.J. and Sheila. So he busted out the window, climbed in dragging blood through the bathroom, up the hall. A trail of bipolar AB negative streaks.

Michael threw the tree over last Christmas, displeased with his present. Sheila's glass ornaments shattered like ice chips.

Michael threatened his sister with a broken beer bottle after smoking dope. She fled the room, begged the parents to send him away.

Michael played first-chair trombone in his high school's stage band. Held one single note for a solo during the bridge of a fast number. Smashed brass over his director's jazzy shoulders when the man complained. T.J. and Sheila sit in the school counselor's office. The man drips concern from a face like a well-meaning pug dog. "We need to work together on Michael's issues." Issues, as if they are chromosomal,

167

genetic, congenital. Listed, categorized, as if a plan can be wrought and executed against them. The counselor doesn't know T.J. has long given up, and that Sheila – bravely countenanced – is not terribly far in tow. And what the counselor actually means, anyway, is *We can really offer no solutions here*. Michael is placed in a special school, lasts two months. Drops out to sail those waves.

That's when T.J. cut off the driving privilege

"O.K.," said his son. "Well then, fuck you."

Also, T.J. steals secretly from his wife, from the reservoir of her fidelity. It is not so different. Layer his infidelity – if in thought only, not deed – over his son's bipolarism. Sins of the fathers visited on the sons, that sort of thing. His head and guts ache when he considers this. He steals, secretly, in these ways: When he makes love to Sheila, he closes his eyes and sees a desert. Sees the shape of *her*, feels the sweat of *her* skin, hears *her* come in the half-light of a high wilderness night. That Roadrunner's rocking. His ears ring with recall.

Who do you love? T.J. knows the answer to this question. He wants to call out her name when he grasps Sheila's fingers. He wants to shout as she opens under him, locks her knees around the force of his hammer. The tip of him soars like planets. He closes his eyes and thinks of the dope man's girlfriend. He unflexes like a slipped cord, stirs through her slick fluid, withdraws. Thief. *Guilty.*

For twenty-two years he's been smuggling secrets.

He crossed the summer desert from Nacogdoches, Texas, to Bakersfield, California, in thirty-one hours once, moving product. A hundred and five, a hundred and eight degrees most of the way, at 85 mph. North through Dallas to Oklahoma City, then west on I-40 through Albuquerque, Flagstaff, crossing into the Golden State at Lake Havasu, further through Barstow. Traversing the flat like an air-breathing ramjet.

In the Roadrunner's trunk, a kilo and a half of dried Colombia, plastic tarp-wrapped but still sweating from its own moist narcosis. The girlfriend of Marquez, his dope man, lounged like an ocelot in the passenger's bucket seat. "She needs a ride out to California," Marquez had said. At the moment of commission, T.J. believed it was to watch over the grass, to ensure the transaction happened with no funky shit going down. Marquez explained he was too busy to go. The dope man held his hands up, palms cupped, shrugging: "There's a whole new crop of freshmen at Austin." That was enough explanation for T.J. That and the fact the dope man was willing to pay him solid dollar for the move. As for the girlfriend, T.J. didn't care – she was small, friendly, stunning. Her eyes – my God, T.J. remembers those brown eyes, that black hair, red merlot-pulp lips in his dreams, at the job site, in the shower, in bed when Sheila joyfully collects him.

The girlfriend was a roadhouse bartender outside Nacogdoches city limits, down on the road to the reservoir. T.J. never learned how she got mixed up with Marquez. She was Mexican, Spanish, maybe Brazilian he assumed – she later corrected that assumption with the claim she was third-generation, her grandfather Nicaraguan.

They'd crossed the New Mexico state line, Bad Co. and Skynyrd pounding from oversized speakers, and stopped for beer and wine at a service station. Then they were finished pumping gas and popping bottle caps. He opened the door for her. She settled in the seat sienna-skinned, with calves like creamed cocoa. Her thighs sucked an already short skirt higher and he flashed on white cotton. Took a good long look, which she saw. Slowly, with a smile aboard, she let him see, *made* him see, and then smoothed down the delicate fabric with fingers of promise. He bulled around the Roadrunner's rear deck pushing a horn. Glancing through the back window, T.J. caught the sweep of her eyes in the rearview mirror.

They made it thirty more miles, almost to Tucumcari. She flirted like a kite in gusts, slouched in the seat, the skirt riding up again. She wanted to know what "T.J." stood for, but he wouldn't give that up. The airstream roared through the open windows and he had to shout at her to be heard. He could swear she kept looking at the gearshift, then at his midriff. She raised an eyebrow, licked her thick lips, shouted back.

169

"What?" he yelled.

"It's hot!"

It's hot! She shrugged, pulled her shirt up and off, flung it in the back seat. Her breasts pulled him off-road on a cattle trail. He drove through the rough to the base of a mesa, pawed at her. *Back there*, she nodded, at the rear seat. There he tasted her beery mouth and the honeyed sweat of her skin, her bright nipples. He breathed in the exotic pollens she gave off. He pulled that skirt up and that cotton down, parted that flower, sluiced through her like a blade, dropping dew everywhere, exploding like a small nova.

Her name was Marta. He never forgot her name; he never will forget. *Marta...* What alchemy she performed across the Southwest, through Arizona, across the Mojave. Turning him to gold, every part of him, under a blue sky that faded brilliant white at the horizon. Riding him across the heat, across twenty-two years, across the dopamine-producing pocket of his brain.

Doing the deal in Bakersfield, then gone.

Can he honestly say, now, that he's weary of this old story? He daydreams constantly about finding her – even now – more than two decades later, denying his own culpability for the reason why that is not possible.

Sometimes he wishes it never happened. Really, with all his heart. He denies it, this high desert pre-AIDS, pre-political correct, mid-70s, high on marijuana and beer and red wine fandango. And what followed it, in Bakersfield.

T.J. lifts the framing hammer and strikes. Every time the hammer hits the nailhead, every time that slim nail drives pine studs, he blinks a new past into existence. He raises the hammer for another blow. He blinks away perspiration.

It's been three and a half weeks since T.J. discovered the smashed-up pumphouse. He and Sheila have reported Michael's disappearance to the cops, to his shrink, to the parents of Michael's known friends. To the school, in case Michael makes a contact there for some bizarre reason. They have plastered Tacoma and the University District and Fremont with flyers T.J. made on the computer. Two reams of paper and a print cartridge later, Michael stares from a thousand telephone poles: *HAVE YOU SEEN ME?*

But even in the midst of this, T.J. can think only of Marta. While a house goes up around him it's four weeks, five weeks, six weeks – a change of season – and Michael's flyers run with ink and the rust of their own staples. The bond sheets fail at the corners. They are rain-soaked, wind-dried. Michael's picture flutters, tears at corners, floats to asphalt. Passing cars throw him up to the sky again. He hovers and spins in their passing wakes, falls with leaves, clogs drainage grates.

Sheila is crying in the front seat. She and T.J. are driving through the U-District on a Saturday in light rain. Traffic is hosed because there's a Husky game, Brigham Young in town, fresh-faced Mormons everywhere coping with the un-Utah-like rain. New paper occludes what remains of Michael on the poles: The Wild Debbies are playing O'Hennessey's. Some sort of grunge cum 70s/psychedelic rockers, if the paisleys that decorate the flyer mean anything.

Sheila is dismayed that Michael's flyers are gone, or ruined. Her guts are cracked in half for her son, shredded like the seasoned paper. She suggests they layer more Michael flyers on poles.

T.J. wants to be through. "What the fuck for?" he snarls. God help him, he wants only to get back to *her*. Sheila recoils against the passenger door. His rage – spat like a sleek, steaming missile – ricochets inside the car. Fire, smoke and propulsion, it overroars the blower jetting through shark gills above the dashboard. T.J.'s muscles and tendons want to rise through his skin. His eyes are bugging, no lids.

"Jesus Christ, Sheila." He stares like Charlie Manson – all he's missing is the tattoo swastika. "He left, but you don't get that do you? He left – he didn't want us. He didn't fucking need us. The little shit-bag motherfucking cocksucker just up and left. Fuck him! Shit!"

T.J. looks up at brake lights.

There is a substantial bang of steel and glass. The airbag blows up in his face, a flour explosion. Sheila stars the windshield with the side

171

of her head just above the right temple.   Failed hoses shoot fluid everywhere. Neon-piss antifreeze flows a runlet into the gutter. Lookie-loos point.   Some do-gooder tries Sheila's door, yanks it free with a metallic crack. Blood oozes down her cheek as she lolls stupidly. The do-gooder encounters her bleeding concussion and a pasty T.J., tears streaming down pancake-meal cheeks. Salt rivulets flay open nude flesh on the dusty face of this man.

    The smell of an accident in rain hovers above the sidewalks.

    T.J. is with Sheila in a shared hospital room. The other occupant has a concussion too – they're in the smashed-head ward. The bellows of pumps and sucking pressurized tubes sough across a cubicle the nurse pulled around them, fabric hanging from ceiling tracks. This is a privacy for the slightly maimed. Sheila's temple is bandanged. She trails nasal tubes, intravenous spikes. T.J. thinks in all of this she has taken on the appearance of an appliance, plugged in but cooking nothing.

    It's funny, how she lays there in a gown, inert: she never sleeps on her back, yet this is the way she rests now. T.J. recalls Marta sprawling in the Roadrunner's back seat. This is different. The doctor keeps repeating Sheila should pull out in a couple of hours. *This is not a coma, but a deep, deep sleep.* But a couple of hours and more have passed. T.J. has kept this vigil for two days now.

    As T.J. watches, he wonders about Sheila's dreams. There aren't any, he knows. He's been watching her lids. There is no REM flutter, not one instance. The nurse comes in to tell him visiting hours are almost up. Will he go home or fill out a special form to stay? He takes her clipboard – writes his name, address, phone, other coordinates, again, like last night, on the form. Then he stretches out in the chair and scans Sheila's bruised face. He pulls a blanket around him. He relives an urgent moment cycling deep in him, where he lifted Marta's legs and slipped the underpants up over her thighs and calves, pulled them in a cotton tangle from her feet. How can he conjure that image and its fundamental scents here, now, in the presence of his not comatose but deeply sleeping wife? Can he recall the first time Sheila let him see her there? The first time she made a gift to him of *that*? He smiles: yes, he can. The memory is not as vivid as that of Marta, but is nevertheless there. He is relieved. His guilt, which he has – years now – so carefully managed, finds a sort of tentative mitigation.

He remembers Sheila from a job site. She is the daughter of the man who had ordered the house built, come around to stare at the structure going up and the men who were putting it there. They had completed framing and were moving to installing the trusses – tough, sweaty, fucked-up work. T.J. remembered it was a morning straight out of Indian Summer – some time mid-September when the sun piled in as insistently as it had on any day during August or July. Sheila had arrived with her father, stood under T.J. while he made truss connections.

"Excuse me, miss," T.J. had said, with politeness and managed reserve, from the rafters. "It would be great if you'd stand over there." He pointed with his hammer across the plywood floor to a place near a framed load-bearing wall – it would form the division of dining room and kitchen. "I'd hate to drop anything on your pretty head."

Sheila pretended to not understand. She looked up at him, squinting out sunlight. "Then don't." She folded her arms under her breasts. Pushing them toward him, he thought. But she got it, smiled, backed away. She reached the retaining wall, watched him work.

She made repeat visits to the site, the pair more interested with each completed step in the home's raising. In October they arranged a date, to smoke grass and drink Annie Greensprings in the unfinished basement. It was a harvest evening – she harvested him and he her, on blankets spread over the hard concrete floor. He closed his eyes – the blankets became Roadrunner seat fabric, the walls and joists around him desert. That was in 1979. Did he love her then, at that moment? They married in 1980, had Michael a year later. Surely, by then he loved her. T.J. worked jobs all over the Seattle area, rose to foreman. He opened his own general contracting company but mismanaged it into the hands of high bidders. Sheila held him aloft out of shit during this time – was it then that he loved her? Kendra arrived in 1989, just as Michael began exhibiting inexplicable behaviors. They were weird episodes of disconnect – he runs a pencil into a schoolmate's palm, swipes change from his second-grade teacher's desk. At home, he starts pounding ants with his daddy's hammer on the cement sidewalk that runs from the driveway to the front door. He unzips on the playground and tells a girl she ought to touch his penis. The school had attempted a progressive response, requesting a meeting with T.J. and Sheila in which recommendations were bravely whispered. Michael's pediatrician was more straightforward: he needed counseling, even at eight.

But counseling required money T.J. couldn't sustain on a hammerer's take. They took Michael to two appointments, made a pair of late rent payments. The counselor's idea had run into eight, maybe ten, sessions. Missing the third appointment, T.J. strained under the notion of failed fatherhood, stacked this atop his unrelenting fantasies and guilt. How would he have raised Marta's child? What would he have done differently? While Kendra grew up perfectly, Michael grew out spasmodically. The boy suffered sleep disorders, trouble eating, outrageous highs, crushing lows. He walked in his sleep, captured and broke animals, beat up neighbor kids after the bus stopped, laid in bed all day scarcely able to move. T.J. turned up the gain on work, twelve, then fourteen, then sixteen hours a day. Sheila dealt with Michael alone. When cash began to go missing, T.J. adapted the idea that force must be met with force. Michael denied the theft; T.J. threw him against a wall, held him there slightly off the floor. Spat invective in his son's face. *Not here! Not under my roof!*

T.J. flounders in half sleep, lacing these memories with those of Marta in the desert – he's in Michael's face, then between Marta's legs. He's at Michael's principal's office, then tasting Marta's slick skin. Michael's trombone slide bends itself around the director's shoulders, and there's the fine peachy down of Marta's upper thighs, New Mexico sun glinting off the energy of each hair, and draws him to the unforgettable locus of those legs. *I'm sorry Marta, God as my witness, I'm sorry.* The fabric he weaves in the chair at Sheila's hospital bedside is shot through with failures of his own, everything a pale shadow alongside the raunchy Nacogdoches-to-Bakersfield route. Could he go back and undo it, reverse the trip? Take Marta and the dope from California to Texas, unscrew her, un-fuck his mind?

"Marta," he mumbles.

"Teej?"

"Marta." He is floating above the desert floor, all erection and remorse at once.

"Who's Marta, Thomas? Who is she?"

Sheila is conscious, talking funny with the tube shoved up her nose. In fact she has been awake for more than an hour, cracking through thrumming ice cloud, a hammering in her right temple like T.J. has visited framing blows upon her. He's heard him mutter the word *Marta* numerous times, as well as speak Michael's name. She remembers Michael is missing, for weeks now maybe, but that's all she remembers, and wonders what – no, *who* – is Marta.

"She's a woman I loved once." T.J. emits this stark admission from a state between sleep and waking.

"Once?"

"Still," he whispers.

T.J. and Marta arrived at Bakersfield with her fluids still drying on him. Thirty hours from Nacogdoches, no sleep, just the pot and beer and wine and sex, the last a pull-over on this side of Barstow. She fucked him on a jacket spread aside the Roadrunner, next to a gigantic irrigation pump. Neither of them entertained any notions this wasn't the last time. So they made it hot and long like a storm. They stank and held grit in the folds of their skin. His beard was coming in.

The Bakersfield pusher peered through blinds after T.J.'s second fusillade of knocks. The man's eyes wandered over Marta, out onto the street, casing the Roadrunner. Marquez, the Texas dope man, had said to look for the '74 Runner – the kilo and a half, plus Marta, would be inside. "And we'll be square?" Marquez had asked. "We see," the Bakersfield pusher said. "Depends if she real nice to me."

The pusher cracked his front door, released chains. He stood between the frame, jeans and motorcycle boots and a silk shirt that hung unrestrained by his belt. The man made a quick assessment of T.J., took another lingering draught of Marta. His veined eyes left trails on her.

The pusher looked at T.J. again. "You got my shit?"

"I'm here from Marquez," T.J. said.

"Who this?" The pusher nodded at Marta.

"This's Marta, Marquez's lady."

The pusher appraised her more closely. "Marquez, he a lucky fucker."

"That's right," Marta said, stared him down.

The pusher laughed from his guts. "You can come on in," he said, waving them across the threshold. "Smoke a bowl with me, we talk about it."

T.J. and Marta entered the front room, filled mostly with a long couch, an end table and a scratched-up coffee table with a waterpipe on it. There was a huge beanbag chair in a corner next to stereo speakers, a poster of Jim Morrison and the rest of The Doors pinned to the wall above the stereo components.

The pusher pulled up a single chair and sat opposite the coffee table from them. He fished a cellophane bag from his jeans pocket, retrieved some pot from inside, loaded the bong. The trio passed it around.

"I could use a shower," T.J. said.

The pusher ignored T.J.'s icebreaker, instead broaching the subject of business: "Marquez say you bring me one-point-five kilo."

"Yeah."

"Where the one-point-five?"

"Trunk of the Roadrunner. You want me to get it?"

"Shit no, fool. Not till it dark out, man." He looked over at Marta to share that he believed T.J. to be an unschooled, unsophisticated lightweight. Surely she must have noted this on the drive over. She refused eye contact.

"Marquez say she part of the deal, too."

Marta's eyes snapped from her skirt to T.J., then to the pusher. "I don't follow you," she said.

The pusher laughed. "He say you product, too, little girl." He held his hands up in the air as if to indicate none of it was his idea, that it had all come from Marquez. But that nevertheless, a deal had been made.

176

To modify it now, even with the authority he possessed as its prime beneficiary, seemed to him unbusinesslike. Seeing that neither of his guests understood, even now, where he was going with this, he elaborated: "Marquez tell me you the ginch come with the dope." He turned to T.J.: "He makin' somethin' right to me with this bitch."

T.J. just then understood. Marta had been sent with the dope as some sort of reparation, a peace offering between two dope men with a beef. Over what, he couldn't imagine – money, some score gone awry, cars, other women. "Marquez never said nothing about this to me."

"Call 'im up, man." The pusher reached at the end table for the phone.

"Look, man," Marta said, stopping him. "You ain't touching me."

"Fuck I ain't." Then the pusher took another nonchalant hit. He turned to T.J.: "Sit down here and help yo'self. I'm gonna go upstairs and fuck this whore – see whether Marquez and me's even."

Fear immersed Marta, then a broiling outrage. She pleaded with T.J. with those eyes, as if blood were flowing from them. *Do something!* He looked away from her. *I have to think, I have to think, doesn't she understand I have to think?*

"Look," T.J. started, stopped. He gathered himself again, cast a reassuring glance at Marta. "Look, that ain't goin' down here tonight," he said. The dealer exhaled smoke, placed the bong back on the coffee table.

"It ain't?"

"No."

The dealer pulled a pistol out of his belt and set the piece on the coffee table, snub nose pointing at T.J. The two men looked up and locked gazes. The pusher nodded at the weapon.

"You sure?"

T.J. was silenced. The dealer turned to Marta. "You sure?"

"Asshole," she said. The comment could have been directed at either the pusher or T.J., or, most likely, both.

"Yeah, and I be all over yours in a few minutes."

There was stillness in the room as densely packed as if all the desert and flatland T.J. had traversed with her, all the cacti and mesas and hoodoos and small dry-gulch towns they had passed for thirty-one hours, all the delicious sweaty sex and sucking and salt, were shoved rudely into its confines. T.J. forced his own breath to inhale and exhale, his own heart to bang. He sought to muster some manner of solution, some brave internal courage he had a feeling wasn't there – never had been there – but shriveled in the raw presence of the pistol. The power of the Bakersfield pusher seemed like omnipotence. T.J. slumped in the couch.

"You go on an' get that shower you was askin' about," the pusher told him. "You," he picked up the piece and trained it on Marta, "come with me."

She sat with her arms across her breasts, staring straight at him. Abandoned, she made a vow: "Never."

The pusher attempted a semi-precious pleading that was really, at the core of it, simply cruel: "Come on, baby. You so fine, you like it with me."

Marta lifted herself off the couch, stood grinning. She wrenched her skirt and panties down. She pulled the top over her neck and stood in a pool of clothing. She flung hanks of un-shampooed hair around behind her.

"See this?" She smiled like a hooker.

"Yeah, baby, I see."

Her smile snapped off. She tucked her lips, folded them up with hate. Her eyes fired shells of her own while his cock rose at his fly.

"Look at me, my eyes," she said. He tore away from her pussy, her flat stomach, her breasts, locked on, saw her rancor. "You will never, ever fucking touch this," she said. "Marquez touched it – I made him crazy for it." She giggled without smiling. "He touched it." She gestured at T.J. on the couch. "All the way from New Mexico to here." She watched the pusher glance T.J.'s way. "I made him into a child," she said. Her breasts lifted high and perfect, the nipples erect like bright rubies. A bead of mercury sweat rolled down the lovely cleavage between, rolled clear to her navel.

"But you..." She waved a single finger at him and barely whispered. "Never."

178

He shot her through the chest. Blew her back out in carmine spray and bits of bone and organs and flesh onto the dirty wall behind the couch. The blast threw her onto the sofa, next to a flinching T.J. She looked toward him, saw him trembling like a schoolboy, tears of fear beginning to form, saw he still refused to witness this.

"Look at me." She aspirated through strange, glottal fluids. "Look," she insisted, throat welling. T.J. turned slowly, met her indicting gaze. Then she died.

"Help me clean this up," the pusher said. T.J. brought the dope into the house and helped the pusher wrap Marta in the empty tarp. They threw her body into an arroyo out west of Bakersfield. Covered the tarp with busted-up wood and stones. T.J. remembered asking, "What about Marquez?"

"I take care of that fucker," the pusher said. "You just book."

And T.J. did, he booked, in the Roadrunner with Marquez's advance to San Francisco, then Portland, then Seattle. Every time he passed California Highway Patrol, or an Oregon state trooper, he was sure they knew and mystified they didn't give chase. He called his mother in east Texas and told her he was taking a break from school. He held odd jobs all the way north: the stuff of his own private diaspora. And then that surety – that he would be discovered – faded with months, and years, then Sheila and two decades. He never knew another thing about what happened in California, or Texas.

T.J. makes this confession to Sheila in their dining room, hovered over coffee and cigarettes. It is the second morning after she's out, the stitches above her temple look like an insect where her hair was shaved back. His wife draws this secret, two decades worth of smuggled product, from him. She is unwilling for his sake to let go of the name *Marta. Who is she? What is she to you?*

At first he says *Don't worry – she's long in the past.* But that doesn't seem enough. Truth is, Sheila's heard this name before at odd moments. In their bedroom washed backward through the prism of his

179

dreams, compressing color into black mottled light. She has felt the word before, not spoken, but emanating from his pores as he labors over her, inside her.

Above linoleum, on a Formica tabletop, he tells her the story. A Nacogdoches-to-Bakersfield high desert run. That's all it was supposed to be. Sheila doesn't interrupt and Kendra is still sleeping, so there's time for all of this to emerge. There it is, on the table, like an excised carcinogenic organ. It beats once there between them, a dull-red throbbing heart or kidney, and stops. The two of them stare at it. T.J. believes Sheila's silence means he is, in her sight, ghoulish. She thinks maybe she has to leave. Admits so to the top of T.J.'s head as he watches wisps of steam rise and curl over his coffee cup. He lights another cigarette, the ashtray is mounded with them. There is a long silence, which he breaks: "Don't give up on me, Sheila." It is all he can think of saying.

"You gave up on Michael." She states this as if there is some connection. And there is, he knows, now.

"I know. But I need you now."

"Michael needed you."

"I need you *and* Michael now. And Kendra."

T.J. feels indescribably dark. He needs his wife to shine a light in the dark places of him, this awful hole. "I'm sorry," he says, finally.

"You have to call someone."

"I know."

"In California, I mean. The police."

"Yes."

There's a wall-mounted telephone in the kitchen. The cord hangs like a helix, a beige kinked strand connecting a handset he soon will collect and ask for Information in California. It is the same phone that will ring in seven weeks, just before Christmas. Sheila will answer, accept the charges. It will be a collect call from Hartford, Connecticut. "Michael," T.J. will hear her say, hear her sobbing. "It's Michael, Teej." T.J. will take the phone. "Michael?" His voice will shake. "Come home, son. We've missed you so bad."

Today, though, the phone waits for him. California waits.

Marta... He takes a drink of coffee, rises, lifts the handset. Hears that immutable tone... raises a resolved wrist. His fingers dance penitence. There will be lawyers, weeks, months of trial, maybe jail pr prison –

In a California canyon, bleached bones in a nest of fluttering plastic call out in a newly configured morning: You are forgiven.

A Ball for My Son

Saturday, and my son and I go to Edmonds County Stadium and watch the Channel Cats play.

I have started doing this "date" thing with him. Because months ago, our family crisis having cycled to a certain point of distension, it seemed necessary to drag ourselves in to see a relational therapist for a few sessions.

Our therapist was a short-haired, humorless, notebook-clutching woman whose eyes were not kind. Although she seemed weirder and more maladjusted than even us, there was a solitary sense-making gem that came tumbling randomly from her thin lips: dedicate time to each other. One-on-one time. So every Saturday, I take my son somewhere. It might be a coffee shop (where he will sit and stare at the froth on his cappuccino). It could be breakfast at the Bob Evans (his fork moving cold scrambled eggs around on a plate). Some Saturdays we'll go to the Krispy Kreme on Highway K (silence as sugar mixes with our blood). Or, sometimes we just take a walk through Fort Denny Park (quiet usually unbroken).

But this week, I got a free pair of Channel Cats tickets at work. So here we are in Section 24, Row 6, Seats 10 and 11, tucked in the shade back in under the overhang, watching ball-playing on the brilliant green diamond.

So far, this is how the year is shaping up: the Cats will be just over mediocre. May even get us all worked up late in the season for a pennant race. But in the end, we know there's no hope, all of us, each red-garbed fan in the park. We know it; we've known it since spring training. Not deep enough in the bullpen, only a few standouts. And then all those errors, one after another. Come October, we'll be watching the Plainsmen or Sabers or Silvertips in the newspaper. And, of course, the goddamned Buffs.

I'm trying to interest him in the game. Bottom of the third, Cats leading New Peters 3 to 2. One away. I point out that Ed Burgess is on deck. "Check it out, the dude up next is batting best in the whole league."

He looks at me as if I have sent him a cryptogram. Trying to speak his language ("check it out"; "dude"), I have only succeeded, once again, in mystifying him. He doesn't give a crap about batting averages, nor about this stud horse Burgess who wields that wood with absolute authority. Nothing could interest him less than this fact: Any time Burgess gets up it could go out of the park. But this doesn't reach my son, either.

I have to remind myself that being here has nothing to do with Burgess or the Channel Cats or the whole league. These seats, this odor of shelled peanuts, the truncated hip-hop blasting from speakers, the eight furling pennants bragging league championships, the retired numbers – all of this is beside the point. I have to remind myself that I'm the grown-up. That I have to keep trying.

The margarita man comes bawling down the aisle, that big tank stretched around pit stains that leech up over his shoulders. A careful balance informs each of his steps, and I can't for the life of me understand how he pirouettes and hollers "Tequila!" simultaneously. It would be interesting if he took a header, all that piss-colored alcohol bursting in a fluid bomb over my fellow spectators.

On the diamond, Dom Stephanina goes down watching a very nasty change-up. For a second, it looks like he wants to reshape the umpire's cranium with the bat. But then he folds it under his arm and struts away from the box, making a brassy show of removing his batting gloves. Burgess passes him on the way to the plate.

Ed gets in his stance and Torres – the Pirates' hurler – goes into a windup. Almost as fast as it leaves his fingers, the ball is on Burgess's bat. And then very slowly zooming in our direction.

Those paying attention rise collectively. Anticipation moves like a wave as people perform split-second triangulation, see the foul ball isn't coming to them after all, and move to sit. Others stay standing, including me. But at the last microsecond, it splats into the hands of a guy eight seats over and two rows down. Not really prepared for the impact, he can't hold on. The ball caroms off a seat back or two, slips in under another seat. A fat-faced kid grabs it and holds it up. His mouth twists into a near-growl of victory. He pistons his arm into the air, that ball fused to his pudgy fingers.

After all these years, I think, that's the closest foul ball that's ever come in my direction. I tell my son so. He shrugs.

The guy who didn't catch it is clenching his right hand, working those shocked fingers, shaking his wrist. "Sonofabitching HURTS!" he shouts. And no one minds the language, because who cares anyway. It's muggy, a real sweatbox in River City.

I watch Burgess strike out. My son is staring straight ahead.

Maybe he's doing the math. Figure twenty balls hit into the seats per game (fouls or home runs), an average of 4,000 fans in the park. Odds are long. If you go to three or four games a year, they're never really even close to favorable. So you can't just stand there and not catch it – the one with your name on it. It's not coming around for a while. And this guy knows it, you can tell. He looks like he could use that margarita man. But that dude's long gone.

Yeah, that's it: he's doing the math. I tell myself this.

But what if it came my way? What if I caught it?

Metaphysicists delight in the notion that any given moment branches. That is, at every instant there are an infinite number of possibilities. These blooming universes only become finite (or seemingly so) with our next action, and our next, and so on. They tempt us with the succulent semi-truth that the future is unwritten. In a way, they are like alchemists or workers of miracles: they propose not one tomorrow, but sets of tomorrows that fall on a continuum from ignominy to ecstasy. Lead into gold. Water into wine.   For instance, if I caught it, tomorrow I could walk with a new, confident step at work. In time, the power of my ideas will persuade my colleagues. The authority in my voice will carry the day. No one will push me around. I will become my boss's favorite. And not because I behave as a sycophant, saying yes to his every idea. But for my competence, my stretching, victorious form.

For instance, tomorrow my wife could see a different spirit

184

burgeoning forth from me. Soon, all her doubts and disappointments will recede in shadow. She'll recognize and appreciate the wisdom of my ideas. She will cooperate with each decision I make. And not because I am bearish and remote and an emotional taker of hostages. But for my ability to lead, to function well in a confused world.

For instance, tomorrow my son could talk to me.

Or, life could be this nullity of lead and water. For another day, and another.

Back in a spiral of time:

While I'm at my cotton candy there's a commotion overhead. People in seats to either side, and in front of us and behind us, are clapping my father on the back. Grinning big, stupid grins. I blink up into the light, see my dad is holding something. As if he can't believe it, he's standing there with a hockey puck in his hand. Those about us go on something fierce. He says my name, holds it out to me. I reach out with my sugar-sticky hands and take the puck. It's still cold from being slapped around the ice for a period and a half. My father has caught a puck – incredible! I look up and around. The whole ice center is staring at us, clapping, hooting. Even the players on the ice, action stopped, are looking at us as they skate lazily in figures, giving my dad the thumbs-up. I hear the organ blast, and the referees already have produced a new puck. There's a fresh face-off, and our team – the Portland Buckaroos of the semi-pro Western Hockey League, skate away with possession. Everyone near us sits again. It's over that quick.

My father has achieved the impossible – caught with his bare hands a slap-shot puck arcing into the seats at X mph – who knows how fast? But he caught it. This giant of a man.

I didn't even see it.

My wife calls me at work. My son has broken his arm. Skateboarding during recess, she says. On the way to the hospital I think of all the times I have alternately praised him for his increasing skateboarding skills and warned him of the hazards. Of course he doesn't wear any protective equipment – and it's not clear that would have helped him in this circumstance anyway. My cell phone chirps. My wife asks whether I am far – he's in a lot of pain.

"Aren't the doctors giving him anything?"

"Yeah," she says, "but he says it still hurts like hell."

I tell her I'm a couple of miles up the freeway, and I should be there in five minutes.

At Emergency, a harried receptionist takes my name and asks me to sit. A few minutes later, a nurse leads me through a maze of halls and windows. Hospital workers pass me in scrubs. The rubber soles of my shoes make a soughing sound on the linoleum floor. The nurse presses a door release chest high on the wall, and a set of double doors unfolds. A right, and down the hall I hear several sets of pained voices – moans, sharp cries, audible intakes of breath – as new injuries are probed, tapped, assessed and treated.

We enter a room with curtained partitions, rollaway carts, instrument trays. There are several tall, wheeled apparatuses for suspending IVs. About half of the curtains are drawn shut; the others are open. I wonder briefly what prompts hospital staff to decide either way. Open or closed? I listen for my son's voice.

Second to the last partition on the left, and there they are – my wife and son. And a young, bearded man whose face is intent on my son's arm.

My son notices my arrival. "Hey," he says. My wife had said he was in pain, but he'll show me only a false, stoic front of indifference. Too cool to hurt.

"You O.K.?" I feel stupid as soon as I speak.

"Your son has experienced a traverse fracture of the ulna close to where it connects with the radius to the humerus," the man says. "I'm Dr. Elvrum." He stands and offers his hand. I shake it.

"He's going to be fine," I state. But it's really a question.

"I believe so," Elvrum says. "We're going to do some additional X-rays, though, to be sure."

"To be sure," I repeat. He beckons me outside the enclosure.

"It's a fairly significant break," he says. "I want to see whether we can simply set it, or whether surgery is indicated. I think it might be."

"I see."

"You need to stay with him, and with your wife. I'll get the X-ray tech to do this in the next twenty minutes or so. We'll know inside an hour."

"Thanks," I say, and turn back into the partition.

They're both looking up at me.

"He talk to you about more X-rays?" I ask my wife. She nods. "You?" I ask my son.

"Yes," he says.

"He tell you why?"

They nod together.

We gather in the surgery prep area. I've already phoned my boss's secretary to tell her I have to be out a couple of days. My guts are in a knot one minute, and then I dismiss the odds and tell myself everything's going to be all right. We've signed the release forms, initialed the paragraphs detailing rare but conceivable complications. At this point, we must trust the practice of medicine.

I have said a prayer. It feels silly and hollow to me, praying only when there are extraordinary circumstances. I wonder whether God honors entreaties of this desperate variety – those uninformed by a long, regular track record of constant communion about matters small as well as large, about gratitude as well as need. So I amend the prayer with a quick addendum of thanks for my son, my wife, my life.

The anesthesiologist is about to put him under. I'm standing there at the side opposite the busted arm. My son reaches out to take my hand.

His fingers twine with mine. In his eyes are not fear, but longing. And, perhaps, the most remote sense that a need he has chosen to leave unspoken has, or is, being met.

"I'm glad you're here, Dad."

"Me, too. I'll be right here when you wake up."

187

He smiles. Whispers he loves me.

Manny Renteria steps to the plate, knocks the dust from his cleats, drops into a stance. The Buff's Aaron Harang winds up on an 0-and-2 count and throws a screaming fastball. Manny lays the lumber: there is a pop like the report of a rifle as he finds the sweet spot. The ball sails in a fantastic parabola toward center field.

There is never any doubt. Despite the mid-day sun, it can be seen precisely and unmistakably through its entire trajectory. The ball pauses in its arc – stitched seems spinning crazily – then drops straight toward Section 7, Row D, Seat 15. Into my bare hands. I don't even feel it hit.

As Manny rounds second, I am handing the ball to my son.

His eyes are wide. And bright as diamonds.

Viable

I did not want a killer's heart. I told them. I had been very clear about it. The surgeon, hospital administrators and even my wife begged me to reconsider. In fact, they wore me down with their arguments and I capitulated. Now my old, malfunctioning heart is somewhere in the hospital's garbage. This thing beating in me is another man's heart, the core of a dead man, the center of a murderer.

Jolene came into the recovery room after I woke up. A chartreuse breathing mask covered her mouth and nose, so that her eyes and cheeks were all I could see of my wife's face. A gown the same color as the mask draped her shoulders, and her hair was constrained in a scrub cap. Her pupils were inky, like the nibs of pens. She moved to the edge of the bed and stood, looking down. I was still stuffed with tubes, trailing fluid lines and plugged into all manner of monitoring hardware. Moving would have been impossible for me, yet what would I have done at that moment to have been able to flee, to get away?

"Baby, I'm so happy." They were the same words she had said when I finally agreed to the transplant. Intubated, I could only blink in response. The tiniest tear dropped down Jolene's cheek and hid itself inside her mask. As quickly as it had appeared, it disappeared. This thing women do – crying when they are happy. I suppose that some men also do it – but if I had shed tears at that moment, they would have been tears of dread. In the short time I had been awake, I already had developed a new perspective.

For instance, when one of the nurses came in shortly after I first reawakened, I am sure I closed my eyes and thought of harm coming to him. Whether I was or could be the agent of this harm I couldn't say. But it was there nonetheless – this insidious grim tugging at the part of me that had always trapped violence in a net and withheld it from the world. I squinted at the nurse and his clipboard from my jumble of tubes and wires, and my new heart pumped a tiny but unmitigated rage. Who can say why? He looked from the clipboard to a monitor above me, then made a note. Plunging the pen through his carotid artery occurred to me. That's when I wanted to cry, entertaining this inexplicable, wicked thought. When I was a boy I had a Sunday School teacher tell me that the devil put those kinds of thoughts in people's heads. She said if I ever had them to get on my knees and pray. How could I do that with all this stuff plugged in?

I recall Dr. Takagawa's early efforts at persuasion. "I encourage you to get over any squeamishness regarding the source of this heart." A diminutive, beautiful man with a warm face that typically radiated affability, his demeanor had grown staid and businesslike. "I will acknowledge that this is unusual, but I am not exaggerating when I say you have a heart that will not see you through summer. One in twenty hearts that become available may be a match for you. We know this heart will become available. Another may not. Almost four-thousand Americans are waiting, right at this moment, for a heart." The doctor stopped to let me absorb these stark facts. Of course, it wasn't the first time I had heard them. I myself even had recited – in my head – these proofs again and again. I knew, for example, that I had no more than six hours from the donor's death until transplantation before a donated heart would be unusable. Knowing that the heart was going to be available here, in my own state just two hours away by light airplane, was an argument in its favor. It was silly to reject the chance at life. In the last blue, gasping stages of congestive heart failure, beggars cannot be choosers. Jolene was counting on me. Sidney, my daughter, Zachary, my son. Compared with their needs, what could matter so much if the new organ came from a convict's chest? And against what standard did I derive my unease? Still I couldn't shake it then, and it was elevated in a sort of logarithmic way when I awoke.

I researched the donor. While I was struggling as a boy with what Takagawa would, years later, diagnose as childhood rheumatic fever, he robbed his first bank. His second and third robberies came the year I had my first partial stroke – I was seventeen; he was twenty-nine. A year later, surgeons opened my heart to replace a valve; he placed a snub-nosed pistol against a savings and loan clerk's head in Olympia and jerked the trigger when the clerk still refused to open the safe. As my condition devolved toward viral cardiomyopathy, an enlarging of the heart, his legal options evaporated, appeals met with no success. Time began to run short for both of us.

I thought of him often in those terms – both of us – as if we were in a symbiotic relationship. Brothers of a sort, or cousins. People for whom time is a finite resource. Even so, I believed his decision to make a "gift of the body" was motivated not out of any sense of rightness or recompense but, rather, was simply a public-relations gimmick his legal team manufactured to influence the possibility of a last-minute telephone call from the governor's mansion.

At night when I found it impossible to sleep I would think of him. Would he too be staring up into blackness, calculating the moments remaining? Did he have a dream – similar to mine – of intervention (his gubernatorial, mine from some divine source in which I held only the smallest semblance of faith)?

My "transplantation team" surrounded me with encouragement and support. In the vernacular of the severely challenged underdog everywhere, they kept me "up." Takagawa was a man of cheer, with something funny to say about everything. But when he proposed the convict's heart, it was with clipped diction and awful efficiency. "It is time for you to make a decision," he said. "What I am about to describe to you is exceptionally irregular." He had my attention. "There is a man whose heart we know will become available." I cocked my head but the equation of his words didn't seem to sum properly. "All of the signs are that this will be a healthy heart. A viable heart." Was he telling me someone living now was to lose his life to benefit mine? Naturally, every ill person in need of an organ knows the extension of his life comes at the bleak expense of another's. Yet these are accidents – no one is prepared for them. Every one is utterly sad, because a life not fully lived has been cheated. Yet before I fully appreciated his meaning, it seemed to me that the doctor was saying there was to occur some stranger deviation from a solution that would normally have been borne out of the most anomalous circumstances. "No, you do not understand." He grinned, but there was uncertainty behind it. "This man is on death row. He is to be hanged. We know the date. We know the place. We'll have an airplane waiting."

The little color that remained in my face color must have drained completely. His perfect hands folded like origami on his desk blotter. Volumes of medical sciences, catalogs and journals filled the shelves behind him. Jolene's hand clenched mine; I recall feeling distinctly the diamond of her wedding band bite into my finger and it was painful.

"I don't understand," I had said.

Later, both Jolene and Takagawa understood my uneasiness. It was a nasty solution, this. Sticking a killer's heart in me. What if the heart truly is the seat of the soul, as some whimsy has posited? Could another's rotten core infect me from within? It had always been enough for me to contain anger just at the lip. My resentments and disappointments in life had kept from spilling over only by agency of surface tension. I became more and more convinced that evil would leach from the heart and spread corruption through me, slowly metastasizing until I exploded in vicious flames.

And then there was the other portion of me that despised my reticence. Dr. Takagawa's slightly chastising frown slapped at the middle of this sensibility as wavelets slap against the hull of a boat. And Jolene had merely to mention Sid and Zack to propel me into an abyss of guilt. Yet no one admonished my ingratitude with greater fervor than I. So the intellectual in me mocked the superstitious, which faced, at first, trepidation. But as the execution neared, that trepidation took form and wing. It flew across a landscape of fear. It ascended on winds over a mountain range of loathing. Until it hovered over a landlocked, parched desolation.

I used to oppose the death penalty. Lucky for me in this state we hang. It's the only form of execution practiced in the United States that leaves organs in decent shape. Lethal injection and the gas chamber would warp the pump with poison. Electrocution presumably leaves it a charred little pit. And of course, firing squads such as those still used in Utah aim for the heart, so it goes without saying.

On the eve of my transplant protesters held vigils outside the penitentiary walls. Lawyers made perfunctory statements. News people reported with their helicopters overhead. Someone somewhere deep in the guts of the penitentiary undoubtedly waited with a sweaty hand on a telephone's handset. But the call never came. And I awoke with the heart of a man who would rain another's brains over the carpet and stainless steel vault of a bank.

I had wanted to reach up with my hands and drag Jolene down onto the bed with me. After that tear fell. Wrap my fingers around her sweet throat and squeeze. Dr. Takagawa came around to see how his patient was recovering. He wore a smile so broad that it forced crows' feet to deepen at the corners of his eyes. His cheeks were fat and red, and his teeth clacked so merrily I wanted to smash his happy face in. Jolene brought Sidney and Zachary to visit after school and I thought of many times they had disappointed me. When they all had left I asked for the hospital chaplain.

"The heart of a killer," he said. "Hmmm." He was Roman Catholic, and wore a cleric's white collar with all the rest black. A Bible, also black, was in his hand. His eyes were gray like flint. "Yet it beats in you."

I nodded from my tubes.

"You're worried its inherent evil will leak into you."

Yes.

"That wickedness will stain you from within."

Yes.

"That what is in the man's heart is the man."

I nodded again and sent him a plea.

"You believe it is already happening."

I wanted to destroy him for discerning the truth. His eyes moved over the terrain of my face, the gowns and light blanket, the tubes, bandages, the mess. He let escape a minute sigh, so small that it could barely be distinguished from an average exhalation.

"You're afraid." And because this was so terribly true my hands and teeth clenched, and I squeezed together my eyelids so tightly that my vision flashed stars and supernovae. When I reopened them, tears of bitter salt carved canyons in the skin of my face.

"But you fear what every man fears." The chaplain opened his Bible. "Look." He tapped a page with his forefinger. "It says every man has sinned. It says every man falls short of the glory of God." He closed the book. "There is not one man who is righteous." He paused and looked straight into me. "What makes you think your first heart was any better?"

I let him pray with me. When he left, I closed my eyes and listened to the monitors sigh and hiss. I felt solutions enter me intravenously and commingle with my fluids. I sensed my blood rushing through new, unfamiliar chambers and already becoming accustomed to them. The nurse came in to run some diagnostics, or check I.V. levels, or observe something I could not have fathomed. He made a note on his clipboard. I felt nothing bad toward him.

About the Author

Brian Ames is a Missouri writer whose previous story collections include "Smoke Follows Beauty" (Pocol Press, 2002); "Head Full of Traffic (Pocol Press, 2004); and "Eighty-Sixed" (Word Riot Press, 2004). Pocol Press published his first novel, "Salt Lick," in 2007. His work has appeared in such magazines as *North American Review*, *Glimmer Train Stories*, *The Massachusetts Review* and *Night Train*.

www.ingramcontent.com/pod-product-compliance
Lightning Source LLC
Chambersburg PA
CBHW051655260626
47170CB00004B/1511